D0980894

WORDS
OF
ADVICE

FAY WELDON

BALLANTINE BOOKS • NEW YORK

1

We all have friends who are richer than ourselves, and they, you may be sure, have richer friends of their own. We are most of us within spitting distance of millionaires.

Spit away, if that's what you feel like.

But after the manner of these things, Elsa, who has not a penny to her name (except the remnants of last week's pay packet) knows Victor, who is an antique dealer, who knows Hamish and Gemma, who are millionaires.
And Victor and Elsa, one Friday evening, cursed or lucky things, sit in Victor's big new light-blue Volvo at the gates of Ditton House, where Hamish and Gemma live, and wait for the great teak-veneered doors to open and let them through.

Victor is forty-four. Elsa is nineteen, and his mistress. A year ago, when Victor was still a tax accountant, he fished Elsa out of his typist's pool. She flapped and wriggled a little, and then lay still, legs gently parted.

Some technological inadequacy righted, the great gates swing open. Victor starts the engine; the car moves for-

1

ward. The house stands in all its brand-new colonnaded majesty before them. The sun sets red and large in the trees behind.

"My God," says Victor. "What a nightmare."

"Why?" asks Elsa.

"Use your eyes," says Victor. "Now what style would you say that was? Tudor, Regency, Victorian, Spanish villa, ranch, or unfinished Mediterranean hotel?"

"All of them," says Elsa.

"Exactly," says Victor, and Elsa glows with the pleasure of being right. She loves it when he says "exactly."

Elsa and Victor walk up the steps to the brass-studded front door. The steps are lined with stone Disney-style beasts, who regard the pair with cold eyes.

"Notice the concrete ramp," says Victor. "Now why is that there?"

"For Gemma's wheelchair."

"Exactly. And remember not to stare at her, Elsa. In the presence of the disabled behave exactly as if they were like anyone else."

"Yes, Victor."

"And don't try to flirt with Hamish."

"Of course not, Victor."

"But on the other hand, don't go too far the other way."

"I'll try not to, Victor."

Hamish, following the completion of Ditton House, and at Gemma's request, is seeking Victor's advice about the most profitable disposal of certain articles of family furniture. And at Gemma's suggestion, both Victor and Elsa have been asked to stay for the weekend. Both are flattered and excited. It will be the first time Elsa has met any of Victor's friends.

"For God's sake," says Victor. "Do up your zip."

"Sorry," says Elsa. She had undone it earlier, in the

car, for Victor's benefit. Victor, driving at illegal speed, found pleasure in further disturbing Elsa's equanimity by a pinch and a fondle here and there with his free hand. And why not?

Stopping to do up her zip, Elsa stumbles over her own yellow and crimson platform heels and drops her shoulder bag. Its contents roll down the steps: hair rollers, pay slips, brush, old underground tickets, deodorants, contraceptive pills, her change of clothes—pink satin shirt, yellow cheesecloth blouse, clean red bikini panties—and so on.

Victor helps her pick them all up. He loves her.

Elsa is abundantly lovely. She weighs a hundred and seventy-two pounds and is five feet eight inches tall. Her swelling bosom and rounded hips give ample promise of pneumatic bliss. Her skin is white; her cheeks red; her hair browny-gold, and thick and long. Her face is perhaps rather heavy, and her expression sleepy; but whether that is good or bad depends on what you want her for. Her blue eyes, when she can be induced to raise them, are innocent enough. This evening Elsa is wearing her best: old jeans whose every tattered seam she knows and loves, and a faded mauve shirt with a button missing. Ah, she's beautiful; lush and not louche.

Another button pops now, as she bends.

"You would have forgotten these," says Victor, handing her the pink case of contraceptive pills. He'd picked them up from where they were hiding, between the claws of a five-foot Yogi Bear.

"I wouldn't," she protests. But she would if she could.

Victor rings the front-door bell. Organ chimes sound within. Victor waits, tapping a powerful foot. If Elsa is poor, weak and young, Victor is rich, strong and old.

Not quite so rich as usual, mind you, since he abandoned corporate life and started trying to make a profit for himself, and not for other people. But stronger than ever since he took to Elsa's bed, macrobiotic food and Yoga. Old? Forty-four, old? No, it is merely middle age, but Victor is undoubtedly old by comparison to Elsa, who still believes that she will live forever, that nothing is final, and that what is done tonight can be undone next morning.

What a gift, what a blessing, are such beliefs. Once we all had them. Can anything recompense once they are gone? No. Ask Hamish, Gemma, Victor. No, nothing. The nearness of Elsa merely underlines the loss and aggravates the melancholy.

Elsa is young; therefore Victor is old.

Victor is six feet two and weighs a hundred and ninety-six pounds. He is a powerful man with a high-domed head and a smooth bald patch, flanked by downy hair running up and over it—like some spiritual landing strip (Elsa's fancy) for flights of mature imagination. His soft brown eyes are deep-set; his nose is long and hooked; his penis long and sturdy, easily moved to stand erect. No trouble there. No trouble anywhere, except for the occasional cold in the nose or a white-capped pimple erupting on his chin, the better to display his inner juiciness.

The studded doors open; the maid is Vietnamese, middle-aged and intellectual-looking. She does not smile.

And behold, gliding down the long panelled hall to meet them, her powered wheelchair moving with the silence of the most expensive machinery, comes Gemma. Seen from a distance she is a child, her smile radiant and full of expectation. As her chair approaches, years pass. She is twenty, twenty-five, thirty, thirty-five—older, older still. Or is that just a trick of the light? Because she lives in pain or longs for death? And that is all her expectation?

Gemma stretches out her pretty hand to greet first Victor, then Elsa. She is young after all. Barely thirty.

"Victor," she cries, in her soft, sad, kitten voice, "how wonderful to see a real human being again."

Her thick pale hair, cut short and square, falls in a fringe to reach her pale grey eyes. Gemma's chin recedes slightly; her bold teeth push her top lip forward so she seems to pout. Gemma's beauty is warped. It is an almost-but-not-quite affair, something imposed by force of will on flawed constituents. Gemma is very pale; it is the unhealthy pallor of some hothouse orchid, valued and admired by many and liked by none. But she smiles: how often she smiles—a mixture of love and malice beamed out at the world and those who go about in it more easily than she.

Altogether Gemma has a clever and a knowledgeable look. Victor likes that. He admires a clever woman. Elsa is somehow in spite of himself.

"Don't you see many real people?" enquires Victor, taking her hand. It trembles within his, which moves him.

"Anyone with any spirit," complains Gemma, removing her hand, "stays away. They either like me and Hamish is rude to them; or they like Hamish and I'm rude to them. But you know what marriage is like. And you've brought Wendy! How lovely to meet you, Wendy. How were your A-levels, after all that? Your father was so worried."

"This isn't Wendy," begins Victor. Wendy is Victor's daughter. She failed all four A-levels—art, English, Latin and sociology.

"No? I am sorry. It must be the concealed lighting; one can't see a thing, really. But Hamish likes it. Of course it's Janice, looking absolutely wonderful, and young enough to be her own daughter. You've put on little weight, Janice. I'm so glad. You were looking ever so thin, as if you had some secret worry. Is it over now?"

Janice is Victor's wife. Janice is dark and weighs a steady hundred and fifteen pounds. Janice blamed Victor because Wendy failed her A-levels.

"This isn't Janice," says Victor, laughing. "This is Elsa; you asked me to bring her down. You know perfectly well."

Or as Victor says afterwards, admiringly, to Elsa, "If I had brought Janice she'd only have asked how her typing speeds were. Stop crying! Gemma's only playing games. The rich do play games with other people. They have nothing better to do."

"Everyone plays games with me," says Elsa despairingly, but the guest room soon cheers her up. It has white fur walls and a ceiling frieze picked out in navy and pink. The carpet is magenta (nylon, however, not wool, as the tinny feel between the toes presently betrays); the curtains are crimson-flowered, the furniture is black-lacquered and the round bed is covered with a spread composed of serried layers of mauve and grey gauzy flounces.

Victor pushes Elsa back upon the bed, the better to complete the unfinished business in the car, but the couple are disturbed by the arrival of the Vietnamese maid Annie, accompanied by her husband Johnnie, who wears glasses and looks to Elsa much like the headmaster of the college of further education where she took her secretarial course.

"Excuse, please," says Johnnie, "but a mistake has been made. This room is for Mr. Dawlish and Mrs. Dawlish. Miss Secretary's room is elsewhere."

And Elsa, embarrassed to the point of tears (how she overflows, always, bubbling and erupting into the outside world; she blushes, she cries, she stumbles, she is sick; she gets diarrhea or cystitis at the drop of a hat; she coughs up phlegm, her nose runs, as if there was far far more of her than could ever easily be contained)—Elsa, snivelling, is obliged to follow Annie and Johnnie along ever-narrowing corridors to a small room overlooking the central nexus of the house: the work area, where the kitchens are, and the dustbins, and the compost heap, and the coal cellars. This room, as chaste and ordinary as the other was luxurious, has cream walls, green-painted woodwork, a narrow bed with white sheets and grey blankets, a locker, a basin, a plain white towel on a peg and a small yellowy piece of soap in the washbasin. There is no mirror, but under the window stands an old brown office desk, and on the desk is a new typewriter, manual, not electric. On the desk are stacked reams of typing paper: top, carbons, and flimsy in assorted colours. There is a tin filing cabinet (full of empty folders; waiting, but for what?)and a small wastepaper basket.

Elsa throws open the window and leans out. She is four stories up. Her long hair falls over the sill and down over empty space. She is frightened.

Elsa lies on the bed and shivers. She does not like being alone. She is one of seven children. She is not a good typist. She tries, but even if she gets the words correct, sheets emerge from the machine crumpled, untidy and smudged. The typewriter sits on the desk like some unfair challenge; the filing cabinet like some test she knows she will fail; the drop from the window an unspoken threat. Defenestrated!

A fairy story comes to Elsa's mind: that of the incompetent peasant girl who boasted of her prowess at weaving, and was shut up in the castle by the king and set to work weaving hanks of straw into gold, on pain of death. Has Elsa likewise claimed to be what she is not—a secretary, when in fact she can barely type a line without smudges and mistakes? Is her presumption now to be punished? And who is her Rumpelstiltskin to be, the dwarf who visits by night and performs the impossible task, claiming her first-born child unless she can guess his name?

Oh, guilt thus harshly punished! Poor ugly Rumpelstiltskin, fit only to be used and abused! This and many other bitter tales Elsa would tell her brothers and sisters at bedtime.

Or perhaps she is being too gloomy: perhaps the typewriter is coincidental: perhaps her nightly visitor will be the prince whose face must never be looked at, in case he's seen to be a toad after all. Well, easy enough not to look. Just to lie back and accept, in the dark. Or perhaps, since she is clearly imprisoned in a tower, snatched out of Victor's double bed and whisked away by the witch Gemma, her prince will come to rescue her, using her yellow hair as a rope to climb the tower? But how did that one end? Alas, he was toppled from the tower by the witch, and blinded by the brambles below, never to look on beauty again.

Elsa shivers. Although there seems little forbidden to her about her own beauty, perhaps God has other ideas?

The door is pushed open. The prince? The dwarf? The toad? But no, it is only Victor. He has to bend to enter the room. His high-domed, much-scarred head catches, nevertheless, on the lintel; he cries out in pain. Blood flows. Elsa laughs. He carries folders in his hands. Recompensed, he is brisk and businesslike.

"Gemma wants these in triplicate, Elsa," he says. "It's an inventory of what she wants sold."

"You mean it's a working weekend?" Elsa is plaintive, dabbing his bald landing strip with tissue. "I thought I was a proper guest."

"Well . . ."

"They wouldn't ask Janice to type."

"Janice can't type. Women should be useful. You are. It's a compliment."

Elsa is slightly mollified.

"I'll make a dreadful mess of it. I'm much too tired now."
"She wants it by morning."
"I'll do it after dinner."

Even as she speaks, Elsa has the sensation that some fixed pattern of events has moved into place and is now firmly locked, and that whatever she says or does now in this household will be according to destiny, and not in the least according to her own desire.

Or is it just that throughout her childhood, whenever Elsa said "I'll do it later" her mother slapped her? But no, our feelings of doom, our intimations of immutable fate, must surely be deeper than this.

"What will you do *before* dinner?" Victor asks Elsa, and supplies the answer by falling upon her once again, peeling off her jeans, removing her shirt and occupying her body, her brain, and the whole range of her sensual responses.

Before Victor leaves Elsa, the better to change for dinner, he looks out of the window.

"The business end of the house, I see." He laughs. Then the smile fades from his face.

"If that's what I think it is—" says Victor, whose talent it is to discover beauty and history in what to others seems just an old worm-eaten piece of wood— and to Elsa's surprise he is on the window sill and shinning down the drainpipe, regardless of any danger to himself, to examine more closely what to Elsa's careless eye looks like a rather stout and shabby curtain pole, left behind, no doubt, by the painters, and stuck in the corner where the coal-cellars and dustbin shelters meet.

And it is, of course, what Victor thinks it is. Working some hidden brass catch, he unfolds the pole into two hinged parts, joined by the most elegant series of wooden slats.

"I knew it," he calls up. "A library ladder. Late eighteenth century."

To climb up the drainpipe again seems impossible. Victor closes the ladder, tucks the resulting pole under his arm, and goes back into the house through the kitchen without a further look upwards to where Elsa's long hair glints palely in the dusk.

2

Other people's tables!

Gemma's table is round and made of rosewood, and seats twelve people. The chairs are mahogany and heavy late Victorian. The cutlery is silver and Regency. The glass is Waterford; the place mats are embroidered with alpine scenes. The walls, almost entirely curtained, portray embroidered episodes of Haitian history in hot reds and oranges.

As a child, Elsa ate at many tables, but seldom sat to eat. Her stepfather being a sergeant in the RAF, and there being nine in the family, there was seldom enough room for all around the tables provided by the Air Force, let alone time enough in any one house to acquire a sufficient number of chairs. Elsa, being the eldest, served as waitress.

Well, why not? Someone had to. In any case, Elsa always liked to make herself useful, and as everyone observed, she hardly looked like someone who needed feeding up. On the contrary.

Now Elsa's stomach is uncomfortably full of spinach quiche, boeuf Bourguignonne, courgettes, pasta tossed with olive oil and basil, mixed green salad, profiteroles with whipped cream and chocolate sauce—not to mention gin and peppermint, liebfraumilch and Côtes de Beaune.

Elsa stifles a belch and the one remaining button pops off her yellow skirt. Johnnie, acting as waiter, his headmaster spectacles glinting in the light from the Venetian glass chandelier, retrieves the button from the foot of a life-size statue of the Buddha and politely lays it on Elsa's side plate, where the last scraps of biscuit and Danish blue, pressed upon her by the ever-hospitable Gemma, still wait to be eaten. Can she?

"No cheese?" asks Gemma, bending forward, perturbed. Gemma wears white silk. Her cheeks are delicately rouged. She has eaten little and drunk less. Unfair.

"I couldn't."

"Never mind." Gemma smiles kindly, and surveys her dinner table and guests as a birthday child might survey the careful icing on its cake before devouring it.

Hamish and Victor are locked in happy combat (and have been since the quiche was removed) over the future of the library ladder.

Hamish! Gemma's husband, millionaire, manufacturer of flowerpots, and unhappy with his lot in life. Elsa eyes him covertly throughout the meal; whether he sees her through his pebble glasses she cannot be sure. Certainly he behaves as if she were not there. He is a thin, scrawny, elderly man, much Adams-appled, who eats ravenously, as if he could never in all his life get enough food, and who twitches and jumps if anyone speaks suddenly. Hamish seems to enjoy Victor's company. Victor, who could make two of him, moves easily about the world; has his finger on mankind's pulse; beauty, art and history.

Hamish's bank balance, on the other hand, could swallow Victor's a hundred times or more. The fact worries both of them; it would be idle to pretend it didn't. In the meantime, Hamish is happy to allow Victor to bully him.

"But I don't want to sell it," says Hamish, adding butter to his Cheddar cheese. "I'm very fond of that library ladder. It belonged to my mother. She used it to get apples from the loft."

"Then what was it doing put out for the dustmen?" enquires Victor. He is feeling slightly sick. It has been a long time since he has eaten meat, and tonight he had even accepted the second helping Gemma piled upon his plate, without asking. Normally, Victor follows a macrobiotic diet, but for reasons of health rather than principle, so he had no scruple about accepting so delicious a boeuf Bourguignonne. His body, alas, is not so quick to adjust as his mind.

"It wasn't out for the dustmen," protests Hamish. "It was waiting for the restorer, wasn't it, Gemma?"

"Of course, Hamish," croons Gemma, in the tone of one who knows she lies. Victor raises his eyebrows.

"I should change your restorer," says Victor. "Whoever he is, he does a rotten job."

"Everything he does comes back perfect," says Hamish.

"Exactly," says Victor. "Shockingly over-restored."

There is silence; Johnnie clears the plates. Has Victor gone too far? No.

"I expect you're right," says Hamish gloomily, a drop of chocolate sauce falling from his long nose, where it had accidentally lodged. "I've got no taste at all. Better face it."

"No such thing as no taste," says Victor cheerfully. "You like what you like, so long as you're prepared to pay for it. I just don't like to see a good library ladder put out for the dustmen, and the rungs used by painters to wipe their brushes on. I'll give you fifty quid for it."

Hamish laughs.

*　　*　　*

"It belonged to my mother. I'm not selling."

"Seventy-five."

"It's worth two hundred at least," puts in Gemma.

"Be quiet, Gemma," say both men, together and sharply.

"Besides, I might want to use it one day," says Hamish. "A library ladder. It cost all of twelve thousand to furbish that library."

"You don't read books, Hamish. Don't pretend you do. When are you ever going to climb a ladder to read one?"

Hamish smiles. He enjoys rough treatment.

"You're quite right," says Hamish, "I leave all the reading to Gemma. She's the cultured one. I just make money. Hasn't she done wonders with the house?"

"Wonders," says Victor, and Elsa echoes "wonders," but nobody hears.

"I only did what you wanted, Hamish," murmurs Gemma, again in the tone of one who knows she lies. "I just hope I didn't overdo things. Why don't you let poor Victor have the ladder? He's set his heart on it, and I'm sure I'll never climb a ladder again."

"True," says Hamish.

"So you'll sell," says Victor, triumphant. "I'll write a check for fifty pounds here and now."

"You said seventy-five."

"Did I? My mistake." Victor takes out his checkbook.

"Now what about the eight dining-room chairs?" Hamish stays his hand. "I asked you down here in the hopes you'd take them off my hands. Set of six and a mother and father. Sotheby's offered five hundred pounds."

"Then take it."

"A ridiculous offer. Even I know that. Rooked right, left and centre, but I know those chairs are worth at least one thousand two hundred pounds. Saw a set exactly like it in Bond Street. You won't raise it, Victor? A good profit in it for you."

"Certainly not. Not without the ladder. I don't like your chairs."

"You don't have to like them, Victor. Only sell them."

"I can only sell what I like. That's how the trade works—at least my end of it."

"I don't like plastic flowerpots," protests Hamish. "But I sell them by the million."

"You don't have to look into the eyes of the person who's buying them," says Victor. "I do. I tell you what: I'll give you six hundred for the chairs, and throw in the ladder."

"I'll keep the chairs," says Hamish, closing his eyes, but not before a real dart of malignity has glinted from them, "and the ladder."

"I shouldn't have mentioned the ladder," says Victor. "I should simply have put it in the boot of the car. No one would ever have noticed." And he too closes his eyes, before the real distress within can be seen.
Impasse.

"Well," says Gemma brightly to Elsa, "shall we take our coffee to the library before the men start bargaining again? And you can tell me all about yourself. I'm dying to hear how the young live now . . ."

Elsa looks across at Victor for help, but none is forthcoming. She has no option but to follow Gemma's wheelchair as it cruises, at a speed so brisk that Elsa has almost to run to keep up with it, along window-lined corridors lit by electric torches held in glowing onyx hands, to the library, where bound books bought by the yard, unopened and unread, line the walls, and a mock coal fire, electric-powered, leaps and sparkles redly in the stainless-steel grate.

Johnnie runs after them with Elsa's missing button. She'd forgotten it, hidden amongst the Danish blue and biscuits. To take the button from Johnnie she has to let go of her waistband, which she has been clutching, and nearly loses her yellow skirt. It is made of old-fashioned artificial silk, cut on the cross, and crumples and stains easily.

Johnnie and Annie lift Gemma from her wheelchair into the deep softness of a purple leather armchair; she settles herself snugly in, like a kitten in a feather pillow. Elsa sits upright on a high-backed Jacobean chair, complete with hard tapestry cushion.

"So you're Victor's assistant," says Gemma. "What fun it must be. And how clever to know all about antiques. Hamish is always buying antiques; he can't resist them. We have no children—my fault, I'm afraid —so we have to make do with things."

"I don't know all that much about antiques," says Elsa. "Mostly I just do the dusting. I'm trained as a typist, actually."

"Yes, so Victor said. I hope you don't mind me giving you the inventories to type? I do like things done properly. I used to be a secretary myself once. In the days when I walked upon two legs and had a full hand of fingers."

And she holds up her left hand for Elsa's inspection. The ring finger is entirely missing. The stump is well healed, smooth and white, but all the same Elsa feels sick and faint. Will she faint? No. Gemma kindly pours her some brandy.

"And you live at home, Elsa?"
"No. I've quarrelled with my parents."
"What about?"
"Victor."
"Oh dear."
"I live with Victor, you see. In a room behind the shop. We love each other. He's such a wonderful man, not old at all. He's given up everything. He's renounced his home and his job and all his past life, just to be able to do his own thing."

"And you've given up nothing?"

"No."

Gemma meditates.

"For a man who's given up everything," says Gemma eventually, "Victor has a very large car."

"He needs that for his work."

"I was only quoting poor Janice," says Gemma lightly, "who makes such a meal of a simple thing like paying off the mortgage. And will you be staying the whole weekend, Elsa?"

Elsa would run home that very moment if she could. Batter against her mother's door, pleading for forgiveness; break into Victor's shop and hide her head under the late-Victorian satin pillows, beneath the Edwardian patchwork quilt or the Art Nouveau sofa which is hers and Victor's bed, and a very dusty one at that. How she wheezes and sneezes, these days! She lives her life in a cloud of dust. Well, better that than in the typing pool, where the mustiness of new concrete walls covered with acrylic paint, and the long expanses of nylon carpet, created such a degree of static electricity as made many a poor girl jump and cry out at least ten times a day. In the managerial offices they applied an anti-static spray to the carpets, but the cost of general application was reckoned far too high. Girls in offices always jump and cry out for one reason or another.

"I thought I'd been asked," murmurs Elsa unhappily.

"My dear, of course you were. Victor's assistant. We were going to have the whole house and contents valued, and will, so long as Hamish and Victor remain on speaking terms. Victor's so clever about everything, it makes Hamish quite cross. But I had no idea that you and Victor were so close, and Janice is bringing Wendy to Sunday tea. It's her eighteenth birthday."

"It's my birthday too on Sunday," says Elsa eventually. "I'm going to be nineteen."

"What a coincidence! Sharing Victor's daughter's

birthday! I daresay you feel destiny has a hand in your relationship?"

"Yes," says Elsa.

"And Victor feels that too?"

"Yes."

"Of course if you *want* to stay, and Victor doesn't mind, I can make a cake for the both of you."

"Does Victor know Janice is coming?"

"You must ask him that yourself. I'm sure Victor would never deliberately wish to hurt anyone."

"Of course he wouldn't," says Elsa. "He's the kindest man in the world."

"And now you and he are to be married!"

"Married?" Elsa is startled. "He isn't even divorced. Why bother? If two people love each other! Marriage and divorce are only about property, after all."

"Who says so?"

"Victor. In a perfect state there wouldn't be marrying or taking in marriage."

Gemma ruminates.

"Do you think mostly what Victor thinks, Elsa, or do you have your own thoughts too?"

"Victor teaches me everything. I was very ignorant until I knew him."

"You remind me of myself when young," says Gemma, and ceases to be censorious, and becomes—or appears to become—quite easy and friendly. "I'm sure it's much more civilised for you and Janice to meet," she says cosily, "and I daresay you and Wendy will get on. You must have so much in common."

Elsa nods, as if fearful and modest. But she is not. Something has hardened in her heart. She wants struggle, conflict, victory. She has the scent of triumph in her nostrils, the taste of sexual power between her soft red lips. Something instinctive and nasty surfaces, hardens, takes possession: other women are her enemy, she perceives. Men are there to be made her allies, her stepping stones to fulfillment and worldly success. Herself, her children cradled in luxury and safety. (Well, how else is she to do that, with a typing speed of 35, and shorthand 53?) Elsa looks sideways at Gemma and thinks, Why, if I wanted, I could have Hamish too. Then where would you be, helpless in your chair, with your unworkable legs and mutilated hand! Sitting there patronising me.

Johnnie fills Elsa's glass with more brandy. His dark head bends until it all but touches her white bosom. You, too. If I wanted.

"You aren't going to stay a typist forever, I daresay," murmurs Gemma.

"No," says Elsa.

"Be careful," says Gemma, suddenly and sharply. "I know what you are thinking and I know where it can end. To be wanton—and yes, you are wanton—with your life, your sexuality, your future, is a dangerous matter. You are greedy and careless at the same time, and have made yourself a hundred times more stupid than you need be. Women do; they have to, if they are determined that men shall be their masters, if they refuse to look both into the faces of men and into their own hearts."

Elsa opens her mouth to speak.

"Be quiet. I know it isn't comfortable. I know that self-knowledge is painful. I know that to think you are a princess and find you are a beggar girl is very disagreeable. I know that to look at a prince and find he is a toad is quite shocking. I also know, and you will probably never have the opportunity to find out, that to think you are a beggar girl and will end up a princess is perfectly dreadful."

Elsa blinks, startled.

"I can read your heart, Elsa, because I can read my

own. I have a story to tell. It's a fairy tale. I love fairy tales, don't you?"

"Yes."

"I thought you would. Princes, toads, princesses, beggar girls—we all have to place ourselves as best we can. This one is the story of Mr. Fox and Lady Mary. Lady Mary the High Lord's daughter was betrothed to the noble Mr. Fox. And the message was written in letters of fire in Mr. Fox's house the day before her wedding, when she stole into his house to see what she could see. 'Be Bold' written above the first door, and all within was grand and quiet; 'Be Bold' above the second, and likewise; but 'Not Too Bold' above the third. But in went Lady Mary on tippy-toe, and there she found a charnel house, and her beloved Mr. Fox feasting with his friends; a robber baron, that he was, her Mr. Fox, and feasting on human flesh. And as she crouched in her dark corner, a finger flew across the room and fell into her lap, and on it was a ring. So she slipped the ring from off its finger, and crept away, and showed it to her brothers. And when the next morning came and with it her marriage day, and handsome Mr. Fox came up the aisle, her brothers fell upon him and killed him, and so justice was done."

Tears stand in Gemma's eyes. Bewilderment shines from Elsa's.

"Do you think it was justice? Or did it just mean that more were dead than were before? I don't suppose she ever married after that. Well, would you?" enquires Gemma.

"What's so interesting about that story?" asks Elsa. Where's Victor? What's he doing? What can Hamish offer him by way of company and entertainment that she, Elsa, can't?

"What is so interesting about it," says Gemma firmly, "is that I heard it one night on someone else's tran-

sistor radio, read by Dame Edith Evans. I was on a
train; I had a sleepless night in front of me. And the
very next morning I met a Mr. Fox, and fell in love
with him; and rings and fingers, or the lack of them,
featured prominently in my life thereafter. Have you
never noticed the way the secret world sends out signs
and symbols into the ordinary world? It delivers our
messages in the form of coincidences: letters crossing
in the post, unfamiliar tunes heard three times in one
day, the way that blows of fate descend upon the same
bowed shoulders, and beams of good fortune glow per-
petually upon the blessed. Fairy tales, as I said, are
lived out daily. There is far more going on in the world
than we ever imagine."

"Just a coincidence," mutters Elsa, disbelieving.
"*Just* a coincidence! I love Mr. Fox and you say
just?" Gemma is outraged. "It was many years ago, as
they used to say at the beginning of fairy tales, when
the world was fresh and young—and so was I—but it
was not imagination. It was in 1966."

1966.

Not, as Gemma observes, that the year made men any
kinder or girls less foolish; all that can be said of it for
sure is that skirts were definitely worn shorter by the
fashionable, and a good mini-skirt was referred to as a
pussy valence.
Picture Gemma in the year 1966 at the age of nineteen,
arrived in London from the distant provinces, where
time stood still—as could be seen from her green tweed
skirt, which reached down to her knees, and the twin-
set—pullover and cardigan—which blurred the outline
of her chest. The twin-set was in dusty pink, and round
her neck she wore a metal pendant, heart-shaped, set
with an artificial pearl. So her mother had walked before her, though never in London, city of sin. (Sin

enough in Cumberland, where she had lived, without looking abroad for it.)

Now her daughter Gemma, more adventurous, five good fingers still on each hand, walked on two good slender working legs down Carnaby Street, London, and saw her contemporaries with their skirts high above their knees, and breasts clearly outlined beneath thin fabric, and even, here in Carnaby Street, at the heart of the world's fashion events, a few going braless, precursor of what was to come.

This is the world for me, Gemma thought. But even while she thought, she stopped in a doorway and took off her mother's pearl pendant, and put on the crucifix her great-aunt had given her on her sixteenth birthday.

"Gemma," Great-Aunt May had said, "you'll need this too." Though quite what she meant Gemma was not sure. Gemma's mother had died when Gemma was four, from (some said) too many late nights and too much rackety living, and (others said) from TB aggravated by self-neglect. Be that as it may, Eileen was certainly dead, and had left her arthritic Aunt May to look after Gemma, which that lady did, willingly, if painfully, until her own seventieth year and Gemma's sixteenth birthday.

On that day, after giving Gemma her mother's pearl pendant (symbol of sin and excitement; Eileen had been wearing it the night Gemma was conceived, pressed up against an alley wall, fully dressed in twin-set and necklace, but her skirt up and her knickers down—the alley cat!) she had produced her own great-auntly crucifix, as if the second gift might somehow neutralise the power of the first. And then she had added another blessing, and had rung up the Council to take back the cottage (rent 17/6 a week) in which Gemma had spent her childhood, and thrown herself

upon the mercies of the National Health service, and
Gemma into the care of the local Children's Department.

For the young to be free of the old—this is a blessing
indeed. Great-Aunt May knew it; and knowing it,
relinquished Gemma without a thought to the loneliness
of her own old age. Such courage, such sacrifice is not
uncommon; it is taken for granted and goes mostly unnoticed. It is remembered by its beneficiary only in
dreams, if then, but has its results, perhaps, in those
small unexpected ripples of family kindness that over-
lap from generation to generation. The good we do lives
after us, for ever and ever. Great-Aunt May died; Gemma did not go to the funeral, but never mind. If Gemma had the crucifix now, she would hand it on to Elsa.
She has lost it long ago. She talks, instead.
Elsa listens, and wonders why Victor and Hamish talk
so long, and Johnnie fills her glass again.

With her pendant in her handbag and her crucifix
around her neck, Gemma stopped at the foot of the
building where the Gallant Girls Employment Agency
had sent her for her first job, and looked up and up its
glass façade and marvelled that technology could con-
struct a solid building out of a substance so essentially
fragile as glass. Coloured lights played upon the surface
from within, so that even at 11:10 on a Monday morning it seemed to demonstrate that work could be fun,
that man need not waste his substance in seriousness,
but could get by just as well by having a good and
colourful time.
Even as Gemma stood and gaped, a yellow Rolls-Royce
slowed up beside the building and a young man in a
white suit leapt out and ran past Gemma, and up the
pink-veined marble steps and into the Art Nouveau
gold-embossed lift and was gone, leaving an impression
of pale good looks, lithe body and perfect teeth behind;

and Gemma took off her crucifix and put her pendant back on, and followed him inside.

When Gemma was taken over by the Children's Department she was kept for a week or two in a Children's Home and then found employment, by a kindly social worker, as mother's help to a widowed vicar's wife in a remote Northumbrian village. Gemma had distinctions in eight O-level subjects, and would perhaps have benefited from further education, but the vicar's wife, Mrs. Hemsley, had five daughters and was desperate. Gemma was disinclined to return to school, and the pressure for places in the Children's Home was great. The closing of railway stations and coal pits in the area, in the undoubted interests of efficiency and progress, had resulted in considerable local unemployment, and the consequent breaking up of families and the taking of children into care. Gemma merely happened to be there at the time. Let us not think that we get what we deserve, any of us; some of us are better at triumphing over obstacles, that's all.

Gemma worked for Mrs. Hemsley for two years. She had her keep and thirty shillings a week pocket money. During the day she and Mrs. Hemsley together looked after Hannah, Hermione, Helen, Hortense and Alice. During their evenings, the two of them washed, ironed, mended and tidied. Gemma was not unhappy at first; the little girls were fond of her and she of them. Mrs. Hemsley was generous with everything except money, which was understandable because she had so little of that to spare, living as she did upon a widow's pension and the precarious kindness of the church. She made up for it by giving a lot of advice, which Gemma ignored.

Gemma's bosom, over those two years, grew whiter, plumper and more munificent, her waist more slender and her skin more translucent. Her large eyes, purple-lidded, grew dreamier. She lived without sexual activity or overt sexual interest, or as the dentist's wife said of her to the doctor's wife, "What you don't know you don't miss, I suppose." It was, more or less, true. If Gemma dreamed, it was of pale knights upon pale horses in dark forests; her excitements were romantic, not erotic. Other girls of her age fumbled and sweated and kissed; Gemma dreamed and sighed.

Gemma's menstrual periods were regular, though painful; she suffered at night from vague aches and pains that kept her sleepless. The doctor, visited on this account, asked a few searching questions about the absence of boyfriends, and Gemma left, embarrassed, though not before the doctor had given her an internal examination, which since she was a virgin turned out to be both painful and surprising, but was presumably necessary. The doctor prescribed aspirin and the pains went away. Later that year the dentist dropped amalgam down inside her summer dress (a shirtwaist, picked up for two shillings at a jumble sale) and had to retrieve it, again an embarrassing experience. The dentist's wife, who acted as his assistant, had been asked to leave the room for more pink mouthwash. It seemed to Gemma that his fingers lingered and tweaked where they had no business.
How, lying away at night, Gemma scorned the doctor and the dentist, and her own body's response to them. How she pitied Mrs. Hemsley, and resolved not to end up like her, as drudge to her own descendants. The purpose of life could not merely be to hand it on? She scorned her own generation too: the sweaty village girls, the mumbling boys who stood about in jeering groups remarking on the size of her breasts. She was grateful to be spared any more subtle attention from her contemporaries, hurrying round the shops each morning as she did, obtaining as best she could food for seven on money sufficient for three—lentils, oatflakes, stewing lamb, turnips, rutabagas—the sound of lewd catcalls in her ears. She was accustomed to frugality—

life with Great-Aunt May had been austere—but could never become used to vulgarity.

Gemma was not like anyone else; she knew it: she had been told so often enough at school—she was a love child, and so was her mother before her. And this Gemma saw—at any rate on good days—as a matter of pride, not shame. Her father had been a visiting repertory actor, and wasn't that better than being fathered in wedlock by some black-nailed farm worker? Her mother's father was never known. Better an unknown possible prince in disguise than a known toad of a station porter, surely!

Gemma, though grateful to the many people who showed kindness to her, was not content. Gemma, cleaning, sweeping, mending, chiding, was merely biding her time. She was ambitious, though for what she did not know. She took a correspondence course in shorthand typing.

And so one Monday morning in a hot June, Gemma was able to present herself at the Gallant Girls Employment Agency in Regent Street, London. She had with her a suitcase, five pounds fifteen shillings in her purse, and a certificate of competence in shorthand and typing from the Courtley Correspondence School. To acquire the latter document she had spent many late nights hard at work, burning up Mrs. Hemsley's precious electricity, wearing out Mrs. Hemsley's deceased husband's ancient typewriter—all that poor lady had left to remember him by apart from Helen, Hannah, Hermione, Hortense and Alice. With Mrs. Hemsley's somewhat relieved blessing, Gemma had come south to London to make good.

"Gemma has her head screwed on the right way," Mrs. Hemsley confided to the dentist's wife. "She'll be all right. Secretarial jobs are two a penny in London, and I've given her the address of the YWCA. I only wish it was me who was going."

"I think our Gemma will be better suited to office life than child care," remarked the dentist's wife, thus putting in words what Mrs. Hemsley felt, but scarcely liked to say.

Gemma, Mrs. Hemsley feared, had lately been showing signs of irresponsibility. As her shorthand improved, so her sense of domestic vocation deteriorated. Even though faced, as could only be normal in the day-to-day care of five children, with emergencies such as broken limbs and crises such as high fevers, she showed a marked reluctance to call in the doctor. She had, moreover, developed an astringent style of talk that smacked, or so Mrs. Hemsley feared, of cynicism. She hardly set a good example to five growing girls.

Hannah, Hermione, Helen, Hortense and Alice. Alice was born the day before her father had his first and last heart attack, leaving his wife to seek in vain for a tolerable name beginning with H.

Gemma lost her address book in the train on the way to London; in it were the names of the YWCA and the various charitable organisations she was to contact if in any trouble. But Gemma had the courage of the very young. Undaunted and unafraid, she left the train at Euston as dawn broke. She sat on the steps outside the station until breakfast-time had come and gone, and then started to walk to Piccadilly, which she had heard was London's epicentre, and which she could at least locate on the station's street map. London seemed larger than she had imagined; that it was dangerous she did not then know. Danger, in any case, is only relative. The alley where Gemma's mother encountered Gemma's father might be considered more dangerous yet.

As Gemma pushed her way through the crowds where Regent Street meets Piccadilly and the flower children of the world meet up, her attention was caught by a

shriek of noisy laughter issuing from a first-floor window. Lettered on the glass were the words "Gallant Girls
Employment Agency."

Well, thought Gemma, at least they're happy; and in
she went and up the stairs, there to meet Miss Hilary,
senior interviewer, from whose very lips the laugh had
burst.

The laugh had not in fact been particularly happy,
being Miss Hilary's normal Monday-morning response
to any request for staff from an employer, or for work
from employee. Miss Hilary knew from long experience
that anyone not suited on a Friday evening—or married
by the age of thirty, for that matter—was either hard
to please or born unlucky.

Miss Hilary was fifty-six; her hair was neatly coiled in
blonde plaits, black-rooted, at the top of her head. Her
voice was loud, her laughter raucous and despairing,
her eyelids blue as a summer sky, and her heart as deep
and sad as sin. Miss Hilary sat glinting behind upswept
glasses like a spider at the centre of its web.

Miss Hilary regarded Gemma with the harsh derisive
pity of one who knows the world for the one who
doesn't. She helped herself to a jam-centred biscuit
from the plate brought to her with her morning coffee,
and offered Gemma one made of decent wholewheat,
which Gemma accepted gratefully. It was her breakfast.

    "Hungry, I see," said Miss Hilary.
    "Yes."
    "And I daresay you've just arrived in London, have
lost your purse and have nowhere to live."
    "How did you know?" asked Gemma, startled.
    "In London," observed Miss Hilary, "no one is
unique. Girls take this route from Euston every Monday morning, and there are pickpockets on the trains.
What did you say your name was?"

"Gemma James."

"Pretty. I go a lot by names. If the mother has imagination, sometimes the child has as well. I suppose you learned your shorthand typing by correspondence course? No, don't show me the certificate. It will be from Courtley and means nothing."

"Then give me a test. I can do forty typing and eighty shorthand. Really."

"Take off your sweater, dear."

"What for?" asked Gemma, startled.

Miss Hilary pushed Gemma another biscuit, this time a chocolate finger. Gemma took off her sweater, and then ate the biscuit. Her bust, in its 36C St. Michael's bra (white) showed to advantage beneath the size 34 jumper. The matching cardigan was in a size 38, the twin-set having been sold cheap on account of this discrepancy.

"That will do," said Miss Hilary. "You'll have to wake up your ideas on clothes, of course."

"Do for what?"

"Let's face it, dear. You need a job starting this morning. I've got a nice one going at Fox and First."

"Who are they?"

"Never heard of Fox and First? Don't you read your Sunday supplements? How ever do you think you're going to get on in the world? On forty typing and eighty shorthand? Self-taught, at that? Leon Fox is London's most eligible bachelor. He's a society jeweller and man about town. Most artistic! Rings for the toes and pendants for the nose; circlets for the bosom and studs for the naval; gold manacles for dainty wrists, male and female, and goodness knows what else for goodness knows where, but nothing under a thousand pounds. They're asking for a nicely spoken girl of good appearance for light reception and modelling work."

"Modelling? I'd rather be employed for my skills than my looks."

"Beggars can't be choosers," said Miss Hilary sharply. "Start today and in here Saturday ten sharp for your wages. Twenty pounds! Lucky girl! Get your card from my assistant. Next, please."

"Excuse me," said Gemma, "but how much do they pay you for me?"

"It is not customary for my girls to ask that question. It is confidential information."

"I'm sorry," said Gemma, abashed.

Miss Hilary looked full at Gemma once again.

"If I die poor," she said, "it will be the fault of girls like you, making me feel sorry for them."

And no doubt Miss Hilary thought herself generous to a fault, considering she had her own way to make in the world and only her own efforts to sustain her.

"I'm ever so sorry," said Gemma, meaning it. "I really am grateful."

"Yes, my dear," replied Miss Hilary, astounded. "I believe you are."

And Gemma set off for Fox and First, and there on the steps, as he leapt pale and lithe from a yellow Rolls-Royce, she caught her first glimpse of the man she was to love forever: Leon Fox

Mr. Fox, Mr. Fox, Gemma loves you. Love struck like a shaft of sudden light from heaven, striking down into the narrow alley of Carnaby Street and into Gemma's heart, and shifted and changed and reassembled the very particles of her being, so that forever after part of him was contained in her.

"Love's one thing," says Gemma to Elsa in the library, years later, "and once love has struck no wonder the body craves to have even this crude physical manifestation of the new constituent lodged within it—dur-

ing the act of sex, that is—making its presence felt even
if only for short intervals. But gratitude, that's another
matter! Beware of gratitude, Elsa. Young girls so easily
feel grateful, and it always leads them into trouble.
Remember always that your good fortune is yours by
right; you do not have to feel obligated to those who are
the mere catalysts of your fate. Do you love Victor or
are you grateful to him?"

"Both," says Elsa firmly.

If Gemma had the use of her feet no doubt she would
have stamped one of them.

"Do you think your meeting with Victor was destined?" she asks presently. "Or was it mere chance? Or
was it perhaps merely your nature, and if you'd been
working in a different office you'd have fallen in love
with the first married fatherly knee you sat upon?"

Elsa is indignant. She stares full at Gemma, the light of
true love beaming from her blue eyes, illuminating her
life.

"Don't be angry," says Gemma sadly. "I only ask the
questions I asked myself. And I am so sorry for Janice,
because she loves Victor too."

Elsa wishes Gemma would not talk about Janice. But
as Victor later explained to Elsa, the rich lack the in-
hibitions of the poor when it comes to the discussion
of delicate problems. The poor know there are no solu-
tions. The rich have the experience that there generally
are.

"Janice only loves her carpets and her bourgeois com-
forts," says Elsa. "She's so hung up about possessions
it's unbelievable."

"Perhaps when you meet her on Sunday you'll be
able to help her to a better understanding of life" sug-

gests Gemma kindly. "You're not afraid Victor will decide to go back to her? No?"

No.

The ladies are joined by the men. The matter of the library ladder has not, it seems, been resolved. Conversation concerns itself with inflation, the tides of commerce, the possible profit in marketing ecologically conscious organic potting compost, and the necessity of tax evasion under a Labour government. Elsa's eyes close. It has been a long and tiring day. She was up cleaning the antique shop at seven in the morning. The first customers were expected at eight-thirty and all traces of her and Victor's occupancy of the back room had to be removed: her nightie and his pyjamas tucked as usual into the case of a grandfather clock waiting for its works to come back from the menders; all their clothes, that particular morning, transferred from a linen press awaiting collection by the shippers to one marked up to £1,750 and unlikely to find a quick buyer. The shop was perhaps overstocked—Victor had raised a large second mortgage on the matrimonial home, as well as selling out his accountancy partnership, to set himself up in the business—and free movement was a little difficult. Although, as Victor remarked, Elsa was perhaps more accustomed than most to cramped quarters, and one of the things he loved most about her in any case was the way she seldom complained.
Janice always complained.
Although Elsa did not, could not, with the best will in the world, on account of her lack of knowledge and experience, actually transact sales, she was kept busy enough at the telephone, running messages, shifting furniture, placating disappointed customers, confirming credit-card viability, and so on. For lunch she had cooked Victor buttered brown rice, served with sardines drained of oil: a perfectly balanced meal of 80 percent carbohydrate, 10 percent fat and 10 percent protein,

and rich in nucleic acids for longevity and prolonged youth. On this particular day there had also been the strain of the car ride, sex before dinner, the dinner itself, sudden acquaintance with the rich and eccentric, and the worry of Janice's arrival on Sunday.

Sunday.

Sometimes Elsa wonders if she might not have been better off in the typing pool. Except of course for Victor.

Wonderful Victor, so much at ease in every company! Listen to him now. Prince among men.

Elsa sleeps.

When she opens her eyes there is silence. All three of them regard her with a kind of sad speculation. Elsa blushes.

"Time for bed," says Gemma kindly.

3

"It's out of the question," says Victor. "It's quite impossible. I couldn't bear it. I'm as sexually liberated as the next man, but there are limits."

Victor is striding the length of Elsa's room. He wears the bottom half of his pyjamas as a concession to his age. His naked shoulders are broad and well muscled. His midriff flat. He is handsome; he is troubled. It is two-thirty in the morning. Elsa keeps drifting off to sleep.

"Do wake up," he implores her.
"Let's talk about it in the morning."
"You take your virtue very lightly," he protests. "Though of course that's a concept unknown to girls of your generation."
"It's not that. I just need more sleep than you do. I'm younger."

Victor sits down gloomily at the end of the bed, on Elsa's feet.

"So now you're holding that against me. I knew that would happen sooner or later."

Elsa wriggles her feet out from under him. She has difficulty manoeuvring under the tightly tucked grey blankets. Somebody has remade the tousled bed while they were at dinner, and even, she fears, had to change the sheets.

"On the other hand, if it's just the same to you, all that extra stock would really get the business going. You should have seen Hamish's billiard room, Elsa! He's like a magpie. A lot of good Jacobean oak, and I'll swear the clothes press was Elizabethan! Spode, Wedgwood, early ironstone."

According to Victor, Hamish has offered him the contents of the billiard room for two thousand five hundred pounds, and will even throw in the library ladder if he can have Elsa for the night.

"Perhaps he was joking," ventures Elsa now.
"How am I to know?" asks Victor, distracted.
"Or it might be some kind of test," she suggests, "to find out the sort of man you really are."
"That occurred to me too, but would passing the test be saying yes or saying no?"
"Anyway," says Elsa, "it doesn't really matter because I won't do it."
"Doesn't he attract you? I thought girls were always attracted to millionaires?"
"You're so old-fashioned," she complains. "Anyway, I love you, so you oughtn't even to think of it."
"Ought?" he enquires, pouncing on it like a dog on a rabbit. "What do you mean by ought?"

Elsa sleeps. When she wakes at four-thirty she has pins and needles in her foot. Victor sleeps, kneeling, with his head upon her knees. She shakes him awake and makes room for him beneath the blankets.

"It's not as if we're married," he says, cold beside her. "You owe no kind of duty to me. You must do what you want. I take advantage of you too much anyway."

"No you don't, Victor."
"Yes I do."

Victor sleeps. He warms up quickly. Soon Elsa is too
hot and cramped to sleep. His large limbs are flung
happily over hers. At five-thirty Victor wakes and says,
"Did you do Gemma's typing?"
"I forgot."
"Then mind you do it before breakfast. She's expect-
ing it. I don't want this deal mucked up for something
stupid like that."

Victor sleeps again. At six, when the dawn light shows
the angles of the room, the door creaks open. Elsa lies
motionless wide-eyed, pressed up against the wall.

And here, first peering, then ducking, then scuttling
across the room to the desk comes Hamish, Rumpelstiltskin, in a silk dressing gown, colourless in the early
light. And here until dawn is well established in the sky
and his dressing gown is revealed as crimson silk, Hamish sits and types the reams of work that Gemma's left
for Elsa—or does Elsa dream? Does she see, or does
she dream, that Hamish, as he takes his departure,
pauses beside the bed and looks down upon her in a
manner both indulgent and lascivious? Whether she
dreams it or whether she doesn't, it really makes no
difference; she is certainly conscious of a wave of erotic
excitement as he stands and stares, the like of which
she has never known before. It is the desire of the helpless for the powerful, the poor for the rich, the weak
for the strong; it has its roots there in her womb, and
from it, one might well believe, grows the whole structure of human society.
Elsa feels it. She sleeps. The notion is too strong to keep
in consciousness.

"You did the typing, I see," says Victor, at seven-
fifteen. He means to slip back early to his own room

so as not to disconcert the servants. "You're really getting quite good. Perhaps it's the machine? I must have been tired; I didn't even wake. If you keep on like this, Elsa, you'll be able to type my invoices, which will save us quite a bit."

Elsa says nothing. What can she say?

"Something rather awkward," says Victor, running his firm hands down her naked backbone so that she shivers. "Apparently Janice is coming down on Sunday. I'd no idea. We'd better get you back to London on Sunday morning. What a lovely strong back you have. Janice was always slipping discs."

Elsa cries.

"But darling, it's for your own sake. I want to save you embarrassment. It's very bad of Gemma. Except, poor soul, she has to live her life by proxy at the best of times. One has to forgive her. If I play my cards right, she might even commission me to do her antique buying for her. She could certainly do with someone. A good eye and no discretion. Hamish, on the other hand, is all discretion and no eye. Why is it that money always ends up in the wrong hands?"

"Why won't you come back to London with me?"

"I'd love to; you hardly imagine I like it down here? Not our scene, is it, and the diet will take years off our lives. But it depends how the deal's going; you must see that. And if Hamish is after you, the sooner you're safe back in the shop the better."

"With the other furniture? Why don't you just put a 'sold' sticker on me?"

"You're very ungrateful," says Victor. "I'm doing my best for you."

"If you're staying I'm staying," says Elsa narrowly and with finality, and Victor looks quite distressed, as if a lobster he had thought was dead had suddenly started waving claws at him.

And Victor departs, having pecked Elsa formally on the nose, to save the servants more distress.

During the course of the morning they change the sheets again, although as far as Elsa can see there clearly is no need. It had been a restless night, but one far from passionate.

4

"Gemma has no natural taste," complains Victor at breakfast. "Whoever heard of boil-in-the-bag kippers served on a silver salver?"

The breakfast chafing dishes are munificently displayed on a late-Victorian mahogany sideboard: porridge, cereal, rather thin cream, the guilty kippers, stewed kidneys, kedgeree, sausages, toast, marmalade and dusty honeycomb. Hamish has already eaten—oatmeal porridge and salt, Elsa deduces from the traces left behind. Gemma takes breakfast in her bedroom.

"The coffee's Nescafé, too," Victor groans. "The rich do have such extraordinary areas of meanness. Of course, neither of them was born to it."

Victor's father was a dentist, and his mother a librarian. They lived in Winchmore Hill, a prosperous outer suburb of London, and although the family was poor by comparison with the neighbours, its members were not strangers to the finer things of life. Vivaldi played on the gramophone, de Buffet reproductions hung on the wall; for a time, in the thirties, Victor's family house was a refuge for professional people and artists in flight from Hitler's Germany. There had been an excitement

39

to life then quite missing from it now—or at any rate until the previous year, when the convulsions in his life had started: his wooing of Elsa, his forsaking of wife and child (in their interest as well as his own; what use to anyone is a marriage founded on hypocrisy?) rendering him alternately elated and anxious, but seldom bored.

"Gemma was a typist like me," says Elsa proudly, piling her plate high with the kedgeree, which she eventually favoured. "She was telling me."

"Gemma would tell you anything," says Victor, "if it suited her purpose. Hamish is no better. Did you hear him say the library ladder was his mother's?"

"Wasn't it?"

"He didn't have a mother, let alone a father. He was brought up in an orphanage with his sister. She's dead now."

"Poor Hamish."

Victor eyes Elsa narrowly.

"You have quite a soft spot for Hamish, Elsa, in spite of what you say. It doesn't surprise me. I know full well I'm just a rung on the ladder in your journey up in the world."

Elsa's mouth gapes at the unfairness of it all.

"You do have a lot of fillings," he observes. "I suppose your early years were spent awash in a sea of blackcurrant juice and ice lollies."

Victor's childhood had been severely regulated so far as diet was concerned: brown bread, carbohydrates and protein never presented at the same meal; vitamin supplements and thyroid extract pills taken as a general tonic, until his heart raced and his brow sweated.

"You're in a horrid mood," complains Elsa.

"You're not behaving very well, Elsa." Victor lays down his fork amongst the orange scraps of dyed kipper skin. Elsa gets up and leaves the table. Her rather heavy jaw is set in mulish fashion. So her mother's would set on occasion, in obstinate defiance of her fate, her husband, anything that stood in her way.

"Where are you going?"

"I forgot to take my pill," says Elsa, an excuse which will take her anywhere.

"Dear God," he groans. "You're a madwoman."

"I don't suppose Wendy ever forgets *her* pill," says Elsa as she leaves. Wendy, in fact, needs to take no contraceptive measure, inasmuch as she is a virgin and likely to remain so for some time.

Elsa goes, but not to take her pill: rather to make a phone call to her friend Marina, from the furry seat of a sedan chair converted into a telephone booth and set cosily in the panelled front hall beneath antlers, gargoyles and crossed swords. Marina is a former school friend of Elsa's who now lives with a married sister, shares a room with her four-year-old nephew, has a clerical job in a department store and gets much pleasure from Elsa's worldy exploits.

"What's it like?" breathes Marina. She is a dumpy girl with a pale face, wild brown eyes, legs without ankles, and a high, piercing voice which she modulates, not always successfully, to a sexy whisper.

"Wonderful," hisses Elsa. "Guess what we had for breakfast?"

Marina guesses correctly.

"You do manage to play your cards right, Elsa. I'm eaten up with envy. I had the last of the Weetabix. All crumbs. And now their washing machine's broken down, so I have to go to the launderette while you go swanning round this millionaire's house. Is he away?"

"No. Why should he be?"

"Rich people usually are. I suppose he fancies you?"

"Yes. Well, I think so." Elsa giggles.

"Good. Wake Victor up a bit. That man takes you for granted. You must take every possible opportunity to make him jealous, Elsa."

Marina was Elsa's head girl at school.

"But I love Victor. I don't have to play games."

"Yes, we all know about you loving Victor. But what about when Victor goes back to his wife?"

"He won't go back to his wife. We're together forever."

"Not unless you watch your every step. Now, Elsa, you're to sleep with this millionaire if you possibly can."

"Why?"

"Because you never know when it might come in handy. If you're born a femme fatale—and you clearly are, Elsa—you owe it to yourself to make the most of it."

"How's my mum?" enquires Elsa, changing the subject. She admires Marina's enthusiasm but is beginning to doubt the extent of her worldly wisdom. Marina lives down the road from Elsa's family.

"She's all right. Saw her in the pub last night with your dad. She had a new hairdo. Streaks. I was out with Petie—you know, the one with bad breath—and all he could afford was cider, so I've got a splitting head this morning. Haven't you made it up with your mum yet?"

"No," says Elsa.

"Quite right," says Marina. "All they ever want you to do is what they did, and look how they ended up."

"Did she look as if she missed me?"

"No. You should worry—shacked up with an antique dealer and fancied by a millionaire, and all I've got is Petie and his bad breath."

"Look, Marina, I've got to go."

*   *   *

Victor stands outside the sedan chair, his bad humour evaporated, beckoning.

"Is it Victor?"

"Yes."

"Thought so from the change in tone. Randy, is he? Kippers have that effect on men."

"I thought it was supposed to be me."

Elsa puts the phone down. She had meant to ask Marina's advice about whether or not to meet Janice, and what to say if she did, but as usual had been deflected.

"Come for a walk," says Victor importunately, putting his arm in hers, leading her past the kidney-shaped swimming pool, where Elsa catches a glimpse of Hamish, black-trunked, skinny-limbed, floating upward in the water like some bloated fish, and through the rose gardens, where long-haired young gardeners work, and through the woodlands to a clearing where they can be alone, and where stands an ivy-clad (the ivy pot-grown and still in the nursery containers in which the plants were delivered) plaster statue of the Goddess Diana, Queen of Chastity. Here the sunlight catches Elsa's lovely, tumbling hair (how Marina envies it; how, gazing at it, she sees the manner in which her own life might change, but never will), and Victor bears her to the ground beneath him, and for once she does not notice—or at any rate makes no complaint about—the rocks in the small of her back or the nettles against the backs of her knees, but is caught up in his passion— which, observed, somehow dampens his own.

"What's the matter, dear?" she asks, concerned. He rather wishes she would not call him "dear." So his mother called him, in her absent bookish way.

"Nothing's the matter."

"If you'd rather I didn't see Janice, I won't." She is never difficult for long.

"It's not that."

"What, then?"

"Do you know what I really want?"

"Anything," she says valiantly. "Only isn't it rather public here? I mean, for anything extraordinary."

Victor has versed Elsa in the many varied tactics of lovemaking; she is always obliging, if seldom enthusiastic. Well, she is young; she will learn.

"I want you to make love to Hamish."

Elsa does not reply. Her limbs go dull and heavy.

"Don't be upset, Elsa. Not if you don't want to."

"But why?"

"I don't want to own you. I want to share you. You're too much responsibility."

"Not because of your deal? The library ladder?"

"What do you take me for?" He is hurt. "Besides, I know you fancy him. You told me so. You don't know how wonderful it is to be able to tell you what I want. I never could with Janice! So many important things that could never be said. Not like you, blessed Elsa; under the sun or the stars, indoors or out, it's all the same to you. Please, Elsa."

"If it means all that to you," says Elsa doubtfully, but she feels the life flowing back into her limbs under the pressure of some excitement in her head, not her womb: a kind of bold eroticism mixed with fear, as if she stood on the threshold of some new world that one step might carry her across, but once taken, could never be retraced.

"What about Gemma?" she asks finally, when his mouth is lifted from hers and she can speak.

"You never said what about Janice, as I remember," says Victor firmly. "Too late to start thinking that way now. I'll look after Gemma, anyway."

He could hardly mean what she thought he might mean.

"You won't think less of me afterwards?" she asks.

Victor laughs. "You're half my age," he says, "and twice as old-fashioned. I do love you."

Victor departs by himself, to save any possible embarrassment and to start work in the library with Hamish. Elsa follows a few minutes later, flushed and happy. She pauses in the rose garden, to admire. Around her, still wet from their early morning sprinkler, red and white hybrid tea roses burst into their unnatural, multipetalled life. Little White Pet, she detects, and Ena Harkness.

"How pink you are, my dear," observes Gemma, appearing from the other side of a crimson floribunda in an antique garden chair (with its original caning), which she propels by virtue of small brass handles set in the plump leather upholstery. "So different from Janice, who always seemed so pale and distraught. Thank you for the typing—excellently done. I was afraid I might have kept you up too late, and you'd neglect it. I've left another pile for you; I hope you won't mind. I couldn't sleep last night. I stayed up till early morning making an inventory. I have become anxious about property; I know it's unreasonable, but I can't help it. Money is such a tyranny, you've no idea. Did you sleep well?"

"Yes."

"The sleep of the virtuous! Did you have the kedgeree for breakfast?"

"Yes."

"I thought some of it had gone at last! We refreeze, and reheat thoroughly. It's supposed to be safe, but one sometimes wonders. Food's such a price, though, and it's a crime to waste food, don't you think?"

"Yes."

Gemma is wearing a pale-yellow blouse which reflects unkindly on her complexion. She seems sallow and tired. The morning light, which makes Elsa seem at one with the bounding, procreative universe, merely puts

Gemma out of tune with her existence: makes her seem herself like something often frozen, often barely re-warmed, after a previous night's feast.

"You don't have to agree with me all the time," re-marks Gemma. "I expect it was Victor who told you to say yes or no and nothing else?"

"Yes." Elsa is surprised.

"And you paid attention to him! How wonderful! You do remind me of myself when young, Elsa. Come and sit with me by the pool, and the servants will bring us iced coffee and sugary biscuits, and I'll go on with my story."

"I think Victor wants me in the library."

"You've done quite enough for Victor already this morning," remarks Gemma tartly.

Elsa blushes. Was Gemma there watching? Can she have heard what was said? Perhaps the statue of Diana hides a microphone? Hardly. If Gemma knew the tenor of their conversation, she would not now, surely, be so friendly? She would be hysterical, after the manner of Sheila, Elsa's mother, on discovering a love letter in her husband's pocket, reducing that nice, much-pursued man to instant, abject apology, total remorse. Wasn't that how wives behaved? Or were the rich different?

Gemma sits Elsa on a tapestry cushion at her feet and continues her story, occasionally stopping to pop a sweetmeat into both their mouths. Elsa has the uncom-fortable feeling she is being fattened. But for what?

1966. Interminable years ago! What have we not suf-fered and learned since then?

Gemma's first job. First and last, as it turned out.

The Fox and First offices were on the top two floors of the narrow building in Carnaby Street where we last observed Gemma falling in love with the tight-buttocked back of young Mr. Fox. On the seventh floor were the showrooms and Mr. First's office; on the penthouse floor, reached by a narrow wrought-iron curving staircase, circa 1860, was Mr. Fox's flat.

An expensive conversion had turned poky rooms into glass-lined expanses where psychedelic fantasy ran riot, sprawling over walls and ceilings in brilliant streaks. Far below, anyone who had the courage to stand near the sheet-glass window wall and look down could see the flower children wander, not yet discredited by time, events and the emergence of their own natures.

The theme within was, as it were, curvaceous. The office desks, lime green, were shaped like giant eggs; the filing cabinets were concealed in a series of pink plastic balls, heaped one on the other, as if laid by some other-worldly hen. Fox and First jewellery was displayed in the holes and crevices of mock Barbara Hepworth pieces, in transparent yellow Perspex, or suspended from the ceiling by gold chains.

In the midst of this, health shoes (especially built for the comfort of wide feet) firmly planted in the orange and mauve-streaked carpet, stood Marion Ramsbottle, twenty-eight, stocky, desperate and determined, dressed in cheap black skirt and white blouse; the outward expression of her inner fantasies focussed only, one might imagine, in her black net stockings and bright green, satin-bowed, French-heeled shoes. Marion's hair was teased and lacquered into a stiff fuzz, resilient to the touch, that stood like a halo round her head; angel-like, she wore an expression composed of kindness, self-righteousness and patience sorely tried upon her pale and frankly spotty face. In her plump hand was a starry Perspex watering can, with which she attended to the many pot plants.
Gemma was half relieved, half disappointed to see so

familiar and reassuring a person. If you ignored the
shoes and stockings, Marion might have been one of
twenty girls in the soprano section of the local Handel
choir back home.

If one *could* ignore the shoes and stockings, of course.
Perhaps one couldn't. Shouldn't.

"So you're the new girl," said Marion in her weary
voice. "The agency rang through. At least you're a
blonde. The last girl they sent—Ophelia, she called herself—had red hair. It clashed with the furniture. Mind
you, she only lasted a week."

"Why's that?" asked Gemma as she followed Marion
round the pot plants, learning their names and daily
watering requirements. Crocus, *Maranta, Passiflora,*
oleander, stephanotis. How sadly the names fell from
Marion's lips. She had to project her voice over a background din that Gemma could not at first identify, but
presently concluded to be the raised voices of a host of
parrots, whose aviary, gold-latticed, mosque-shaped, was
placed like a fragile dome over the splashing indoor
fountain.

"The work doesn't suit some," replied Marion, "nor
quite frankly, does this style of office. The flimsy's always damp from the fountain and the ink runs on the
files, and the parrots get loose sometimes and shit all
over the outgoing mail. But I think it was mostly that
she thought she might put on weight from all the tast-
ing. Mr. Fox does a lot of experimental cooking and
likes to have a second opinion. I don't much care for
foreign foods myself—not outside their country of ori-
gin anyway. It spoils one for abroad, don't you think?"

"Oh, quite!"

"Be careful not to overwater the *Salix serpyllifolia.*
It's the devil. It's crazy to try and grow it indoors. As
they say, you don't have to be crazy to work here but it
helps . . . I work mostly for Mr. First. He's the brains

behind the organisation, and the money. Mr. Fox is just the talent. You'll be working for him."

Mr. Fox! Mr. Fox, whoever and whatever you are, Gemma loves you. Are those your footsteps overhead? Yes. What are you thinking, feeling? Do you know about me?

"But doing what?" persisted Gemma.

"Any job's what you make of it. They keep me for the heavy work: typing, filing, and so on—what nobody else can be bothered to do. That's my fate in life. Yours is more on the P.R. side. Customer relations— and a bit of modelling, of course. Mr. Fox likes to try out his pieces."

"Not with my clothes off?"

"Not if it's earrings. But you can hardly model a naval stone or a pubic gem fully clothed, can you? Don't worry. Mr. Fox doesn't regard working girls as human. You have to be someone special—have a title, or be a famous model, or immensely rich, or in the gossip columns—before he thinks you belong to the same species as him."

Mr. Fox, this is Gemma. That is not how you're going to think of me. Do you hear?

Gemma went to the window and cautiously looked down. Toy people and clockwork cars moved below. There was no guardrail, or any sill, to the bow-shaped sweep of window, with its squares of thin glass set in fine lead frames, that curved out from floor to ceiling. Through any one of the squares a man or woman might easily fall.

"Keep away," said Marion sharply.

"It doesn't look very safe."

"It isn't."

"Someone might have a nasty accident."

"They have, and I'd rather not talk about it, thank

you very much," snapped Marion. "Turn the amaryllis daily, or else it grows crooked."

"What sort of accident?"

"I was only joking," said Marion, but Gemma knew, from long experience with Hermione, Hannah, Helen, Hortense and Alice, that Marion was lying. "One of the panes was broken when I came in one morning, that's all. It was a week before anyone would come to mend it: everyone said it was too dangerous. We couldn't even sue the architect. He'd gone bankrupt because Mr. First kept him to the penalty clause in the contract. Late completion. These are my hyacinths. I keep them behind the duplicator in case Mr. Fox sees them. He might drop them out the window. Well, they're ordinary, aren't they? And now you know the flowers, you'd better get familiar with the stock and prices in case any of the public call. They do sometimes. Not often. There's a lot of mail order. Mr. Fox spends half his time at Ascot or Lords or house parties, making useful contacts, and the rest of the time upstairs in the penthouse working out designs. He doesn't like to be disturbed."

Mr. Fox, this is Gemma. You won't mind me disturbing you. Mr. Fox, I will disturb you to the roots of your being.

"The trouble is," said Marion dismally, "I can't keep a straight face. When I see a water-soluble brooch at four thousand pounds it just makes me want to laugh."

"It wouldn't make me laugh."

"Mind you, the prices do mesmerise. If you see a lot of pieces at eight thousand, four thousand begins to seem cheap. That's how it works. Mr. Fox designs mostly in solid gold or spun sugar. This headdress here is in the middle range. Barley-sugar flavoured, polyurethane-coated for display purposes only. He sells a lot of manacles like these: that's for the kinky lot. And personally I don't like looking at the armpit jewels too closely for fear of what I might see. Not that I'm shocked—I'm as broad-minded as anybody—I just don't like to be reminded of what doesn't apply to me. Sex, and all that."

Marion looked as if she were about to cry. "I just make myself useful," she said. "There's always room for someone who likes to be useful, don't you think?"

So the dentist's wife back home had once, sadly, spoken to Gemma. The dentist's wife worked as her husband's receptionist; she mixed the amalgam for him, and was the source of several of his various income-tax allowances. Her hands were a great deal more deft than her husband's; her business brain just as acute; her response to other people's needs (and her empathy with their pain) considerably more pronounced. But her bosom was flat, her complexion muddy, her teeth protruding, and her legs crooked, so her opinion of herself—at any rate, during her lifetime—was low. "Always room for someone who likes to be useful!" And Gemma, looking at the dentist's wife, had marvelled that she put up with a husband who would dive between the breasts of young lady patients on the shallowest of pretexts; just as she marvelled that Mrs. Hemsley put up with having five unwanted daughters in order that her husband might have the son he deserved. Gemma, mind you, was young, arrogant and pretty.

Now Gemma looked at Marion—that anxious, friendly, unerotic person—and both liked her and despised her. Subtly she altered her own stance, so that both bosom and bottom were a little more pronounced, and the length of her skirt appeared provocative and willful, rather than merely provincial.

Mr. Fox, come to me!

Mr. Fox thereupon came rattling down the iron staircase, took a cursory look at Gemma and said, "You're the new girl. You'll do. Feed the parrots, will you.

Bottled water, never tap. Too much chlorine," and rattled on up the stairs again, leaving behind him a strong smell of garlic and talcum powder mixed—and a general impression of lithe, small-buttocked blue-jeaned masculinity, combined with a face of almost feminine beauty: wide-eyed, red-lipped, clear-complexioned, to which a brown silky goatee beard that seemed to come from another age, and to belong to another person entirely, added a slight touch of—what? Ah yes. The freak show at a touring circus to which Gemma had once taken Hermione, Hannah, Helen, Hortense and little Alice, gaining free entrance under an insecure canvas flap—the price of admission clearly being beyond Mrs. Hemsley's purse—and which had caused such an uproar in all their lives. Little Alice, though sworn to secrecy, had told her mother about the visit, thus betraying Gemma, her guilty love; and although Mrs. Hemsley, once informed, could have forgiven the excursion, she could not easily forgive the degree of deceit entailed in accomplishing it without her knowledge. Hers were the deceased vicar's children, after all, and not just anyone's—and since the new incumbent, a lively, fresh-faced youth, seemed too interested in his choirboys to set about providing the village with another generation of clerical children, the ex-vicar's wife felt her responsibility the more. No wonder she made a fuss. Uproar!

Be that as it may, Mr. Fox's arrival, departure and passing blessing left Gemma breathless with admiration and a strong sense of vindication, as if the disastrous visit to the freak show to see the hermaphrodite, the mermaid and the bearded lady had after all had a richer meaning, a greater significance, than either she or Mrs. Hemsley had at the time realised. Perhaps Alice knew it, somewhere in her heart, and wished then, as always, to protect Gemma from the consequences of her own destructive desires.

"I've done the parrots," said Marion sourly. "I'll

show you the filing. If the names are double-barrelled, and they often are, I file under the last name. Pinks in this drawer, green in that, and whites in here. The parrot cage needs cleaning once a week in hot weather, once a month in cold. Otherwise things start to smell, and Mr. Fox wouldn't like that."

"And Mr. First? What's he like?"

"Don't be greedy," was all Marion would say to that, and there was a look of fear upon her face that Gemma did not understand. What need for fear is there, after all, in those who minister to the needs of the powerful, be they kings, bishops, business executives, the designers of spun-sugar jewellery? The barber survives the palace revolution, the chambermaid the coup, and the good clean typist is always in demand although blood may flow on the boardroom floor. And Marion, her button eyes efficiently if sadly focussed on the complexities of the Fox and First card index, the columns of matching figures which to her had the sanctity of beauty—this side balancing that in proper harmony—would be abused, exploited, over-worked, underpaid, but truly valued—as long, at any rate, as her eyesight lasted. So why was Marion afraid?

Gemma pauses in her tale. Victor comes striding out of the house from the direction of the library, and passes out of sight amongst the colonnades and statuary.

"What a handsome man Victor is," says Gemma. "Some men get so much better looking as they get older. I take it you don't much care for your own generation?"

"No."

"Who would? I do sympathise. Nevertheless, it seems hardly fair to your elder sisters."

"I'm the eldest."

"I was speaking of the human family, not your mother's."

Elsa blushes, and grinds her tiny teeth. She is becoming tired of being condescended to. Some revolutionary spark ignites within her. If she can bed Gemma's husband, by God she will. To serve her right, if nothing else.

"Never mind," says Gemma, patting Elsa's large white knee. "I know just how you feel. And I know I'm very old-fashioned, speaking of men as goodies to go round. But remember the dark ages in which I was reared—in which man was one's future meal ticket. But you have been reared in the brilliant light of self-awareness; you have all the advantages. You are free from the fear of pregnancy, free to choose an equal as a mate, to live with him as and when you please, by mutual consent. You can be as sexually active or idle as you wish, and no one will think any the worse of you for that. You can stand on your own two feet. It just seems rather unfair of you to stand on Janice's toes. She's not nearly as agile as you. Though I grant you, half the size."

Victor, to Elsa's relief, now approaches them. He is in a good humour.

"Love your chiffonière, Gemma," he says. "The one in the library room. But why have you painted it with scarlet enamel?"

"Because I like scarlet enamel." She is stubborn.

"You're a big girl now," says Victor indulgently. "You're too old to know what you like."

"Advice about what I like and what I don't like comes expensive."

"Not mine."

"Is Hamish selling you all that boring stuff in the billiard room?"

"So far."

"Good. I suppose it isn't boring at all, but valuable, and you're laughing at us?"

"Only out of the side of my mouth you can't see.

And did you know that your ironing table is oyster oak?"

Gemma laughs merrily.

"Elsa," she says, "perhaps you'd better go and see if Hamish needs you in the library. I want to talk business to Victor."

"Yes, run along," says Victor, just as he used to say to Wendy, "run along," from the very first day she rose from crawling position to sway on her tiny feet. Eventually she became good at running, and made a very good wing at hockey, and later even occasionally captained the school team.

Elsa gets up—her knees creak as she does so—and walks towards the library. Her heart hurts. The kedgeree weighs heavy in her stomach. She is conscious of the pair of them watching her, and of the movement of her buttocks in her jeans. Before breakfast, since clearly it was going to be a hot day, she cut off their bottoms to make knee-length shorts. Now she wishes she hadn't.
Gemma calls. Elsa turns back.

"Elsa," she says, "how many are there in your family, of which you say you are the eldest?"
"Seven."
"How wonderful! How fertile! It runs in the blood, I suppose. Hamish and I are such dead ends. Childless. It's a matter of grief to both of us. But it makes us rather more vivid people, I daresay; so much natural energy dammed up inside us!"

Elsa opens her mouth to speak, but Gemma nods her dismissal and Victor declines to meet her eye. Elsa goes to the library. Hamish sits at the head of the table in a tall Jacobean side chair. He wears an open-necked shirt, as if to emphasise the informality of the occasion, but his movements are still and agonised, and his face is coloured with embarrassment. He toys with a carved ivory-handled paper knife, but carefully, as if to illustrate the sharpness of its cutting edge. Hamish smiles, with difficulty. Smiling does not come easily to him at the best of times, but he has seen other people do it and he knows it has to be done.

"So you deigned to come." His voice is harsh.

"I was sent." Elsa stands first on one foot and then the other. So she stood before her headmistress, who had the same difficulty with smiling, the same rasping voice, harsh with the genuine attempt to be kind.

"You girls are all the same. None of you are prepared to accept the slightest responsibility for your actions." So says Hamish now, as once the headmistress said.

"If we're all the same, why pick on me?" Did she say that then? Or did she merely want to and lacked the courage?

Hamish stops smiling. He waves Elsa towards a polished pig bench, on which she sits.

"Well?" she asks when his silence becomes oppressive.

"You don't seem to like me very much," he complains. "What was Victor talking about? You know he had the nerve to offer me two hundred for this table? Two hundred for a really majestic piece of oak like this. I've seen one like it at Sotheby's go for over four thousand."

"Perhaps it's a reproduction. They sometimes are." She knows that much.

"Nonsense," he says. "Just look at that wood. It's got a nice bit of age to it, you can tell . . . Can't you?" He's unsure.

"They beat them with chains, sometimes, to age them."

"People like Victor?"

"Of course not!" she cries. "Victor's the most trust-worthy man in this world. He has his hang-ups, more than I thought, but he wouldn't ever lie about furniture. He loves furniture as he loves . . ." Her voice trails away. What does Victor love? Hamish smiles his cracked smile.

"—loves his life," she finishes.

"He loves you? Does he?" How he grates!

"He'd do anything for me, and I'd do anything for him," she says, but again her voice dies away, its power and passion fading. These are yesterday's truths, not today's. Yesterday she loved Victor, childishly, as a child might love its father, with the glory of omnipo-tence; today she is left with his reality, and yesterday's words still leaping to her lips. Tears start to her eyes.

"You are crying," says Hamish, and turns his own head away. Tears glint behind his thick glasses. So, occasionally, her stepfather would turn his head, stum-bling unexpectedly into self-pity, saying "The men don't like me. I have no natural authority. All they notice are the stripes on my arm."

"You shouldn't cry," says Hamish. "Something as beautiful as you shouldn't cry. I love beautiful things. I reach for them, but they're always just beyond me. Do you understand? I'm crippled."

Elsa stops crying, interested. What does he mean?

"I'm not much good at the things I want to be good at."

Sex, does he mean?

"You can make money," she consoles him.

He shrugs that off, irritated. A smell of hot oil fills the air; a dark mist swirls before her eyes. Some of the lamp wicks, she notices, are burning unevenly; others are too high. Elsa is familiar with the problem. Her mother Sheila would light the rooms by oil when the electricity supply, as frequently happened, was disconnected for nonpayment of the bill. Now she attends to the lamps. He watches, marvelling.

"I did your typing," he claims. "Doesn't that make you like me?"

"No. It gives me the shivers."

"There'll be some more tonight. Gemma will want it done."

"Then I'll do it myself."

"She won't think much of your typing."

Elsa hesitates; she wants Gemma's good opinion. But then she wants everyone's good opinion. Some girls do. She knows it, and knows it gets her into trouble.

"I enjoy typing," he says. "I love to see it emerging clean and neat upon the page. It's the nearest I get to painting pictures. To be an artist—now that would be to be a man. To write a book, to have a finger on the pulse of humanity . . . You're laughing at me?"

"No," she says, and she isn't. He takes off his glasses and rubs his tired eyes. She looks at him, safe in the knowledge that now she can at least see better than he can. Without its glasses, his face seems vulnerable, his eyes tired and sad. Yes, I could, she thinks. I could make him better. I could please him, and please Victor, and please Marina—and Gemma need never know. And if I don't particularly please myself, does it matter?

Once Elsa, as a consequence of wearing tight jeans and nylon knickers, and taking antibiotics, developed a nasty case of vaginitis. The ensuing inspections, probings and treatments, in a teaching hospital and in full view of thirty medical students, had perhaps eroded her romanticism, and the notion that penetration by the male, whether with the scalpel, the probe or the penis, must necessarily be accompanied by love.

If I could put up with all that, she thinks, I can surely put up with Hamish. It would be selfish not to.

"All right," she says. "If you want to do my typing tonight, you'd better."

"I look forward to it," he says. "I really do. I'm not just doing this on medical advice."

"Medical advice?" She pauses on her way out into the sunlight, the patio and the swimming pool.

"I have some small trouble with my prostate gland. The doctor says sexual activity is the best remedy."

Elsa blinks, but whether from the sudden strong light or from astonishment she scarcely knows herself.

5

"Hamish started life as a shorthand-typist," says
Gemma. She and Elsa sit companionably by the pool
and wait for lunch. Gemma has recovered her good
humour; Victor has gone in to talk to Hamish. Elsa is
at ease, sad in her heart, but confident that she at least
has only her own pain to put up with, and not the
added burden of other people's.

"He was in the army. They trained him for it. When
he came out he used his demob money to start a
secretarial agency. Then another, and then a chain of
them, stretching nationwide. He very seldom smiles,
have you noticed? It makes people take him seriously.
Soon he diversified and started a chain of low-calorie
sandwich bars to feed the girls he'd found jobs for, and
then into the house-plant business to provide greenery
for their window sills. There were other enterprises of
an artistic nature on the way. My husband loves beautiful things. Have you noticed?"

"Yes."

"He prefers them inanimate to animate, by and large.
He likes to know where he is. Girls and appetites and
vegetation are all difficult to control, being likely to wilt
and fade for no apparent reason, so eventually he concentrated on plastic plant pots: the solid basis in which

others more easily creative than he can root their aspirations, and watch them grow and develop and blossom —or else die, of course, from lack of some essential nourishment. Sometimes I think that is happening to me."

The pain in Elsa's heart swells and bursts. She cries.

"You're not crying for me, I hope?" enquires Gemma. "How sweet of you, if you are."

"I'm crying for all of us," says Elsa, and so she is. For the things she should and could have had, and never did and never would.

"That's very generous of you," says Gemma. "It seems to me you are rather too generous, one way and another. Has something in particular upset you?"

"No."

"Perhaps you are worrying about meeting Janice? Would you like me to telephone and put her off?"

"No."

"Did Hamish say something to upset you? He can be tactless. I love my husband very much, but I am not blind to his faults. I'm sure he can't have criticised your typing; you're so very good at it. I do envy you. I never had the opportunity to put mine into practice, as I was telling you. Was it Hamish?"

"No."

"You weren't in the library very long. Well, never mind. I had a nice little chat with Victor. He's so fond of you. What are you going to do about Victor?"

"Do? What do you mean?"

"You shouldn't let him exploit you. You've given up everything for him and got nothing in return."

"I've got him." Yesterday's truths again, not today's.

"Of course. How silly of me. You have Victor, and that makes up for everything—family, job, flat, future."

"It wasn't much of a family, or a job, or a flat, or any kind of future: not without him! I wanted to start everything fresh. I wanted to be something and do something."

"Ah, yes, Victor said. A rung in the ladder in your clamber up the world."

"Victor said that?" Elsa is tremulous.

"There's nothing to be ashamed of. I was no different."

Gemma proceeds with her tale. And although, like any tale told in retrospect, heightened in the telling, purified of pain, reduced to anecdote and entertainment (as a thin stock, boiled away, becomes a thick and tasty sauce) it comes to Elsa more like a burnt offering to the gods of fortune and misfortune than as a solid meal for the nourishment of the self, she is nonetheless able to gain some fortification from it.

1966.

Gemma took off her mother's pearl pendant and put on her great-aunt's crucifix. Everything, she feared, was going too well. In less time than it took the earth to go once around the sun she had escaped from the Hemsley household, found an interesting job, a friend in the form of Marion, and fallen in love. If she stood clear of the window she would not fall out. Now all that remained was to find somewhere to live, as her suitcase, brown fibre with feeble bolts reinforced by string, reminded her. Perhaps God would help her in this, as the pendant had helped her so far. She fingered the crucifix.

Marion regarded the suitcase with disfavour, and presently hid it behind a curtain woven out of silver string.

"It wouldn't do for Mr. Fox to see that," she remarked. "Mr. First will see it, of course, when he goes through to his office, but that doesn't matter. Mr. First is a bit like me. We're neither of us much good in the showroom. Him with his dandruff and me with my spots. The customers are beautiful people like you."

"Like me?"

"Yes. So you'll take over the selling, if you don't mind. I can't stand the customers, to tell you the truth. They waste hours of your time and never buy a thing."

"But I've never done any selling. I'm trained as a shorthand-typist."

"Who wasn't? It's perfectly easy. Just never let them take anything on spec, and never accept a check without ringing the bank first. I wish I worked in a solicitor's office, I really do. Or if only I could do social work, or train as a nurse . . ."

"I'm sure you could."

"No. It's no use. I'm saving for my next holiday. I always am. We're a three-holiday family, you see. I always tell myself I'll give my notice after I come back, back I never get around to it. And my family likes me working here. It's a privilege. I meet people I never would in the run of things. Elizabeth Taylor was in once. They can't get over that."

Gemma shakes her head in wonderment. So far from Cumberland so soon!

"If I were you, dear," says Marion, "if you don't mind me saying, I'd take off that crucifix."

"Why?"

"It's cheap, isn't it?"

"Yes. Woolworth's."

"If you were a princess you'd get away with it; being what you are, you can't."

Plain, stoical Marion talked with the ease and confidence of a trained economist buying a joint of beef from an incompetent butcher. Gemma removes her crucifix.

"My great-aunt gave it to me," she said. "She's the only relative I have. She lives in Cumberland, in an old people's home."

"Cumberland's ever so nice," said Marion. "We went

there one year. We take our first and second holidays abroad, and the third one here at home."

Gemma dropped the crucifix into the lemon-shaped wastepaper basket.

"I didn't mean you to throw it away," Marion protested.

"But if it's cheap and nasty—"

"Your great-aunt gave it to you—"

"I don't care about the past," said Gemma, and meant it. "I only care about the future."

"It's a crucifix," said Marion. "I'm sure it's unlucky to throw a crucifix away. Stands to reason. I'll look it up under 'Superstitions' in the *Occult Weekly* special supplement. My mother's collecting the whole edition. We're up to T and U, so you're in luck."

So Gemma, indifferent, placed the abandoned crucifix in the top left-hand drawer of her lime-coloured, egg-shaped desk with its starry Perspex top, and on it the IBM golfball in mellow-yellow and pineapple, but without a plug at the end of its cord. In the left-hand top drawer, Gemma found what remained of her predecessor: blue nail varnish, a silver hair spray, two false fingernails, two packets of crisps (the new vinegar flavour), one half-melted Mars bar, a tube of Pretty Feet for the removal of hard skin from the heels and a lucky Cornish pixie.

"Ophelia left her lucky pixie behind," observed Gemma.

"She got herself out of here," said Marion briskly, "that was the main thing." And then, quickly (after the manner of little Hortense when she said no, it wasn't her who wet the bed but a strange little boy had come in and done it), she added, "She was wasted here, that's all I mean. Her speeds were so very good: ninety typing and one hundred and thirty shorthand. She was a nice girl, but she wasn't right. Now I'm just popping out for some fresh coffee. I get freshly roasted beans every day and start grinding them the moment I put on the kettle. That way we preserve its full aroma. Or so Mr. Fox says. He's very particular."

A look of anxiety crossed her face. She hesitated.

"Marion," said Gemma, "is something the matter?"

"Nothing," lied Marion. In just such a tone would Hannah say "nothing"—home from school in tears and with a black eye and a torn dress.

"You won't be frightened when I'm away?" Marion asked.

"Of course not."

"Don't go near the window. If there's a knocking sound it's only the sea gulls. They're such a pest, and half-blind, most of them. Try and ignore them."

"What if a customer comes?"

"Almost no one comes before midday. They stay in bed during the morning, after the night before. It gets ever so lonely here. I'm glad you're here, Gemma, I really am. I wouldn't want to lose you."

And Marion took a ten-shilling note from the smoked-glass petty-cash jar and went out to buy the coffee.

Mr. Fox came rattling down the spiral iron staircase—he had changed into a cream linen suit—and passed through the office with no more than a friendly whistle to the birds, who rose in a cackle, and with not so much as a glance at Gemma.

Gemma, both disappointed and relieved, bent her pretty head over the filing system, trying in vain to remember Part 5 of the Office Routine section of her correspondence course, and presently felt a kind of cold dead breath, only slightly tainted with the warm exhalation of the living, on the back of her neck.

She jumped and shrieked, and there stood Mr. First, grey-faced, pale-haired, ageless behind businessman's rimless glasses, his lips drawn back in the bloodless snarl she had quite happily observed in television versions of the story of Count Dracula, but had scarcely ever expected to encounter in real life.

"Who are you?" he asked, as a squire might address a poacher.

"I work here," replied Gemma.

"No one would mistake you for a customer. What's your name? Or do you prefer to be the cat's mother? Ha-ha!"

Thus Gemma's teachers had been accustomed to address her, with sarcasm and insult mixed. It was not so new to her, nor surprising, though she had always hoped that as she grew older the insults of her superiors would become less frequent, and finally die away altogether. But no.

"I'm Gemma James," she replied with dignity and ease. "The new temp."

"Oh, God," said Mr. First, and showed the whites of his eyes. "Here, file these. In the P.R. file. Do you expect me to walk around holding them all day?"

"They're photographs," protested Gemma. Nowhere in *Lesson Five to Eight, Filing,* had there been any mention of photographs, and Gemma felt, like many an earnest student before her, that the world must be wrong because the book couldn't possibly err.

"File them under the name of the person photographed, idiot."

"But there's more than one person in some of them."

"The person in the foreground. Are you mad? You are certainly incompetent. I hope you are mad. If the agency sends us somebody incompetent that's fate, and a fairly usual one at that. If they send us a mad person we can sue."

"Mr. Fox is in all the photographs. He may not be

the nearest to the camera, but he is certainly smiling hardest. I shall file them under F."

Mr. First snatched the photographs out of Gemma's hand.

"On second thought," he said, "leave the filing to Marion. Tell her to come and see me when she gets back. Is Mr. Fox in?"

"I think so," said Gemma.

"What has thinking got to do with it? You either know or you don't. What a waste of time you girls are."

It seemed to Gemma, however, as Mr. First gazed up the circular staircase towards Mr. Fox's quarters, that he was in the grip of some kind of terrible indecision, and that his rudeness to her had been automatic bluster, designed to mask anxiety and loss. Just so had little Hermione nagged and stamped whenever anything went wrong. Mind you, Hermione had been Gemma's least favourite Hemsley child, Alice the most favourite.

"He's not in," said Mr. First, with what almost sounded like relief, and Gemma—whose face in those days was normally impassive, shot him such a forgiving smile, all white, pearly teeth and brilliant eyes, that Mr. First blushed—purply hue, rather than a rosy glow, creeping unbecomingly over grey skin, but a blush all the same.

"You should smile more often," barked Mr. First, and backed from the room, spectacles flashing in the light reflected from the green spun-glass chandeliers, bouncing off the red wings of a flying, squawking parrot, so that Gemma could not see the expression in his eyes.

Gemma took a half crown from the petty-cash jar and went to buy an electric plug for the typewriter. ("Initiative and Its Rewards," *Lesson Eleven, Office Routine.*)

She forgot to buy a screwdriver. On her return she used her nail file instead. Lesson Eleven, again: *Resourcefulness*.

When Marion returned, she seemed displeased at the event.

"The office should never, never be left unattended."

"But there was nothing to do here."

"That's your good fortune," snapped Marion.

"Mr. First came in and was horrible," said Gemma, hoping to elicit pity.

None came. "That's normal," said Marion. "Ugly men are always horrible to pretty girls. I have a girl friend who's a model. When we're out in her mini, she gets roughed up all the time by lorry drivers and middle-aged men in Volvos. I'm afraid to go out with her. She only asks me along for contrast, anyway. Me, I'm just the plain friend every pretty girl needs."

If Marion was hoping for contradiction, Gemma could give her none. She asked instead how photographs should be filed.

"Under the name of the event, stupid," said Marion, and slammed down the striped electric kettle so hard that the pure water (bottled in France) spilled down onto the flowery formica of the kitchen annex. Then she ground the coffee so furiously in the grinder that the windows shook, and birds on either side of the thin glass rose noisily into the air.

Gemma retreated to her desk and studied the photographs more closely. Most showed groups of young men and women; slender men with shirts unbuttoned to the waist, and women likewise, and each with a Fox and First navel stone glittering to advantage. In all the photographs Mr. Fox hovered, well-buttoned, white-shirted, the king taking pleasure in his court. And he smiled just as confidently as any king might smile who has his paid executioner at his elbow.

Well, a typist can look at a king. If a cat can do it, so can she.
The first photograph was put down, and the second, and at the third she paused.

"Marion," called Gemma, "who's this in this photograph? She looks like the cook, wandered in from the kitchen."

And so she did, her face leering over Mr. Fox's shoulder, out of place and out of fashion, forty if she was a day; fat, grossly fat, with a pendulous lip, bulbous eyes, rolls of flesh spoiling what line there was of her dowdy dress—and her cheek leaning against Mr. Fox's own. And still Mr. Fox smiled.
Marion put down the coffee, took the photograph and tore it into shreds. Her hands were trembling.

"Why did you do that?" Gemma asked. "I only wanted to know where in the file it belonged."
"It doesn't belong anywhere."
"Everything can be filed. It said so in *Lesson Six, Office Routine*. And if things can, people can."
"She can't be, and that's that. Thank God."
"Why not?"
"Never mind."
"Is she someone's relative?"
"Yes she is, Nosy Parker. Mr. First's sister."
"There you are!" Gemma is triumphant. "One would never have guessed," she added. "He's so thin and she's so fat."
"Glands," observed Marion. "Something wrong with her thyroid. And I wouldn't be surprised if Mr. First had acromegaly. That's a disfunction of the adrenal glands. Giant-like excrescences form."
"You do know a lot," admired Gemma. Well, flattery is easy.

"We believe in self-improvement," muttered Marion. "My dad has a teach-yourself-diagnosis manual. He reads it aloud in the evenings. Anyway, do me a favour, just forget Mr. First's sister and forget I ever mentioned her."

"Why?"

"Because she's dead, if you want to know."

"I could file her under C for Corpse."

Oh, Mrs. Hemsley, you were right to get rid of Gemma. You managed it just in time.

Marion, pale-lipped, does not reply.

"How did she die?"

"Never mind." Marion poured boiling water onto freshly ground coffee in a heated pottery jug—a rather ordinary jug, but with a brown French glaze—and stirred with a wooden spoon especially reserved for the purpose.

"But what happened?" Gemma persisted.

"Nothing."

"You don't get dead just by nothing."

Even Mr. Hemsley had died of a coronary, the arrival of a blood clot at the heart, and not just disappointment at the birth of his fifth and final daughter Alice. Everyone knew.

"If you must know," said Marion, driven to desperation, "she killed herself."

"How?"

"I don't want to talk about it."

"How?" So Gemma had bullied Hermione, whose habit it was to come home from school with money from undisclosed sources hidden in her coat pocket.

"She jumped out of a window." In just such a distressed manner would the truth eventually burst from Hermione's lips.

"Why?"

"She felt like it, I suppose."

"What window?" But Gemma turned cold even as she spoke. She knew the truth.

"That window there right behind you, if you want to know, and only last week too, and that's why Ophelia left. She left in a hurry or she'd never have left her fake nails. They're such a price!"

"And everyone else just goes on using the office? Mr. First comes in and out, where his own sister . . . It's dreadful."

"Don't be silly. All you do when people die is just carry on as usual. If people choose to kill themselves they don't deserve any respect. And she didn't die here; she died at the bottom. I daresay Mr. First crosses the road directly now, instead of walking along the front of the building to the crossing, but I wouldn't know for sure, and I wouldn't think it was my business anyway. And I'm not going to give up a good job so near to holiday time, and you can't think what they've invested in this building. It's a swinging London showpiece; they couldn't possibly move their offices elsewhere."

Gemma sat trembling in front of the typewriter. Something more serious than the absence of an electricity supply ailed it: now that it was plugged in and switched on, the warning lights glowed red, but the carriage would not move. She had only a theoretical knowledge, in any case, of electric typewriters: *Chapter Ten, Office Equipment, Its Care and Maintenance*. "A good secretary, like good housewife . . ."

"What's the matter now?" Marion had recovered. Her voice was mean and sharp, like Great-Aunt May on a bad day.

"I haven't been trained to use an electric machine," muttered Gemma.

"No one's asking you to type."

"Then what am I to do?"

"Take Mr. Fox up his coffee."

"I'm not the maid."

"I don't know who is, if you're not. Look, if you don't like it you can go straight back to the agency and they'll find someone else not so squeamish. It's all the same to me. And you can get a job copy-typing in a pool at seven-and-six an hour, where they deduct from your wages if your hands leave the typewriter. Do you want that?"

"No."

Gemma took up the silver tray: the pottery jug, the French green coffee cup and saucer, gold-rimmed. She had pretty hands; she thought these accessories suited them rather well. Then she put the tray down.

"But Mr. Fox went out."

Mrs. Hemsley, did Gemma do that kind of thing to you? Wait until you'd found all five children's swimming costumes and swimming caps and five dry towels, and then disclose that the school swimming pool had been empty for a week? Gemma did, frequently. She was forgetful. Or so she said.

Before Marion could express her anger, Mr. First's door burst open. Mr. First waved his small fist in the doorway. Marion went pale.

"I thought I told you to come straight to my office, Marion."

"I'm sorry. Gemma didn't tell me." So much for loyalty.

"I forgot," said Gemma. "Sorry."

"Yes," said Mr. First. "I imagine it is your fault. Do you think that because you have a pretty face no one will notice you're an imbecile? I am astounded by that agency. It sends in girls better fitted to potato-picking than office work. Marion, come in at once and take dictation. You've kept me waiting at least ten minutes."

Marion, rebuked and docile, took up her shorthand pad and went into Mr. First's office. Mr. First slammed the door. The display mobiles trembled; their chains clanked; the parrots rose screaming in their latticed mosque; lights and colours flashed. Gemma was alone.

Gemma hated.
Gemma hated all employers. Employers could be rude to her, could insult her, and she could do nothing. She must hold her tongue and just stand there and try not to cry. If she wanted her wages, that is.

"If I were a man," thought Gemma, "he wouldn't talk to me like that . . ." And of course he wouldn't.

Gemma, who seldom wept, now cried into her electric typewriter. She remembered that she was homeless; that she was tired and sleepy, having spent an uneasy night in a train; that she was sitting in a room from the window of which someone had recently plunged to their death. She remembered that she was an orphan; that Mrs. Hemsley had proved unkind; that she had nowhere to sleep that night; that in spite of a cheese-and-lettuce roll bought when she went out to get the electric plug for the typewriter, she was still extremely hungry.
Gemma laid her head upon her typewriter. She cried a little and slept a little, and cried and slept some more. Presently she felt a hand upon her shoulder. Young, firm, kindly fingers. Mr. Fox. His cream suit slightly crackling, of so rare and delicate a fibre was it made (from the bark of some exotic tree).
Mr. Fox. His moustache curling, eyes glinting. Mr. Fox.

"Ah, coffee!" said Mr. Fox. "Rather cold, isn't it? That's not like our Marion at all. I hope she isn't falling off."

At least he hadn't said falling out, though for a moment Gemma thought he had. But surely she must have misheard. Mr. Fox!
Gemma loved Mr. Fox.

6

Love!

"Love," says Gemma grandly to Elsa, "is what the nubile young feel when their search for a mate reaches an appropriate conclusion. It is the tool nature uses to perfect her species. We do not, cannot, choose to love out of admiration for the other's spiritual qualities; we love where love seems right, gene calling to gene, as country cats call to each other across fields.

"Therefore!" says Gemma, "Elsa, I shan't ask you why you love Victor; I shall simply accept that you do because you say you do. Perhaps your blue eyes need to match his troubled green ones to produce a serene and grey-eyed child?"

("Oh," says Elsa, "I don't know about that. I don't think either of us want babies: I mean, it wouldn't be sensible.")

"Ah," says Gemma, "so you mean to join the rest of us who, by reason of age, or self-discipline, or common sense, or fear, or a simple malfunction of Fallopian tube or testes, are destined to deny nature its genetic self-expression? Well, well!

"In that case," says Gemma, still grandly, "love will be for you what it is for me—the emotion we feel for

74

those who have the capacity to hurt us. Is that what you want, Elsa? Elsa, are you listening?"

"Does Hamish hurt you?" asks Elsa, horrified.

"Yes. He hurts me because he is so often away making money I enjoy spending. He hurts me because he is sorry for me, and because his inner disabilities are such that they match my more open, more dramatic ones. He hurts me by being tired and ill and unhappy, so that I cannot take credit for making him happy. He hurts me by disliking my friends almost as much as I dislike his. He hurts me by buying antiques himself instead of leaving it to me. I have few pleasures in this world. I love him, so I put up with the hurt he causes me; indeed, it is because he hurts me that I know he loves me, and to live with a husband one loves is good fortune indeed.

"And at least he is not unfaithful to me," she adds, and falls silent.

Gemma smiles at Elsa: the smile of a good and loving wife, albeit in a wheelchair.

Elsa smiles at Gemma, wretchedly: the smile of the daughter who has stolen the love of the father, or means to do so.

Gemma smiles back, all innocence.

Elsa loves! How she loves. She is all love. It is her excuse. She loves her mother, but does her mother love her back? Elsa doubts it. Sheila, drinking gin and tonics in the pub with her husband, Elsa's stepfather, her hair newly streaked; laughing and carrying on, no doubt, as if she wasn't the mother of seven children, the eldest of whom has run off to live with a married man—well, share a Regency sofa with him in the back of an antique shop—and has been forbidden to darken her door again.

"You go with that man if you like," said Sheila. "You're a big girl now. Give up your job and your bed-sitting room and honest folks' good opinion if you must; ruin some poor woman's life, if that's how it grabs you, but don't come back here with your dirty washing for

me to do. I don't know what's come over you, Elsa,
I really don't."

Love.

It came over Sheila once, and there she was, carrying
Elsa. But that was a long time ago—not that she's forgotten.

Elsa's father was a big blond man, a sailor home from
the sea, and Sheila has never forgotten. A golden dan-
delion waved above her nose on the cliffside as Elsa
was conceived. Blue sky, blue eyes; gold flower, gold
hair. The first of seven, and the best, the very best.
Sheila loves Elsa.

"Out you go, Elsa, and don't think you've got my
blessing. You haven't. And don't come back here whin-
ing at Christmas time because he's gone back to his
wife."

"He won't, Mum."

"Don't call me Mum. So far as I'm concerned you're
a motherless child. Double gin and tonic please, and
don't forget the ice and lemon."

Victor dear. Victor my love. Block my ears, shut my
eyes; your tongue in my every opening, blacking out all
memory, all sense. Victor, transport me to other lands
so that what she said can no longer be heard; Victor,
be my mother, my missing father, my everybody, all my
love, forever and ever. Amen.

Elsa loves Victor more than she fears Gemma. But
Elsa also loves her mother. She is a good girl. She opens
her mouth to blurt out Gemma's husband's proposition,
via Victor, and her own acceptance of it. But Victor
stands beside her. Elsa shuts her mouth.

"Hot!" he says. "How do you keep the plants watered,
Gemma? Illegal hose-pipe after dark?"

"We have our own well and irrigation system," says Gemma. "Naturally. Now I must leave you two love-birds together and see about Wendy and Elsa's cake. I will have to make it myself, of course. The trouble with Asiatic servants is that not for love nor money can they make a simple sponge."

How easy it is for Gemma to make an exit, thinks Elsa enviously. She presses a button and glides away. Elsa, using her feet, stumbles, blushes, is misunderstood or fails to understand—and leaves, one way or another, with her own inadequacies fresh in everyone's mind.

"You made quite a hit with Hamish," says Victor to Elsa. "There was no need to be quite so enthusiastic."

"I won't if you don't want me to."

"It's not what I want; it's what you want. If you don't want to, I certainly don't want to put pressure on you. It's the last thing I want; you'd never let me forget it. On the other hand, if you want to make me happy, if you want to demonstrate to me that you're sexually free and truly liberated and that it's not all talk, then you certainly will. I spent twenty-two years with Janice and she was faithful to me and I was faithful to her, and in the end it meant nothing. Except we both missed out. And if I regret anything for Janice it was that: the necessity she felt to be faithful to me. We put ourselves in prison. No one put us there."

"What do you mean, you were faithful to Janice? You were always having affairs with your secretaries. You told me so. You were absolutely frank."

"Faithless with my body, faithful in my mind. You've no idea how guilty I felt, how it spoilt everything."

"And I was just the current one when you left Janice," says Elsa, full of self-pity. "I know all that." Victor looks pained.

"You underrate yourself and you underrate me. I hate it when you talk like that, Elsa. You sound cheap and cynical."

"I'm only trying to face facts, Victor."

And she is, she is, as if all facts were of necessity unpleasant and all truths hard. He takes her hand; she is
trembling.

"I don't want you to be unhappy, Elsa. I don't want
to be responsible for that. I made Janice unhappy. I
don't want to do it again."

Lunch settles Elsa's nerves, as a complimentary meal
served on an aircraft will do much to settle the stomach
of any nervous traveller. It is a gift, something thrown
in for free, and as in our experience good things and
bad things come grouped together, by virtue of the free
gift the plane seems the less likely to fall to the ground.
The meal is served by the pool, on a glass trolley with
gold wheels. It consists of jellied consommé spooned
into Waterford tumblers, topped with artificial whipped
cream and a spoonful of mock caviar, followed by cold
tongue and salad served with bottled salad dressing.

"The culinary taste in this household," remarks Victor, "is as confused as is its taste in antiques."

"Perhaps," remarks Elsa, "you will be able to help
Gemma there as well."

"I hope you are not jealous," murmurs Victor. "It
would hardly be reasonable if you were. Good heavens,
a middle-aged woman in a wheelchair!"

Clearly Elsa is being ridiculous.

"Victor," says Elsa presently, "what's a prostate
gland?"

"Not something I wish to consider. Some men have
trouble with it in later life. Malfunction interferes with
the urinary processes, I believe, and can make one more
or less impotent."

Elsa has not had first-hand experience of a man who

has trouble gaining an erection. Indeed, her only sexual intimacy so far has been with Victor, whose trouble— if trouble it be—has been the opposite: that of confining his manifest erections to convenient and appropriate places.

But Marina's other friend has a boyfriend who is occasionally impotent, so Elsa is not altogether ignorant of the problem. Tales have got back to her of the embarrassment of lying beneath a man whose member becomes unexpectedly defenceless and childlike, and she and Marina have helpfully read and re-read articles in *Cosmopolitan, Playboy, Mayfair, Playmate, Penthouse Forum* and magazines of even more explicit and colourful detail, which analyse the condition and suggest cures, some of which Marina thought her duty to pass on to her friend. They were not well received.

"Why do you want to know?" asks Victor now.

"Never mind," says Elsa.

"It must be very hard for a man not to be able to express physically what he feels emotionally," says Victor. "At least I've never had that problem."

While Victor and his girl friend sit in a rich man's house and eat caviar and jellied consommé, albeit not of the first rank, Victor's wife Janice and daughter Wendy sit in their suburban lounge, on the outskirts of London, and eat fish and chips from newspaper, and use up the last of the sea salt, left over from the days of Victor's husbandry. They eat with their fingers; all the cutlery is dirty and stacked in the double sink with the expensive mixer taps. The radio is on in the dream kitchen although no one is listening to it; the hall light is on although it is broad daylight; the television is on, although it is the middle of the day and only rubbish showing.

Wendy, who is exactly Elsa's age, but who averts her

eyes from newsstands that sell sex magazines, is still in her nightie and bathrobe. She is a plain, plump, peaceful, lazy girl with an interest in embroidery and very little else.

"Mum," says Wendy eventually, "it's rather nice with Dad not here."

"Yes," says Janice after a minute or so's reflection. "I know."

"Once you've got over the shock."

"That's right," says Janice, and she puts down her mug of coffee on the polished coffee table and does not even worry in case it leaves a mark, and what would Victor have to say then? And eats yet another chip without worrying about her figure and the appearance she will make at the firm's Ladies' Night.

"When things happen these days they just happen, and no one has a nervous breakdown," says Wendy. "If I haven't got a boyfriend that's my bad luck, not Dad's. I've got a patchwork quilt in the church sale— I didn't tell you—and I don't have to dread it not selling. If it does it does, and if it doesn't it doesn't."

Wendy hasn't said so much for years.

"Do we *have* to go and meet him tomorrow?" she entreats. "Supposing he decides to come home?"

Just suppose! For the last twenty years Janice has dutifully considered and talked out with Victor every practical and emotional problem that has arisen in the home and in the marriage. Just suppose! What then? I feel this. Do you feel that? Of course you do!
Only talk, and you will see
That I am all in all to thee.

"Is that unfair of me?" asks Wendy, in whom there is clearly something of Victor. "I suppose you must miss him. For sex and all that," she adds kindly, albeit mistakenly.

Since Victor left, Janice has been to bed with the insurance man who came to investigate a claim for a damp bedroom ceiling, and the furniture removal man who came to take away Victor's quadriphonic sound system, with its extension speakers in the bedroom; and others as well she can barely remember. She has discovered the irresistibility of sexual opportunity. It has nothing to do with her attractiveness, or lack of it. If she, a married woman with a missing husband, stands helplessly next to the matrimonial bed, the likelihood is that any man who happens to be in the room with her will bear her down upon it, as if moved by a kind of cosmic sense of responsibility towards her rather than by any base or disagreeable opportunism. She is comforted by the knowledge.

In the meantime Victor's sense of guilt towards her ensures that her bills and the mortgage are promptly paid, and the housekeeping money is almost double what it was when he was home. Nor is she any longer obliged to show him the household accounts weekly, and account for missing pennies. She no longer has to shop and cook for his evening meal; she no longer has to entertain friends she does not like, or wash up after them.
Wendy is companionable and easy. Weeds overrun the garden; dust collects in the house; the milkman has to beg her for the bottles back; she sleeps well, able to stretch over into Victor's side of the bed; she looks younger and prettier than she ever did. Her thoughts, her habits, her child, her bed, her home—they are all her own.

"We'll see what we feel like tomorrow," says Janice. "If you don't want the rest of your fish, can I have it?"

Gemma summons Elsa to her bedroom, which is in the

eastern turret. It is reached by means of an ornamental
lift. Gold doors open as Elsa approaches to reveal an
octagonal room. Sunlight filters mistily through the
greenish opaque glass of its long windows. A tropical
aquarium runs like a broad frieze around the room;
flashes of scarlet fin can be seen in and out of the
bubbles and the stirring water weed. The carpet on the
floor is sandy grey; the ceiling is of rippled, muted blue;
palms and ferns wave gently in the flow of some concealed air-conditioning system. A fountain fills the room
with the gentle sound of splashing water.

"It's like being under the sea," says Elsa.

"I'm so glad you said that," says Gemma. She is
wearing white, edged with bubbles of brown, like the
very summit of a breaking wave. "Because that's what
the designer promised me, and then I thought I could
do it better than he could and took over. I think rooms
should assert the personality and complement it, and
not just be a boring background to one's life. Don't
you think so?"

"Yes," says Elsa.

"At any rate I was told that by the only man I ever
loved—not counting Hamish, of course. You'll have a
taste for antiques all your life, did you know that?
You'll never be able to go back to the patterned carpets
and factory chairs and Woolworth's paintings of your
childhood. First love has that effect. You're very lucky,
Elsa. You might have fallen for a car maniac or a
yachtsman or a dedicated golfer, and learnt something
positively detrimental to your future survival. In later
years you won't regret having met Victor."

"I don't regret it now."

"Sit down," says Gemma, fondly, patting the frondy
pouf at the foot of her chair, "and I'll go on with my
story, my warning to wantons."

"I wish you wouldn't call me that."

"Why not? I don't mean to insult you. The only
sensible thing a pretty girl with no education can do

is live off men and get what she can out of it. Where would I be if I didn't have Hamish? Life for a rich woman in a wheelchair is not so bad; life for a poor one is fairly disagreeable, I imagine. I am only trying to help you to avoid the major pitfalls, the ones I didn't. Consider Miss Hilary, for example, the unfortunate lady in the employment agency who found me my job. I heard later that she killed herself. Miss Hilary worked hard all her life, and no doubt had a fiancé killed in the war—and after that carnage, remember, there simply weren't enough men to go round, and none left over for second chances, not if you had a big nose and a big loud laugh and big feet. Not like these days, when there's a surplus of men and a girl can pick and choose—well, look at you, Elsa! Miss Hilary certainly wasn't wanton, and much good it did her. She kicked and struggled all her life to keep her head above water, but she'd fallen in a particularly cold patch, and when finally she got her head up—a good job, running a department—the air was so damp and misty as to be almost no better than the water: barely breathable. I imagine she just gave up and went under. At least I found a sunny spot. And I daresay she thought that she was wicked, sending off girls of good appearance to model naked at Fox and First for art's sake. Though no doubt they'd have got there, one way or another, without her aid. Would you model jewellery naked for Victor, as I did for Mr. Fox?"

"If he wanted me to."

"You'd do anything he wanted?"

"Yes."

And so, it seems, she would. The coming night looms large in Elsa's mind. She feels already the press of Hamish's poor weak body struggling against her own. She looks forward to it and dreads it as one might a hospital operation: welcoming the appointed time for no other reason than it is appointed, and the attention,

the ministering, the drama; fearing death under the anes-
thetic, and pain on waking, if waking there be.

Hamish, lie close. Do your best or your worst or your
nothing. Give me something of your past and your power
and your wife. Do you lie here at night, Hamish, in
this very room, in the grey gauzy bed pushed back
against the wall as if it were of no importance? Along-
side Gemma, with her lost, dangling legs? Do you part
them by force or by habit, or have you lost heart altogether? Perhaps you never come here at all? Perhaps
you are her polite and daily husband, and not the
instinctive nightly one at all?
Hamish, Gemma is yours and you are Gemma's, by
virtue, night or day, of the grief you can cause her,
which she herself defined as love.

But Hamish, I mean to have you. Victor says so. And
I will afterwards have power over Hamish, and Victor,
and Gemma, and myself.

I will be free.

And afterwards perhaps Hamish will see me right, give
me some money. I could buy some new jeans, some
moisturiser, without having to ask Victor and having
him discuss at length the brand of jeans desired or the
morality of face cream. No, I would send any spare
money at once to Sheila. The new school term is
coming, the young ones will want new shoes and Sheila
is struggling to pay for them. Sheila will not hear of
the handing down of used shoes from older children
to younger. Such a practice is bad for the feet.

Oh mother, what is happening to me?

Gemma smiles at her in a kindly fashion. Elsa cannot
meet her eye.

   "Well, I was much the same at your age; I would

do anything for love. And it was a good job I had at Fox and First, by any standard. Does Victor pay you well?"

"I don't exactly get wages. If I need anything he gives me money. He's very generous."

"Does he stamp your insurance card?"

"I don't have one."

"Of course not. Why should you? Victor is your insurance against an unkind future. So he was to Janice. At any rate, you have somewhere to live not too hot, not too cold, not too damp, not too dry; otherwise I daresay the antiques would rust or warp or split. I was lucky too, in that respect. I failed to find a room of my own and went to lodge with Marion's family. I shared her bedroom. She wanted me to. She was accustomed to sharing with her gran, but when that old lady became incontinent and had to leave, she found herself lonely in a room all to herself. She suffered from night fears, poor girl. Understandably, as it turned out."

1966.

Swinging London! Yellow Rolls-Royces carrying pop stars from recording to recording; mini-cabs with darkened windows to hide the unknown excitements within; housewives carrying psychedelic shopping bags; the smell of marijuana rising in cinemas, public transport, and over polite dinner tables. The first brave schoolboy began to grow his hair long and was expelled for his pains. The barricades were not yet up, but the tumbrils rumbled in the distance. Oh, the fun of revolution before the bombs began to burst! Gemma, of course, heard no distant rumblings. She heard only the pounding of her own heart, the steady timeless pulse of love.

Gemma loved Mr. Fox. What's more, she believed what he said.

When Mr. Fox said to Gemma that first morning, in relation to the tepid coffee, that living was an art, not an experience, she believed him. It was also a selective process, Mr. Fox said, and the more stringent the selection the finer the end result would be. It was important to take a firm stand against the second-best: against tepid coffee, against pink angora sweaters and so on, and all things either spiritually, physically or emotionally lesser than they should be. He, Mr. Fox, was a creative artist responsible for wresting beauty out of the chaos of experience. Beauty was born out of beauty; therefore Mr. Fox tried to look only on what was beautiful.

"What do you do with the ugly things?" enquired Gemma.

"Burn them, break them, destroy them."

"What about ugly people? You can't destroy them." People, Mr. Fox admitted, could be a problem. In the meanwhile he required fresh coffee to be brought up to his penthouse, and would Gemma kindly oblige?

Gemma would.

Mr. Fox went upstairs. Now just as any mortal would, not two at a time, but three. Gemma marvelled. Such godlike energy!

Gemma set about making Mr. Fox's coffee. Gemma failed to close the lid of the coffee grinder properly so that when she switched it on, fragmented coffee beans flew into the air and about the office, as if a volcano had spewed its grit into the heavens. The noise brought Marion running from Mr. First's office. She seemed distressed. As for Gemma, she was laughing.

"It's the last straw! Now I have to sweep it up, I suppose. Who else is going to? I'd hand in my notice," said Marion, not for the first or last time, "if only it wasn't for my holiday pay. As for Mr. First, he's perfectly horrible. He just said he hoped he hadn't made you cry. That means he's glad he did."

"He did *not* make me cry."

"He liked you," said Marion. "But then everyone likes you. Even me."

And she got down on her hands and knees with the green and yellow dustpan and brush and swept and cried at the same time. She was distraught, and reminded Gemma of little Alice crying her heart out in the shrubbery, unmoved by offers of homemade sweets. "Gemma, don't ever leave us. Gemma, don't go. You're the only friend we've got."

But Gemma went.

"You will stay," begged Marion now. "You won't let Mr. First drive you away? You won't just not turn up tomorrow? I couldn't stand another new face."

"Of course I'll stay. I like it here. At least it's not boring, is it?"

"No, it's not. And what's more, if you're looking for somewhere to stay, you can come to my place. We've got a spare bed. My mum and dad would get on with someone like you. I'm a bit of a disappointment to them, to tell you the truth. I'm getting nightmares, you see. I can hardly bear to close my eyes. It's only since Mr. First's sister, and the accident. But I'm all upset, and that's the fact of it."

" 'Accident?' You said she jumped."

"Well, she wasn't dead when she landed and then she was run over by a car, so it was an accident, really. A traffic accident."

"No, it wasn't. It was suicide. Why did she do it?" Gemma persisted.

"She was making a nuisance of herself."

"What sort of nuisance?"

"I don't like to talk about it."

"Tell me!" Naughty Hannah, this time. Refusing to tell Mrs. Hemsley where she'd hidden the tin-opener. Hannah couldn't abide baked beans, which was a pity, since they were her staple diet.

"Miss First fancied Mr. Fox," Marion went positively

red in the face, just as Hannah did when blurting out the truth. "And Mr. First didn't like it. I don't want to talk about it, Gemma. You know what these new buildings are like; the walls are awfully thin. If you offer to pay my mum four pounds a week, she'll be ever so grateful, and my dad can drive us both up in the mornings. Did Mr. Fox really ask you to take up his coffee? Up to the penthouse?"

"Yes."

Time enough. Marion would presently disclose all. Hannah always confessed to the whereabouts of the tin-opener when hungry enough.

"Then I suppose you'll have to. But Gemma, dear, do be careful."

Up the circular staircase, round and round and round in the service of her beloved, Gemma noticed only that she had a broken fingernail. She must be very careful, she thought, to hide such a blemish. Such a falling away from perfection.

Mr. Fox's penthouse was an octagonal structure perched on the main roof of the building. Quick-growing ivy vine extended fronds and stickers over its eight windows. Within, he had contrived a yellowy jungle gloom: palms grew about the room; stuffed jungle animals glared from under and over metal furniture, upholstered for the most part in leopard skin. A flock of hummingbirds darted to and fro amongst the underbrush.

Mr. Fox was nowhere to be seen, but his voice came from the floor. "Is that my coffee? I've been waiting. What took you so long?"

Mr. Fox was in his bath. It was a steamy jungle pool, sunk into the floor, from which the smell of musk arose. The water was murky. Water lilies floated on the surface, through which his white, sinewy shoulders broke. His eyes were little and sharp and gleaming.

"I don't lie in the bath to get clean," remarked Mr. Fox, "but to get ideas. I clean myself first under a shower. Put the tray by the water's edge, my dear. And try not to blink or look surprised. It's rude to notice nudity, not rude at all to be nude."

"Yes, Mr. Fox."

"Do you like my bath?"

"Isn't it rather difficult to clean?"

Mr. Fox sounded quite peeved. "Now how would I know a thing like that?"

"Are the water lilies plastic?"

"To me, plastic is the worst of the four-letter words."

Gemma, trying to spell plastic in her head, put down the tray without remembering to hide her broken nail.

"One of your nails is broken," remarked Mr. Fox. "I hope we are not going to find you slovenly. Every movement, every activity, every object must be given its due; then such accidents don't happen. But you walk well, Gemma, and move gracefully. I like that."

"Thank you, Mr. Fox."

"Anytime," observed Mr. Fox, and sank deeper into his bath so that the water lilies swung gently over the surface, beneath which a rather slight, pale, naked, but clearly male body stirred. Gemma was accustomed to the bodies of females, but had had little contact so far with males, apart from a teacher or so, the doctor, the dentist and poor dead Mr. Hemsley, whose spirit lingered still in the house he left behind.

Little Alice, pulling on trousers instead of a skirt, saying, "That's what Daddy wants. I saw it in a dream."

Little Alice, with a daddy never seen in the flesh, but known in the spirit.

The unusual sight of Mr. Fox, white, gentle, bare beneath the water, moved Gemma to compassion. His body seemed vulnerable, as vulnerable as a girl's might be. Perhaps there was not much difference, after all, between him and her, between the male and the female? Perhaps he felt and hoped and suffered too, just as any woman might?

Gemma smiled at Mr. Fox.

Mr. Fox smiled at Gemma.

The world stood still.

Mr. Fox leapt from his bath, lithe, lily-white and dressed for some reason in red-and-black-striped swimming trunks. Mr. Fox embraced Gemma, so that her twin-set and skirt glistened with moisture.

"Your ear lobes are delicious," he said, nibbling them. "I look forward to a future in which they model many a pretty sugar ear-piece. But that's enough for now. Just go away downstairs and type, or whatever it is you do. And tomorrow, when I see you again, do try and wear something different, something more appropriate to the spirit of the age. There's a boutique next door—at least I think they've reopened; they had to close for repainting after a rather nasty accident in the street outside. Try them, at any rate."

But how Gemma was to afford new clothes Mr. Fox did not say. Nor did he offer to advance her any of next week's wages. Marion, however, offered to lend Gemma any of her gran's clothes she might care to have, and Gemma was able to array herself in some very pretty shawls, lacy dresses and granny boots left over from the days of Gran's youth at the turn of the century.

Marion's home in Finchley was abundantly cosy, and Marion's mother and father as kind as could be. The colours in their semidetached suburban house, with the narrow back garden where the marrows grew and the washing hung, were as vivid as in the Fox and First office and perhaps less unexpected.

Here, in the room where the family sat and ate their supper in front of the television, the carpet was of red Indian design, the wallpaper willow patterned, the curtains of flowered chintz, and the three-piece suite covered in tartan wool. Shelves, display cabinets and mantelpiece were crowded with mementos from holidays abroad: dolls of different nationalities were tacked around the walls, their arms raised, by virtue of the nails that held each beneath its armpits, in row upon row of forlorn entreaty.

On the first evening of her stay, Marion's mother Audrey, forewarned by a telephone call from Marion, came home especially early from the betting shop where she worked and made Gemma a special celebratory mixed grill. Liver, bacon, kidney, sausage, egg, chips and tomato, followed by tinned peaches and a rather strange custard and a strong cup of tea. After supper, leaving the three-leafed oak-veneered table and the place mats with scenes from the Italian lakes, Marion's father, Arthur, a compositor by trade, settled his solid, friendly bulk into one of the armchairs, took out his pipe and puffed a slow reflective puff or so. Audrey settled into the other chair with her knitting, and Marion and Gemma sat side by side on the sofa. Marion, who seemed surprisingly restless for someone who had eaten so much, leafed through holiday brochures. Gemma longed for bed, tried to keep awake, failed, and dozed.

Presently Arthur spoke.

"That was a good supper, Marion's mother. As good as any I remember. That was zabaglione with the peaches, Gemma. Real Italian zabaglione, made with brandy, not even wine. Made you sleepy, did it? Well, no harm done, Marion's friend. You know you're safe with us; that's why you sleep. Shall he who is amongst enemies sleep? Shall we have a drop of slivovitz to round the evening off? What do you say to that, Marion's friend?"

"Drop of what?" asked Gemma, startled.

"Slivovitz. Yugoslavian plum brandy. We were in Yugoslavia back in '61. Still some of the good old slivo in the cocktail cabinet. Gets a bit encrusted, but that makes it stronger. Are you warm enough, girl? You're a pale lass, not like our Marion."

"Boiled beetroot, I suppose you mean!" interposed Marion. "I'd be a shade less red if I didn't have to roast year in, year out in the southern sun."

Arthur ignored his daughter.

"Are you warm enough, Marion's friend? Shall I turn the electric log fire higher?"

"You're boasting, Marion's dad," said Marion's mum, proudly enough. "It's not manners. What will Gemma think?"

"She'll think we're like anyone else, which we are, but we're not ashamed of it. Proud of what we have, and not afraid to show it. Remember those Yugoslav roads, Marion's mum?"

"Call those roads, Marion's dad?"

The talk rose and fell between them; rising on one side of the electric fire, falling on the other. A baffled Marion in the middle supported the net. Back and forth.

"More like ditches," said Audrey. "Bump, bump, bump. And what with the goat's meat churning away inside and the yogurt too, I was heaving half the time. No, I didn't fancy Yugoslavia."

"It's Capri for us this year," said Arthur to Gemma.

"Valerie, that's Marion's mum's sister's eldest—our niece, as you might say—was meant to be coming too, but she went and got herself married to this fellow."

"And now they can't go away at all because of the mortgage," lamented Marion's mum. "Makes you think twice about marriage, doesn't it. And then the kids come along, and you know what they're like in foreign hotels. Especially if there's bidets. Well, you just can't do it. We never had more than just the one, for that very reason. Well, we didn't *know*, when we had her. Feeling all right, Marion? You're looking queasy."

"I suppose so." Marion was sulking.

"Poor Marion," said Audrey. "She's been that depressed lately. Never mind, a nice holiday will bring back the roses."

"It doesn't bring back the roses," cried Marion, with unexpected defiance. "It just makes me peel. Why do we always have to go south? I want to go to Scandinavia. And it's not the holiday doing me good, so much as working for it in that office does me bad. Especially overtime. On top of that great empty building with the birds banging against the glass, and those bloody parrots staring at you with their nasty eyes."

"You shouldn't speak like that of God's creatures," said Arthur, shaking his head at his wayward daughter.

How, wondered Gemma, could the world hold both the Ramsbottle family and Mr. Fox as well? If one was real, how could the other be too? Each so defiant, so certain about its own way of life. The notion came to Gemma that she was at the parting of the ways: she was being required to choose.

Mr. Fox, or Marion and Marion's family.

Mr. Fox and danger. Marion's family and safety.

Mr. Fox, I love you.

Mr. Fox, save me from a fate worse than death; save me from the boy next door, because this is what next door is like. Save me from all the things my great-aunt wanted for me, and poor Mrs. Hemsley achieved, and the dentist's wife as well.

Audrey's voice had become somewhat stringent.

"I don't like to hear you talking like that, Marion. It smacks of ingratitude. It's a good job and lovely people you meet up there, so no more of your stories, if you please, Marion."

"What stories?" enquired Gemma.

But Marion leapt to her feet.

"Shut up, all of you," cried Marion, spilling her glass of slivovitz on both the Indian design and the tartan cover, as if determined to make the most of every spilled drop. "Shut up! I want some peace! There's no peace at work and there's no peace at home."

They were all three on their feet now. Gemma rose too, out of politeness.

"Behaving like this in front of your friend," said Audrey. "What's she going to think of us?"

"It's you who'll shut up, my girl, speaking like that!" added Arthur. "And you won't have a holiday at all if you go round saying the things you do."

"Put me in a home, will you?" Marion shouted. "Like the cat and my poor old gran?"

"You were the one who wanted Gran to go, our Marion, and don't you forget it. It was you who complained about the state of the Slumberland mattress, and don't you forget that either, *and* left it to me to scrub it up."

"Aye aye," said Arthur, steadying the nerves of the group, as clearly he was accustomed to doing. "Tempers all round! No use grieving over spilt milk. Mr. First's poor sister, poor old tomcat, poor old Gran. Life is not without its tragedies. But you've got a good job there,

Marion: good pay and good workmates you can bring home, and a chance to meet the stars."

"You could do that in other places." Marion remained stubborn.

"You can't pick and choose," said Arthur. "You didn't do too well in your O-levels, remember that."

"Only because you took me on holiday the fortnight before I sat my maths, and my stomach was churning from the channel crossing . . ."

Gemma sat and stared at the fire, and was consumed by longing. She longed for the touch of Mr. Fox's hand, for the feel of his lips on hers. In her mind his white and tender body stirred beneath the floating water lilies. Oh Mr. Fox, Mr. Fox, think of me as I think of you. I love you.
See, I send my longing out to you across unknown distances, across uncharted wastes of feeling. I can feel my spirit reach you, encircle you, gain strength from you, and return to me enriched. Mr. Fox, you are thinking of me. Mr. Fox, I love you. Mr. Fox, I want you.
I know what that is, now. Love.

"I know what," says Arthur, "let's put aside the slivovitz—it always did make for an acid tongue—and have a drop of Italian vino, and hey presto, we're on the Isle of Capri already, with our troubles behind us, soaking up the sun and the wine and the friendly faces, and listening to our Marion telling us tales of who came into Fox and First, and what's going on in the world. Our own personal gossip column, that's our Marion . . ."

A morning in May, in 1966.

In Gemma's office the fountain splashed and the birds sang. Outside the sun shone and the minis darted and flower children begged alms and distributed nature's largesse with confidence. The world was clearly going their way. The enemy was in retreat, forced back by peace and love and a little help from hallucinogens. In New York a millionaire's son scattered his inheritance in bank notes from the top of the Empire State Building, and he wasn't even mad. What price honest toil now?

Upstairs in the penthouse Mr. Fox slept in his jungle bed. Down one flight of iron stairs Marion typed and Gemma filed to make his rest comfortable and his waking prosperous. Gemma was properly clothed in a black lace dress and a cream shawl, scarlet-embroidered. She was happy and beautiful and excited. She had slept soundly in the room she shared with Marion. Air-Wick had for the most part deodorised the smell from the Slumberland mattress. It had been well-scrubbed, in any case, by Marion's mother with old-fashioned Lifebuoy soap.

Breakfast had been Continental-style. "We go Dutch on Tuesdays," as Marion's dad explained, jovial even with shaving cream all over his chin. Coffee, boiled egg, cheese and cake were placed in front of Gemma by Marion's mother with the best will in the world. Not once during the meal did Gemma have to get to her feet—Gemma, who for years had breakfast standing up, the better to get Hermione, Hannah, Hortense, Helen and little Alice off to school!

Business, it seemed, was booming. Gemma had to stop filing when a film actress with a known name, wide eyes, a limp look, a slender body and tufts of hair missing from the top of her head came in to inspect a naval stone dangling in one of the showcases. The actress asked Gemma to model the stone, but fortunately, since Marion's gran's dress did not easily open, let alone come off, she changed her mind and wandered out to see if she could buy a meat pie. She fancied a meat pie, she said. She wore a shaggy fur coat with the buttons gone and nothing on beneath it.

Marion said it was just as well she had gone, since it was well known that she was broke, and they would have to have woken Mr. Fox. Nevertheless, it had been an encounter with the great, and Gemma's heart beat faster.

"Famous people have a kind of aura," Marion assured Gemma. "Mick Jagger was in once. He had a blazing white light around his head. I've never seen anything like it."

Gemma nodded politely. Marion, who yesterday seemed so solid and sensible, was showing signs, Gemma thought, of eccentricity, or of what Mrs. Hemsley referred to as "the neurotics." She had woken screaming and gabbling in the night; Gemma had registered the noise through her own dreams, but had been too tired to arouse herself properly. In the morning Marion claimed to have slept the better for her presence, so Gemma did not like to mention the disturbance.
Now Marion typed and made mild statements, and Gemma filed. Happy Gemma, on the brink, the very brink of life. The sun shone; the fountains splashed; birds sang. Life was hers, and youth, and every possible, wonderful future. A shadow fell across her desk. A skinny hand, claw-like, rested on her shoulder.

"Did I make you jump?" Mr. First's voice.
"No."
"Liar," said Mr. First. "Now don't look so cross. And don't mind when I say unpleasant things to you. If you know what you're like, if you have your own vision of yourself fixed firmly in your mind, it can hardly matter what I say. Can it?"
"Well, yes," said Gemma. "Because you pay the wages."

Mr. First, she noticed, held a paper knife in his hand. The edge was so fine, so sharp, as to be almost transparent.

"Sharp!" said Mr. First approvingly. "Brilliant as

well as beautiful. Cutting through the cackle with a mind sharp as a razor. Do you mind me stroking your hair?"

"Yes," said Gemma, "I do." Although the paper knife was oddly near her throat.

"Is there something so terrible about my hand?"

"No." But there is, there is. It is old, and mine is young. And it is not Mr. Fox's hand. That surely is enough.

"You have such soft hair, Gemma. Will you have lunch with me?"

Au secours! Au secours! Gemma needs help. Lost mother, vanished father, where are you now? Mr. Fox, how can you sleep? And where is Marion, come to that?
Slipped from the room, deceiver that she is, at the first sign of Mr. First. False friend! Like the doctor's wife, the dentist's wife, Mrs. Hemsley, Great-Aunt May—all false, false. Her own mother, dead and gone, the ultimate, original, worst betrayer of all. Mother, how dare you die!
Silence. The parrots are quiet. There is a lull in the office. Not a footstep on the stair, not the rattle of a teacup. Silence. No one. Nothing.
Nothing between life and Mr. Fox, and death and lunch with Mr. First, but a knife at her throat, sharp-edged and not so jokey as the twisted smile on Mr. First's face pretended. Again, it seemed to Gemma that she was at the parting of the ways.
Courage and death. Cowardice and life.
Gemma chose death.

"No," she said. "I won't have lunch with you, Mr. First."

Silence. The knife blade trembled at her throat; then Mr. First sighed and put it down. A joke, after all.

Of course. Employers always joke with typists.

"Not even on pain of death," lamented Mr. First, "will a pretty typist have so much as a meal with me!

What a worthless, elderly fellow I must be! Would you like me to cut my own throat with the paper knife? Would that entertain you?"

"No."

"At least we would find out whether the knife is as sharp as it looks. It is very valuable, very delicate. Designed by Mr. Fox for the excitement of us all, and clearly fashioned for the slitting of throats rather than the opening of envelopes. Are you willing to try? Would you do it for me? It would prove its worth, and what is human life, as my partner Leon Fox would say, compared to art? Life is short, but art is long."

Leon! His name was Leon. Thus his mother christened him. Well, perhaps she did. In any case, Mr. Fox has a past, has a Christian name, has a lily pond beneath which his tender body stirs.

Mr. Fox! Love Gemma, Mr. Fox. Gemma loves you.

"No," said Gemma. "Art isn't very long, not these days. It's a flicker on the telly screen, or a splash of paint on canvas."

"I shan't cut my throat," said Mr. First. "I shall stay alive if only in order to hear your words of wisdom. Would you have gone to lunch with Mr. Fox had he asked you?"

"Yes."

Mr. First licked his lips.

"If I might give you a word of advice—"

"Please stop touching me."

"I touch you as one human being touches another, from concern and friendship: not, I assure you, as an employer touching up the typist. I tried that—well, one does have to—and it didn't work. I touch you, Gemma, as a father might touch a daughter. I have no children of my own. I suppose *you* want children?"

His voice is harsh and graty, the opposite of fatherly,

the voice of the forever disgruntled child, who nevertheless has male powers.

"Of course."

"Of course. It is the natural answer. May I give you a warning? The natural world is a dangerous place. You are staying with Marion, I hear. I can't stop you doing so, but remember that Marion is a disturbed girl and has been having psychiatric treatment—the firm has been obliged to pay for it. Well, girls prepared to stay are hard to find; we do our best to help them."

And Mr. First returned to his office.

7

"Sheraton," says Hamish proudly. "An inlaid, cross-banded, mahogany, bow-fronted Sheraton sideboard. I got it for a song. Eight hundred."

"In the style of Sheraton," corrects Victor. "And four hundred would be too much. The legs are wrong, too."

Hamish flinches, as if from a physical blow. In his boastful peregrination of the house and its contents, he has flinched already some eight or nine times. The two men stand in what Gemma grandly refers to as the morning room, an elegant room of Georgian proportions painted in modest white, picked out with gold and green, where the electric fire is lit every morning and where Gemma —if only such were her temperament—would go after breakfast to deal with her correspondence on the mahogany writing table with the U-shaped stretchers circa 1800.

"At least," remarks Victor kindly, "you've managed two pieces of approximately the same date and style in the same room."

"It's Gemma's fault," grits Hamish through his teeth with unaccustomed passion. "If I like something, she doesn't like it, and if I want it in a certain place she doesn't rest until she's got it somewhere else."

"That's marriage," says Victor insouciantly. The two men move up the wide, shallow staircase to stand under the tall windows, with their panels of coloured Art Nouveau glass.

"The panes are moulded, not cut, I'm afraid," says Victor. "I hope you got them cheap."

But of course Hamish hadn't.

"People take me for a fool," he says mournfully. "Money isn't what it was. No one respects you for making it, not any more. If anything, they despise you for it."

Victor raises his eyebrows. Only the rich talk thus, his look indicates. He is discovering in himself a certain animosity towards Hamish.

"Even your lass Elsa is unimpressed," complains Hamish. "She doesn't want me for my money. She pities me."

"Um," says Victor, who would rather not consider the detail of Elsa's forthcoming intimacy with this forlorn buyer of dud antiques. Victor has a marked facility for ignoring matters that might cause him mental distress. His parents were of an altogether different temperament, and thought long and hard about disagreeable matters, and on many occasions the small Victor would be turned out of his bedroom to make way for some distraught refugee fresh from an SS inquisition or a concentration camp. As if to right the balance, to supply the family with a quality that it otherwise might lack, Victor developed a degree of frivolity, a capacity for looking the other way whenever trouble loomed, that finally altogether estranged his parents from him.

"Victor is not serious," they each separately concluded, and presently confided in one another, earnestly
grieving for their son. "Where did we go wrong?"
That was on the occasion when Victor, offered a gramophone record for his nineteenth birthday present, had
specified "Bach for Swingers." They could not bring
themselves to buy such a travesty of a decent aesthetic experience, and bought him a gift certificate instead, and
were pained by the look of disappointment that passed
across his face. He was a hefty, hearty boy by then,
making two of his father. A changeling. Both his parents have died since: his father, painfully, of lung cancer; his mother, shortly afterwards, of sorrow, in the
form of a heart attack. Their loss and their distress
washed over Victor lightly, and drained quickly away.
Janice had cried enough for both of them, sobbing and
sniffing at the funeral. It wasn't that Victor lacked feeling; he merely did not like to waste it where it would do
no good: on the dead, the dying or the destroyed. His
parents had taught him that, however inadvertently,
and would have to put up with the consequences. In
any case, or so it seemed to Victor, they had used up
in their lives their full quota of mourning; there was
none left over to shroud their departing. He walked
briefly about the graveyard, organising.
When the good die they are regretted, but not much
grieved. It is the imperfect we miss so badly, once they
are gone. Apart from Janice, most of the mourners
were dry-eyed.

Once Victor's good parents were dead, Victor lived. Ah,
how he lived! What Elsa most loved about him was his
cheerfulness, his kindness, his positiveness. He woke in
the morning so full of energy, joy and life, while she,
poor thing, had to ease herself, moaning, groaning and
yawning, into the waking world.

"She's not going to change her mind at the last minute?" Hamish persists. "I would find that very undignified, like being outbid at an auction."

"Hamish," says Victor unkindly, "auctions are no places to exercise the ego. Buying in a salesroom is the surest way to acquire rubbish at ten times the price you meant to pay. Leave a sensible bid with the porter the day before and don't go near the place until it's all over. Then you won't be tempted. I take it you bought the stuff in the billiard room at an auction?"

"As a matter of fact, yes. Local."

"Rigged, you mean. I imagine the trade was there in force, a ring was operating, the auctioneer was in cahoots, and you paid through the nose, poor muggins."

"I paid a fair price. I wasn't after a bargain."

"Poor old Hamish. Through the nose again. Well, I'll take it off your hands for a couple of thousand."

"You said two and a half," protests Hamish.

"I've had another look at it."

"And I've had another look at Elsa."

Victor looks both shocked and pained.

"We're not bartering Elsa."

"Then what else are we doing?" Hamish demands.

"You are doing me a favour; I'm not doing you one, believe me. You are relieving me of the indignity, because indignity it is, of being in thrall to a buxom teenage body and a luminous eye. It makes me nervous. Other men look at her. Young men. I'm too old for her. She'll be off presently. I can't stand the strain. I never had it with Janice. I want to get it over with, and she can't wait. She broke a *famille rose* palette plate, Chinese, eighteenth century, authenticated, the other day. Knocked it off the wall with a feather duster. That was a sign and a portent, believe me."

"Um," says Hamish. "She didn't seem all that full of portent to me. She's not perfect, either. Her legs aren't right." He shakes silently. It is the nearest he gets to laughter.

"What's wrong with them?"
"They're too thin for her body."

Victor does not deign to answer.

"Two and a half thousand and the library ladder thrown in," is all he says, insouciant as can be.
Hamish's eyes narrow. He looks now as if he had never laughed in his life.

"That library ladder belonged to my mother. I'm not selling it."
"Hamish, you didn't have a mother."
"We all had mothers," says Hamish. "Pretty young mothers. Mine was a typist, I believe, before she went to the bad. Or so I was told. But perhaps she wasn't all that pretty; she produced a fairly dreadful daughter, my poor sister Joanna, late lamented. Unless she took after her father. I like to think so. I've always fancied typists, for some reason. I like to see them sitting typing away, heads bobbing, fingers flying. That's how I met Gemma."

Hamish is overwhelmed by gloom. He takes off his spectacles, rubs his eyes, and peers out between the purple globes of a glass bunch of grapes as the noise of a passing motorbike swells on the other side of the palisade wall, and then, instead of passing on, turns into the gateway and stops and splutters. The plastic gates open at once, as if the visitor was expected, and the heavy machine skids through the gravel and is brought to a stop at the bottom of the steps, and allowed to drop as if it was a toy discarded by a willful child—unlike the owner, leather-suited, swaggering, curly-haired beneath the yellow helmet, who leaps up the steps to bang heavily at the front door.

"Dear God," says Hamish, the light through the glass grapes casting plague spots over his face, "it's her."
"Who?"

"Some dyke friend of Gemma's. An alleged physiotherapist. Alice Hemsley. Gemma claims to have known her as a child."

"Can't you put a stop to it?"

"To what? How can you put a stop to something you don't even know about? How can a man decently stand between a crippled wife and a physiotherapist."

Hamish is agitated.

"What was it we agreed?" Victor asks cunningly. "Two thousand and the library ladder?"

"I will talk about it tomorrow," says Hamish, speaking for once like a man of decision. "And ask Elsa to check the light bulb in her bedroom. Gemma keeps putting in 40 watts. It's impossible to type properly with anything less than 100. I tell her so, but she takes not the slightest notice."

8

"What price dream kitchens now?" laments Gemma. "Who dreams of kitchens except those who have given up dreams of love?"

What can Elsa reply? She holds her tongue. Gemma has taken Elsa down to the heart of the house, to the kitchen. Here Johnnie and Annie work, in the dignified dress of their native land, in a great sweep of shiny white hygienic cooking areas leading to pantries to utility rooms to laundries—peering with their alien eyes into the detail of Western domestic preoccupation, padding on soft soles, supervising the clumsy work of a handful of dull-eyed servants.

Down here machinery whirs, purifying the air, disposing of smells, sterilising dish clothes, sucking up dust, spewing out ozone—and at the moment shredding cabbage for the evening meal and dripping oil at calculated intervals into churning egg yolks to make mayonnaise.
Gemma is going to make Elsa's birthday cake—the one Elsa must share with Wendy, Victor's daughter.
Gemma points out the travel posters on the walls: distant scenes of golden shores, pounding waves and laughing native women bearing produce on their heads.

"I've been to all those places," she says sadly. "I don't

have to cheat and get them from travel agencies, like some people do. But the places are never quite like the posters. Just rows and rows of new hotels and oil on the beaches. So much better to want than to have! I'm afraid we are all at the end of our dreams. Aren't you?"

"No."

"But what do you hope for, Elsa, in the end?"

"Not to be like my mother," says Elsa, "that's all."

Gemma steers her chair into an alcove especially designed for its accommodation, and waits for mixing bowl, wooden spoon and ingredients to be set in front of her. In her hand she holds Great-Aunt May's cookery book, its tattered pages, spattered with the mixtures of past ages, carefully preserved between Perspex sheets.

Gemma weighs her ingredients with care, taking the weight of three eggs in flour, butter and sugar.

"Of course this isn't a proper sponge," says Gemma. "A proper sponge is made without butter, but is rather dry and rubbery as a consequence."

One of the eggs slips and breaks between her fingers, as automatically she clutches to save it. The shell is unusually brittle and paper-fine.

"What a horrible egg," Gemma cries. "It's unnatural! Nothing's right! Nothing's what it should be any more."

She stretches out her sticky hand for Elsa's attention. Elsa wipes it with kitchen paper, between the slender fingers and around the unsightly stub of the missing ring finger.

Annie fetches another egg and the weighing process restarts.

"Does my finger repel you?" enquires Gemma as she flicks a switch and the butter and the sugar blend.

"No," says Elsa, poor Elsa, and then, "Well, not much."

"I can't really think what I'm doing alive at all," complains Gemma. "Not only am I of no possible use to anyone, but I positively repel people as well. As for poor Hamish, he should never have married me. It is a great misfortune for a rich man to have a barren wife."

"I don't think having children is all that important," says Elsa. "The point of life can't just be to hand it on, can it?"

"But it is, it is," moans Gemma, adding eggs, one at a time. "You're quoting Victor, in any case; I know you are."

"Anyway, Victor and I don't want any children. He has one already, and as for me, I know what I'm missing, don't worry."

Gemma looks quite taken aback.

"I hope not many girls feel like you, or what will my friends do for grandchildren?"

She sifts the flour into the creamy mixture in the bowl.

"I thought you told me you loved Victor? In which case, surely you want to pledge a token of your love to future generations? To join your genes to his and see what happens next?"

"It's not Victor's child I don't want," protests Elsa. "It's any child. I'm not interested in the future. I'm interested in the here and now. There are far too many children in the world, anyhow."

"Not so far as I am concerned," says Gemma sharply. "Though I seem to remember thinking the same when I was your age, and looking after Hermione, Hannah, Hortense, Helen and Alice. But now I begin to feel like one of nature's dead ends. Nature has observed me and decided against me. She will breed eels that give electric shocks, and sea gulls with internal desalination plants, and fish that turn red at the approach of the opposite sex, but she will not let me hand on my inheritance. I am the weakest, and she will not let me survive."

"You could always adopt," says Elsa, with that streak of practicality that both irritates and refreshes.

"It's not the same," says Gemma, not to be comforted. "Though I have tried. But there's such a shortage of babies to adopt; only idiots go through with unwanted pregnancies these days, and who wants an idiot's child? After hostilities ended in Vietnam, Hamish flew me out there—he had a consignment of mutated orchids from the defoliated areas to collect—but I couldn't find a baby I liked. Then I came across Annie, who was widowed and pregnant, and flew her back here to oversee the pregnancy, but I'm afraid her husband turned out to be merely playing dead—he'd been in the Southern government—and the baby was born prematurely and died, and I was left with Annie and Johnnie and no baby. All my life I have been dogged by the unexpected. Nothing turns out right for me. Even this cake I'm making now—I have to take the most stringent precautions, or else it will most certainly not rise. When I was with Great-Aunt May I could throw them together and they never went wrong. Now the light has failed me and I must put my faith in domestic science. My mother could never bake a proper cake, according to Great-Aunt May."

Gemma clutches the pendant she wears. It seems a cheap and shoddy thing to Elsa.

"But at least," says Gemma, "I have never had to endure the swelling up, the grossness, of pregnancy, or the humiliation of giving birth."

"It's not that part I mind," says Elsa. "I think I'd rather enjoy all that. It's just afterwards. Never going anywhere without a bottle and a bagful of bits and pieces, and disturbed nights, and never really doing what you want or as you like ever again."

"I'd have a nanny to see to all that," says Gemma. "If only I had your temperament. If only," she adds, "I had your body."

Speculatively Gemma eyes Elsa, who shuffles her large and shapely feet, none too clean between the toes.

"For all I know," says Elsa nervously, "I'm completely infertile. I've been on the pill since the beginning, so how would I know?"

"I am quite sure, Elsa," says Gemma firmly, "that you are abundantly, gloriously fertile, and if I were you I'd throw away your horrid pills and find out."

Elsa is too shocked to reply. Gemma bears the cake tin, lined, greased and floured (although clearly nonstick), and two-thirds full of a light, white, swirly mixture that seems barely to contain its own energy in its impatience to be rising and hardening, and is clearly of the male gender, to the oven in the wall. The oven has special magnetic doors to prevent any inadvertent slamming and resultant collapse of the rising batter following the sudden loss of carbon dioxide.

"And are you looking forward to meeting your stepdaughter tomorrow?" asks Gemma lightly.

"I mightn't stay," says Elsa. "Victor's not too keen on my staying."

"I hope he's not ashamed of you?"

"No. If he's ashamed of anyone he's ashamed of them," says Elsa, with brilliant clarity. "And since I'm not married to Victor and don't want to be, I'm not Wendy's stepmother. We've finished with all those titles —wife, husband, in-laws, steps and so on. They were the cause of all the trouble."

"You may change the system," says Gemma. "You may do without the bits of paper—the marriage certificate, the birth certificate, the deeds to the house—and the mortgage papers—but the people involved remain much the same. There is really no escape."

Gemma summons Johnnie and says something to him which Elsa cannot hear, and then leads her through to the larder where the evening's mayonnaise is in trouble. A fault has developed in the oil-drip feed, and the egg yolks have failed to coagulate.

"Will you do it by hand for me?" asks Gemma of Elsa. "I'm afraid my wrists tire so easily! It's rather a tedious occupation, but I'll go on with my story while you do."

So Elsa sits with aching left wrist, dripping oil drop by drop from a jug into a bowl of egg yolks held steady at the base by a damp cloth, fetched steaming from the steriliser in wooden tongs, and beats with aching right hand, and Gemma, cursed or blessed, sits and smiles and talks and fingers her cheap pendant.

1966.
Years, years ago.
Mr. First was gone, back to his office.
Gemma's happy mood was spoilt.

She took the paper knife and stabbed it into the lime-green desk, causing flakes of plastic to leap into the air. Again and again she struck, and wished the desk was human flesh. But whose? Her own? Mr. First's? Or even Mr. Fox's? Gemma hardly knew. It was the flesh of all the living world she hated and wished to hurt. And would no one come to stop her?
Surely. Great-Aunt May, where are you now?
No one. Stab, and stab again!
Perhaps the blade would break and fly into her face and blind her.
For such was Gemma's conviction that she led a charmed life that she could afford the luxury of such dreadful thoughts. And where was Mr. Fox? Gemma

had dreamed of him all night, and imagined that surely
such dreams must be reciprocal. Had it meant nothing
to Mr. Fox?

Mr. Fox, where are you? Gemma needs you, wants you.
Her need, her want, rings through the universe. Mr.
Fox, I am unused, I am waiting. Defy my need, defy
your own existence. I am the empty vessel of the Al-
mighty. Mr. Fox, do you hear? Are you deaf? Where
are you? Hidden away upstairs in your penthouse,
watching Wimbledon on the television screen that
nestles in the heart of a great yellow knitted orchid? Or
gone out the evening before, to spend the dark hours
in nameless debauchery, and not yet returned?

Mr. Fox, you are unfair.

Stab, and stab again.

"Destruction is not pretty," a voice behind her said.
Mr. Fox.

"Don't damage things, Gemma. Value them. Temper
fades. Weals in wood endure forever, witness to the
dark side of our nature. People heal. Things do not.
Has Mr. First upset you?"

"Yes."

"He upsets me too, my dear, but holds a purse string
or so, so bear with him for my sake. But perhaps don't
be alone with him too long. A bad temper and a mean
nature is more infectious than an attack of measles. As
with ugliness, it rubs off. Too long exposure to Mr.
First might be dangerous, Gemma, in more ways than
one. See, already, how you are driving the knife into
that poor pretty desk? I'm sure that yesterday you would
not have dreamed of doing such a thing."

Gemma turned slow luminous eyes upon her employer.
Mr. Fox stretched out his elegant, manicured hand and
touched his typist's cheek.

"Gemma," he said. "Gemma. It is a lovely name.

I'm glad we found you, or at least that Miss Hilary did; she is very good to us and understands our needs. Now kindly feed the parrots and give them fresh water. Not from the tap. They prefer bottled spa water from the Midi; they have a natural discrimination that must be encouraged. It keeps their feathers spruce. And at mid-day, neither earlier nor later—you will come up to the penthouse, Gemma, for dictation."

"My shorthand isn't very good."

"I am pleased to hear it, and not at all surprised. Language is too beautiful, too serious, too subtle in its proper form for a sensitive person to easily reduce to scrawls upon a page. Mr. Pitman is responsible for more cultural debasement than was ever laid at poor Genghis Khan's door."

"Yes, Mr. Fox."

Genghis Khan. Who's Genghis Khan?

"All the same, I do hope you are a fast writer. I don't want my words to be lost in thin air."

"No, Mr. Fox."

"Thank you, Gemma. Pretty child."

And Mr. Fox danced away on delicate feet up the circular stairs, coloured lights from the ever-moving chandelier reflecting upon his pale suit with its inter-woven hint of glitter. And his diamonds, or what passed for diamonds, flashed as he went: the lapel pin, the ring, the bracelet, the pendant lurking in the bushy hairs of his chest; could they be real?

Yes. They could. They were.

Mr. Fox, dandy. The absurdity, the glory of the ex-treme.

How Mr. Hemsley would have snorted; how the doctor, the dentist and the butcher would have sneered. Yet how they would all have envied.

Mr. Fox, oh, Mr. Fox, you are an idiot, and Gemma

loves you. She has searched the universe, and found you.

People heal, things do not. So Mr. Fox spoke to Gemma, falsely.

Did Gemma heal after the death of her mother? She was only four years old when her mother died, absorbing sorrow into growing brain and bone and tissue. Did her nature take a twist and a turn, like a gnarled pear-tree branch grafted onto a young apple tree? For all that Great-Aunt May took little Gemma into her own bed after the funeral and consoled the small cold body by night with a warmth of her older, tougher being, did little Gemma really heal?

Little Gemma, waking in spite of Great-Aunt May, would see her dead mother's face pressed against the windowpane, calling to be let in.

Or do you think Gemma withstood, without some alteration in temperament, the sight of her earlier, living mother, coughing blood into the cracked scullery sink, her gaunt face reflected back from a window rattling in the cold north wind? Do you think Gemma survived, unscathed, the anonymity of her father, that roving repertory actor, who scattered his seed backstage or in the alleys round the theatre or in theatrical lodging houses: children springing like flowers where he walked, or at any rate thrust his procreative loins? Growing up to live, and partly live.

Damaged people go on living; hide the damage from themselves; eat, sleep, most fervently reproduce themselves; laugh, cry, even offer up some verisimilitude of love, but are never what they could have been, should have been.

Mr. Fox, Leon Fox, dancing up to his penthouse, partly living, mostly dying, clinging to illusion, power and grandeur with his well-manicured fingernails, how he snatched at the surface of other people's lives!

Mr. Fox, Leon Fox, up in his penthouse room, stared at his face in the Art Nouveau mirror and feared the falling of his hair and the rotting of his teeth.

Downstairs Gemma fed the parrots their daily ration of birdseed and refilled their cut-glass water bowls.

"Mr. Fox's father was a waiter at the Ritz," said Marion, back in the office after making a pendant delivery to the Dorchester, where a visiting film tycoon had touched down on his way to Tokyo; touching here, touching there, living on front money for a film which never would be made. "Only nobody's supposed to know, so don't let on I told you."

"A waiter! I don't believe you." Gemma was shocked.

"A very bad waiter too," said Marion. "He hated food and he hated rich people. They say Leon is overcompensating. It was a very rude pendant he did for that film tycoon. In gold, too. A naked girl sitting on a fat man's knees while he was doing goodness knows what—I didn't look too closely. There was a magnifying glass in the box—there always is—but I didn't use it. Our clients seem to love to be insulted. It was a portrait, if you ask me. Mr. Fox couldn't bear to deliver it himself, so I had to go. You know what he's like about other people's physical appearance. I don't know how he puts up with me. Mind you, it's fat people he can't abide, most of all. And I suppose I'm just stocky, not really fat."

"Mr. Fox must be wonderful with his hands," was all Gemma would say, and it was then that Marion caught sight of the paper knife, sticking point down into the lime-green desk. It quivered as she looked. What made it shudder so? Was it the sea gulls, who now thudded in a sudden spasm of senseless flocking against the convex sheets of glass, or the nearer, gentler flutter of parrots' wings? The birds were lively today. Sometimes they would perch silently on their bare branches hour after hour, beady eyes flickering, sulking behind silver mesh, which they could all too easily evade if they had the wish. Then some impulse of light or noise or distant rhythm would animate them, as now, and they would flutter, squirm, squawk and eventually, defying the symbol of their servitude, fly up and over the silver mesh and about the room and batter against the windows. Sometimes the birds inside and those outside would between them shatter the glass with the clash of their discontent, and feathers and even specks of blood would fly.

The knife in the flimsy flaking plastic toppled and fell even as Gemma turned her attention to it. Marion's stolid face, drained of colour, was given an unexpected pattern of light and shade, of grief and gauntness, as if the marks of daily experience, daily endurance, daily horror, lingered only marginally beneath her pallid skin.

"What are you doing with that knife?" asked Marion in dead tones.

"Nothing," said Gemma, much like little Alice surprised in mischief. And she went across and picked it up and tested the sharpness of the blade.

"Put it down," said Marion.

"Mr. First said he'd cut my throat with it, Marion," said Gemma with haughty blitheness, "if I didn't go out to lunch with him."

Marion neither smiled nor relaxed.

"Then perhaps you'd better," she said carefully.

"Don't be silly," said Gemma, startled. "He's only a dirty old man."

As if dirty old men were not to be pitied or understood, and had no right to the satisfaction of their needs, but could be dismissed out of hand!

"No older than Mr. Fox."

"I can't believe that. Mr. Fox has lots of hair."

"It's woven hair."

"What's that?"

"A plastic surgeon takes strands of pubic hair and grafts it onto the scalp. That's why Mr. Fox's hair is so springy and curly. It's woven. Gemma, I don't think you can go on working here."

"Why not?"

This job, her shared room with Marion, her love for Mr. Fox—these were all Gemma had in life, the foundation blocks on which her future was to be built. Why not? Why not indeed?

"It's not safe." Marion's head was lowered. Again the gauntness, the look of madness. Well, of course, that was what it was. Marion was mad. Her parents knew it. And that was why there had been talk of homes, of putting away; why Marion still lived with her parents, hadn't broken away to start her own life. Marion was mad.

Oh God, thought Gemma, now what have I got into? Will Marion take the knife and plunge it into my heart? It was the kind of thing, in Gemma's experience, that mad people did.

Mrs. Dove had been mad. Mrs. Dove the butcher's wife had killed her two children, and then herself, to save them all (or so she whispered, dying) from the Roundheads. Mrs. Dove lived in a wooden house halfway up a hill at the end of an unmade road; the butcher used to come home in the evenings up to his elbows in dried blood. It was his joke. He had a round, bald head and little puffy eyes, and drank a great deal of beer. Mrs. Dove had a four-mile walk into the village, and suffered from phlebitis; few people cared to visit her. The cottage smelled. The children, girls, had long hair which she arranged carefully, with curling tongs, into Cavalier ringlets. Poor little dead girls, saved forever from the Roundheads; poor dead butcher's wife, mad as a hatter.

Nothing wrong with her, a few said, except him. Poor

him, most people said, married to a madwoman. Worse, a madwoman who gave herself airs, to the extent of putting her death before her life. What arrogance! That's the worst of madness: the arrogance that goes with it. The determination to keep others out, to see the world as you choose to see it, not as others assure you that it is. Peopling the world with Cavaliers and Roundheads. It all ended in death, and more blood than even the butcher had dreamed of; of course it did. Death is the only sensible way out for people who will not, cannot relinquish their belief in a world that others do not see.

"Not safe?" Gemma humoured Marion. She was restored, brave as a blind bat tangling in a lion's mane. Thus she had humoured little Alice when the latter saw visions. Dead Mr. Hemsley at the top of the stairs, shaking his fist at his fifth daughter. Mad!

"But yesterday you were so keen on my staying here."

"Yesterday was different."

"You want them for yourself, don't you?" Gemma was spiteful. "Mr. Fox and Mr. First. You're jealous because Mr. First wants to take me out to lunch, and I took Mr. Fox's coffee up. You just don't like competition."

"It's not like what you think. Please put the knife down. It turns me over to see you with it. Put it back in the desk drawer where it belongs and forget it."

"But there's blood on the blade," said Gemma, and so indeed there was. A few flakes of rusty brown still clung to the pitted blade.

"Don't be stupid," said Marion. "It's not blood, it's rust. It must be rust. I had a dream about that knife, if you want to know. It's been about the office for a long time. It's very sharp. Ophelia, the last girl, broke a fingernail and didn't have her nail scissors, and tried to smooth it with the knife, and it slipped and she cut her finger. There was blood everywhere. But we wiped it really clean, so it must be rust. It was after that I had the dream."

"Tell me."

"Come closer. The walls are very thin. They always are in new buildings. And the ceilings. Sometimes Mr. Fox has model girls up there in working hours. The floorboards creak. Not like my parents' bed creaks, though. A different pattern of noise altogether. I don't know what happens, or what they do. I don't care."

"Your dream," said Gemma, gritting her teeth. Presently she would go up to Mr. Fox and take dictation, and nothing would do but that she, Gemma, would make the floorboards creak in whatever pattern Mr. Fox chose, and the more unlike the Ramsbottles' creaking the better. Gemma would offer Mr. Fox her virginity, and surely that could not be refused? In the meantime there was Marion's madness to be dealt with.

Oh foolish Gemma, foolish virgin.

"I dreamt I was working late—overtime," moaned mad Marion. "I was down in that corner sorting out the bottom filing cabinet. The pink and black one. The drawers stick, I'm afraid. I'd stopped for a cigarette; I was sitting on the floor in the almost dark, having a little think about going to Scandinavia one day and seeing fiords. I've always wanted to see fiords. Mum and Dad love beaches and garlic, but me, I love towering mountains and deep, still water. You never know what's there. In the Mediterranean you know, all right. It's all floating about on the top of the water—French letters and worse. None of your mystic samite swords, mysterious, wonderful. One day I'll get north by myself. I'm not very good at being by myself. I get dreams."

"Is it a dream you're telling me about, or can I get on?" So Gemma chided little Hannah, who chattered night and day. "Because personally it's nearly midday. I'm supposed to be going upstairs to take dictation from Mr. Fox."

And that's not all I'll take. Mr. Fox will undress me, button by button, zip by zip, and stand me naked before him as I have stood before a mirror a thousand times, and his eyes will see what no man has ever seen before, and his hands will go where no hands have been before. Except the doctor. Damn the doctor.

"Oh, yes," said Marion. "The dream. Anyway, there I was in the dream in that corner in the half dark dreaming of still water when I heard a scream and a woman came running in here completely naked; and all the birds flew up suddenly, screaming and battering—though you know they can get out whenever they please —and she had no business being naked; she was very fat and blobbing about, buttocks and breasts, and I saw that it was Mr. First's sister—"

"The one who killed herself?"

"Mr. First's sister, that's right. And he came running in after her, this man in my dream, from Mr. First's office, and he hit her on the head with that lamp. It's alabaster." Alabaster is tricky stuff, prone to marking and discolouration. The round globe of the lamp which Gemma now regarded was veined and mottled, with a darkened patch where a head might well have hit. What a blunt instrument it would make, in the fevered, mad imagination of a disturbed typist.

"It's a very lovely, very gracious lamp," said Marion, "but heavy, I've noticed that. The woman fell, and that seemed to make him angry, as if she should have risen again, seeing stars, like a comic fat woman in a cartoon, and he bent over her and tried to get a ring off her finger, but he couldn't. You know what rings are when you've put on weight. And he just picked up that knife and sliced at it in a temper, and the finger and the ring still on it flew across the room and landed in my lap. I was wearing my best beige skirt. I just crouched, terrified. I thought, now he'll murder me. But he didn't look for the finger or the ring, or see me. He just opened the window cleaner, which pivots them open, terribly dangerous—and toppled her out. There was blood all over the floor from her finger; you can see the marks still, though I've scrubbed and scrubbed and—"

"That was where Ophelia cut her finger. You told me so yourself. You're mad, Marion."

"I'm not mad. It's not mad to dream. It's very good for the persona. And while his back was turned I nipped out, and I heard the squeal of brakes and shouts, and when I got down to the street there was this crowd, and oh, Gemma, Gemma . . ."

"It must have been very upsetting for you, Marion, Mr. First's sister jumping the way she did. No wonder you have dreams."

"But I think I had the dream before she jumped. I don't know. It's all muddled up."

"Perhaps you should see a psychiatrist."

"I did. He gave me Valium. The worst part of the dream was what I did with the finger. I took it home and put it in the top drawer in my bedroom, with all my nice things. You know, scarves, and belts and nail varnish. I wrapped it in tissue, with a bit of cotton wool at the end in case it leaked blood."

"Your mum and dad are right," observed Gemma. "You need a holiday."

"If it *was* a dream." Marion was tearful. "If it wasn't for real. How can a girl be sure? I remember what happened in the dream much more clearly than I remember what happened last year in the Canary Isles. There was this waiter. My mum and dad are always going on at me to have a holiday romance, so I did try, with a bottle of red Spanish and the waiter behind a windbreak, but I could hardly remember a thing the next day to tell them. They do like to be told things. If you could find a fault with my mum and dad, it's the way they like to be told things."

"Of course it was a dream," said Gemma. "You're frightened of Mr. First in real life, so you're frightened in dreams. Now I'm going up to Mr. Fox to take dictation."

Marion opened her mouth to speak, but shut it again; a look of spite crossed her face, as would cross Her-

mione's when she blew down Hannah's card houses
and pretended it was the draft that did it.

"Go on up," said Marion. "See if I care."

You care all right, thought Gemma. You love Mr. Fox.
Clearly, the whole world loved Mr. Fox, since Gemma
did. And with a hardness, a coldness she did not know
she possessed—well, all of us are nice, charming people
enough, until tried by circumstances and hard times,
and then, and only then, do we find out what we really
are—Gemma adjusted her hair in the mirror, pursed
her lips, made, all for poor plain Marion's benefit, the
faces any pretty girl makes in the mirror, took a shorthand pad and Marion's freshly sharpened pencils, and
ran upstairs to Mr. Fox's lair. Round and round, up
and up. Fifteen stairs to destiny.

"Alice!" cries Gemma, here and now, stretching out
her thin arms in welcome. And Elsa's hand slips, so
that a whole dollop of oil falls into the egg yolks, and
the thick mass instantly curdles and thins. "Alice, at
last! How I've waited for you."

Alice Hemsley, bold and beautiful, in black trousers
and white shirt, tall, tanned, handsome and hook-nosed,
swaggers in, hands on hips. Her hair is black, short and
curly, and her cheeks full and pink beneath their bronze.
Her voice booms huskily. Her bosom is high and full;
the eye searches it out in the attempt to define male
or female, and finding it, is both surprised and gratified.

There are tears of welcome in Gemma's eyes. Elsa is
unaccountably jealous.

"I was angry with you," says Alice. "So I waited."
"What for? What have I done?"
"You weren't at your great-aunt's funeral."
"She was dead. What difference did it make?"
"You should have gone."

"I sent money for the burial. I'm crippled; it's difficult for me to get about."

"You get off on holiday all right."

"If I'm going where I want, if there's pleasure and warmth at the end of the journey, I manage quite well. If I don't want to get where I'm going, the pain in my legs is intolerable. Do you want me to suffer?"

"I don't see why you shouldn't." Alice is brisk. "Everyone else does."

"Were there many people at the funeral?"

"The matron of the nursing home and myself."

"You see! I couldn't have borne it."

"You never visited her. You left it to me."

"You're good with the old and sick; I'm not."

"She gave up everything for you, and what did you do for her?"

"Kept her company for sixteen years of my life. My life! A young girl cooped up with an old woman!"

"Now you coop yourself up, since she's not here to do it."

"I'm glad she's dead," says Gemma savagely. "Her whole life was a reproach to me. She was so good, and where did it get her? Ten years crippled with arthritis and two people at her funeral."

"And how many will you have if you go on like this?"

"I'll pay an attendance fee. Then I'll have hundreds."

Elsa is forgotten. She leaves before the state of the mayonnaise is noticed, and goes to her room to take her forgotten pill, quickly, before worse befalls. But she cannot find the packet in the otherwise empty desk drawer where she put it, and though she searches everywhere it does not come to light—which, thinks Elsa, puts an altogether different complexion on everything.

9

"Of course," says Victor gloomily at dinner, "at the first cold snap they'll turn on the central heating and that will be the end of everything."

"In what way?" enquires Elsa. They are dining alone, on thick pea soup, cold game pie served with potatoes duchesse and coleslaw (the sauce a vinaigrette, not mayonnaise), followed by chocolate mousse and cream. The Buddha gazes down upon the two diners. Annie waits upon them, her hands obliging, her mind clearly absent, bent upon some political reflection or another.

"All the good furniture will warp and split."

"They've got to keep warm."

"The Jacobeans managed to keep warm without central heating. So did the Georgians, the Victorians and the Nouveau-Artistes, and not only did they look after the artifacts of the past, they made good stuff of their own. And what's happened to us? Factory-made rubbish and central heating. The dawn of comfort was the sunset of creativity."

"I'm sure you're right," says Elsa, and then, "Couldn't we just go home now while no one's watching? Just get in the car and go?"

Victor has already considered this possibility. It would

be possible to smuggle the library ladder out under the back floor of the Volvo—on penalty, of course, of losing Hamish's friendship and the furniture in the billiard room, but keeping Elsa for himself. The car, however, is now locked away behind electronically sealed doors in one of Hamish's garages. Hamish, no doubt, foresaw Victor's plan.

Victor says as much to Elsa.

"In any case," he adds, "the beds here are comfortable, and I don't think I can face the shop again tonight."

"I could make the shop much more comfortable," says Elsa eagerly, "if only you'd let me. We could curtain off the whole raised dais and have a little cooker and a permanent bed."

Victor laughs, though gloomily.

"You'll be asking for fitted carpets next," he observes. "Scratch any woman and there's a Janice waiting to get out."

"But it was you who said the shop was uncomfortable."

"That doesn't mean I want it comfortable."

Victor is irritated and irritable. Hamish has outwitted him. He does not enjoy it.

"There's a train at ten-thirty tomorrow morning," he says to Elsa. "I'll drop you off at the station after breakfast, agree on a price with Hamish during the day, and be with you by evening."

Elsa raises her blue eyes to his.

"Victor," she says. "I'm going back when you do, and not a moment before."

Victor helps himself to more chocolate mousse. With

Janice, he thought, I used to eat like this nightly. I was not forever rumbling, with a stomach full of brown rice and quick-cooked vegetables and a sprinkling of nuts: carbohydrate, roughage and protein, Yin and Yang in proper proportion, ensuing long life and a cancer-free bowel. But is a long life with Elsa so much preferable to an early death with Janice? If I took Janice to a station at least she would get on the train I thought best.

Janice is my wife. Elsa is the typist.

"Are you ashamed of me?" demands Elsa.

"Not ashamed," says Victor cautiously. He hates to tell lies; he finds the act demeaning and undignified. But neither does he like to hurt, if he can help it. "It's just that Janice and Wendy are serious, and you somehow aren't. I don't want them hurt. It's a great pain to a woman of my wife's generation to see herself supplanted. You have your life in front of you; hers is behind her. And as for Wendy, it is probably disturbing for her, in a Freudian sense, that you share a birthday with her. I hadn't realised it until Gemma pointed it out."

"My life is serious to me," protests Elsa, indignant.

"Dear Elsa," says Victor, "I love you because you aren't serious. Don't you understand? Girls of nineteen aren't renowned for their deep seriousness. Their egocentricity, perhaps."

"I'm only eighteen," says Elsa, "until tomorrow. Please don't be like this. Don't spoil my birthday for me."

" 'Don't spoil my birthday for me!' " Victor marvels. "And please, having said it, don't bore me ever again by claiming to be a serious person. Look how you left home—in a fit of pique. Look how you left your job—on an impulse. How you moved in with me, to share my sofa—on a whim."

"It wasn't pique or impulse or whim; it was love. I loved you."

"Love may have been the excuse, but it certainly wasn't the reason. I notice you put love in the past tense. At least you have the honesty to do that, with thoughts of Hamish in your mind. The lustful millionaire. You can't even be serious about sex."

"All you think about is your library ladder. You think things are more important than people."

Victor takes his cup of coffee to sit outside in the warm moonlight and be away from such petty wrangling. Janice seldom answered back.

Elsa goes to the sedan chair and telephones Marina, and presently feels better, having revenged herself on Victor by discussing his sexual predilections in some detail. Marina raises the possibility of a strain of voyeurism in her girl friend's boyfriend.

"I wish I had your problem," says Marina, "I really do."

The lights of the swimming pool are illuminated, dimming the moon. Where once the spiky shapes of trees could be seen, glowing softly in celestial light against a hot starry sky, now all beyond the pool is a dense, velvet black. Victor returns indoors, irritated by this abuse of nature.

Alice wheels Gemma to the side of the pool. Elsa follows. Alice wears a black one-piece suit, Gemma wears a white silk wrap-around shift.

"You ran away," complains Gemma to Elsa. "Spoilt the mayonnaise and ran away! Young girls find it so difficult to face the consequences of their actions. And you never met my Alice properly. I used to look after her when she was a little girl. Now she looks after me.

She's a trained physiotherapist. She is going to teach
me how to walk again, aren't you, Alice?"

"All you have to do is decide to walk, and then
you'll walk," booms Alice. "You're just lazy and selfish
and spoilt."

"I have a hysterical paralysis," says Gemma, "which
is scarcely my fault. You're so old-fashioned, Alice."

Elsa's mouth drops open. Gemma beams at her.

"There's really nothing wrong with me," says Gemma,
"except that I haven't been able to walk for more than
a decade, of course."

She claps her hands and orders Elsa a glass of cold
milk, and two whiskeys for herself and Alice.
Alice unwraps Gemma from her silk shift.

"I wish you'd take off that ridiculous pendant," she
says.

"It belonged to my mother," protests Gemma, clinging to it.

"Much good she ever did for you," says Alice,
lowering Gemma's white, naked body into the pool
with her massive golden arms. Gemma floats happily,
her body slight and pretty, her arms thin, her legs likewise, but otherwise perfectly formed.

Alice jumps in beside Gemma, turns her on her front,
and supports her waist. Gemma's white arms splash
feebly; her legs trail uselessly, if prettily, behind.

"Kick," cries Alice. "Kick, Gemma, for all you're
worth."

"Can't," moans Gemma.

"Won't, you mean," roars Alice. "I'm going to let
you go. You'll have to kick or you'll drown."

And she lets go of Gemma, but since Gemma seems

perfectly happy to drown, she has to catch her again, and even to raise her head from the water.

"It's the pendant," says Gemma. "It weighs me down."
"Then take it off."
"Shan't."

Gemma emerges dripping and triumphant from the water and is patted dry. She shaves her pubic hair, which gives her an air of depravity and innocence both. Gemma's body seems to belong to a child, yet has begun to show signs of age. Saved from the shocks and storms of pregnancy, it is fading before it has ripened— like sterilised milk kept too long, which will taint and go off, but can never turn suddenly, rottenly sour.

"I left you some typing," says Gemma to Elsa when she is back in her chair. "Did you see it?"
"Yes, I did," says Elsa. "I'll do it in the morning."
"Elsa's such a wonderful typist," says Gemma falsely, and Alice eyes Elsa without enthusiasm.
"You're like the opposite ends of a spectrum," observes Gemma. "Two female bookends supporting between you a whole row of alternative life forms. I am telling Elsa the story of my office days, Alice."
"Which version?"
"Listen and you'll find out."

1966.
Up went Gemma, up the circular staircase, to take shorthand from Mr. Fox. If she tripped—if she fell— but of course she did not. Girls in love do not often fall; they have magic wings on their feet.
Gemma tapped on Mr. Fox's door.
Mr. Fox, dressed in a white caftan and gold chain, opened the door to let her in.

"Don't tap on doors," he said. "Just open them. It's vulgar to tap. Even butlers never tap on doors."

"What the butler saw," said Gemma, bright as a button, "and no wonder!"

"You're late," said Mr. Fox, unimpressed.

"Marion kept me. I'm sorry."

"Never apologise. If accused of a fault, merely compound the offence by an even worse one. Was she chatting on? Marion frequently chats on."

"Yes, she was. I don't think she's all there."

"Really? She seems all too solid flesh to me."

Mr. Fox nodded towards the desk. Gemma sat in a seat shaped like an orchid. It was not very comfortable.

"Don't keep gaping, Gemma. It's irritating. Learn not to be impressed."

"It's just this room—oh-ow!"

A hummingbird tangled in Gemma's hair.
Mr. Fox disentangled it gently, lovingly. Was it the little fluttering bird he loved, or Gemma?
Gemma trembled at Mr. Fox's touch.

"We should write to a client or two, I daresay. Lady Sylvie Whatsit has had her ears altered by cosmetic surgery, the better to accommodate my ear pieces. She complains that gold is too heavy; she wants to know if there is some new lightweight alloy available, some spin-off from the space program."

"It all makes work for the workingman to do," said Gemma brightly. So said the plumber when Hortense had pierced the rainwater tank for the fourth time with a homemade bow and arrow.

"I am not a workingman," said Mr. Fox. "I am a creative artist. When I was a boy of twelve I went to my father's place of employment, and there, sitting at a table sat the begum, the wife of the Aga Khan. The glittering of her jewels will remain with me to the end of my days.

"How hard she worked, I thought, at being herself;

and how triumphantly she succeeded. Where she walked, all eyes turned. My father was a waiter, and quite invisible. I tell you this only because I know Marion will already have let you know the details of my parentage; the insignificant can always be relied upon to diminish those they envy. She did, didn't she?"

"Yes."

"In any case, I determined there and then to be significant, to work hard at my existence. Dictation is very boring. I shall leave it all, on second thought, to Mr. First, who is a very boring person, and fortunately fairly invisible. Apart from his penchant for young girls, of course, which sometimes brings him sharply into focus. I am giving a little party this week for a group of friends; we will eat a little food, smoke a little pot, get a little high. Nothing extreme. Will you join us?"

A party invitation! Oh, Mr. Fox.

Gemma was mesmerised by Mr. Fox's sing-song voice. She lifted her eyes to his; they were blue-green, and oddly blank; they roved to and fro; they reflected (had she but known it) a profound anxiety.

He loves me, was all Gemma thought. He knows I am a princess in disguise, and not really a typist at all. That though I lie on a hundred mattresses, I can detect the pea beneath them all.

Mr. Fox's fingers moved from Gemma's cheek to her breast; it was a professionally inspired gesture, but how was she to know a thing like that?

Though where professionalism stopped and eroticism began, who was to say?

"Pretty," said Mr. Fox. "A good regular shape. I did very well for a time with spun-sugar circlets for the breasts—in the fun-trifle range—but word got round that the stickiness spoiled the pleasure rather than enhanced it, and demand fell off. Well, life is long and art is short."

Gemma, with Mr. Fox's fingers at her breast, standing closer to a man than ever in her life before—except when approached by the doctor and dentist—felt his breath upon her cheek. It had a warm, sweet, Pepsodenty smell, covering up some ranker, ferous odour; she welcomed it, and with it some essential corruption. To prefer what is bad because it is exciting to what is wholesome and pure is most certainly corrupt, and Great-Aunt May had told her so. Mrs. Hemsley had told Gemma so as well. So had the dentist's wife. It was in the Bible, after all. The Book of Judges. Bees nesting in a dead lion's stomach: out of strength coming forth sweetness.
If you have a mind for that kind of thing.
As Mrs. Hemsley and the dentist's wife did.

After the dentist's death, Mrs. Hemsley moved in with the dentist's wife, at first for company and later for comfort as well. The children were grown and gone by then, except for Alice, once little, now big. The dentist's wife presently qualified as a dentist herself, and took over her deceased husband's practice, extracting his old fillings with a shocked and ultraprofessional frown. Mrs. Hemsley's cupboard, once so bleak and bare, was soon stuffed with tinned crab, tinned salmon, tinned cream and such luxuries as the village store could afford. Here presently, where once Gemma had obtained her pound of lentils, her half-pound of oatmeal, her quarter-pound of butter, was to thrive a delicatessen counter, selling grams of smoked salmon and kilograms of muesli the better to please a changing clientele, much reinforced by lady couples of a certain age and income who had taken retirement cottages in the area. Even poor Mrs. Dove's cottage was bought up, converted, given running water and electricity, and the bloodstains on the floor erased with a power sander, to bring up the texture of the fine elm floorboards.

Alice qualified as a physiotherapist and unwillingly left home, her position usurped by the dentist's wife. How unfair fate can be: poor little Alice, training herself so magnificently in mind and body to be her father's vindication, her mother's salvation, to be in the end unneeded! Self-transcendence swept away, overwhelmed by the dynamism of events. The dentist's wife kept Mrs. Hemsley in every comfort—as many tinned black cherries as she liked, as much Heinz tinned custard—so that the money Alice sent home weekly was but a drop in the pool filled daily by the flow from the dentist's widow's practice.

Alice tears south on her motorbike, in the pay of the Avon County Council, peripatetic physiotherapist, sleeping bag and spirit stove in her rucksack, travelling rough, strong hands at the service of the poor, the weak, the lonely and the aged. Gruff, kind Alice. Handsome Alice.

But this is now, and that was then.

Gemma was intoxicated by Mr. Fox's breath, lulled by his finger's peaceful, artistic exploration of her breast beneath its blouse.

"Did Marion tell you anything else?" enquired Mr. Fox.
"No."
"Nothing?"
"She talked a little about Mr. First's sister."
"I was afraid of that. How the vulgar love to batten on tragedy."

Mr. Fox, Mr. Fox, you really do not like Marion at all. Marion is my friend. Well, girl friends must fall when boyfriends push. That's one of the laws of nature.

"But why did Miss First do such a dreadful thing? Did she really jump, not just fall? I could never kill myself. I always want to know what happens next. They might land on the moon or something, and if I were dead I'd never know."

"You are young; you are still curious. She was old. Better dead."

"To be old isn't a crime."

"Isn't it?"

"It will happen to all of us," Gemma protests.

"But not yet. Besides, Joanna First was ugly."

"People don't kill themselves because they are ugly."

"They should."

Gemma gaped. Mr. Fox laughed and bared Gemma's left breast, and thoughtfully stroked her modest pink nipple.

"Typists!" he said. "Don't be a typist for long, Gemma."

Mr. Fox bared Gemma's right breast.

"Quite symmetrical," he said. "That's most unusual. You could usefully do some modelling for me, Gemma. Miss Hilary at Gallant Girls has come up trumps again."

He rebuttoned her blouse; his interest, one might well believe, and more's the pity, had indeed been professional. Gemma, whose instinct it had been, upon her uncovering, to fall into Mr. Fox's arms and have his mouth pressed to hers in passionate and adoring kisses, stood still, swaying slightly in the force of unaccustomed desire, and greatly puzzled.
The fronds of a palm tree drifted gently above.
Presently she regained her balance.

"Joanna First," said Mr. Fox, appearing out of the undergrowth, "was better dead. She was stupid, gross, ugly and except that she was rich, and perhaps provided a little extra employment for the labouring masses, of no use in the world. She did not speak; she whined. She was greedy. Well, we are all greedy, I daresay, but her greed lacked style. She would take my most beautiful jewels, slobbering, and put them on her gross fat fingers and around her pendulous breasts; my navel gems would be invisible in the rolls of fat that swathed her belly. My armpit studs would be lost in a forest of coarse hair, and my sugar pubic-shields likewise. They were not meant for the likes of her. She made my jewels ridiculous. She took the magic out of everything."

"So does her brother, Mr. First."

"We need Mr. First, Gemma, just as we need Marion to do the typing and the filing. But we must not be contaminated. What else was Marion talking about?"

"A silly dream she had."

"Let me guess. It won't be hard. The Marions of this world always dream about their bosses. I hope you don't dream of me, Gemma."

"No. Oh, no."

Great-Aunt May had been right to worry about Gemma's lies.

"Marion dreamed she saw Mr. First murder his sister, that's all," said Gemma lightly. "Saw him chop off her finger, and then throw her out of the window."

"Mr. First did that? How gruesome!" Mr. Fox looked quite startled. "And how phallic. What happened to the finger?"

"She put it in her drawer," said Gemma, and giggled.

"With the ring still on it?"

"It was only a dream," Gemma protested. But Mr. Fox had stopped listening. He had seated himself at his camouflaged desk and was leafing through folders of designs. He did not ask Gemma to sit down. She stood beneath her palm tree like some lost girl in a jungle, and wondered sadly whether she should go or stay.

"Can you cook?" enquired Mr. Fox, out of nowhere.

"Shepherd's pie," offered Gemma eagerly. Mrs. Hemsley's favourite. On Saturday Gemma would buy a bottle of Heinz tomato sauce; on Sundays the girls would be allowed to finish the bottle on their midday shepherd's pie. Their life was not without moments of glory; Gemma saw to that.

"I suppose," said Gemma as an afterthought, "shepherd's pie is not the sort of thing you meant."

"No. Though it might just do on a special evening of English cuisine. If the mince were sirloin and the mushrooms fresh. Mediterranean cookery is the in thing. Garlic, tomato purée, fresh herbs and olive oil."

"You can't buy those things in Cumberland."

"Can't you? No wonder you came south. Come through to the kitchen."

And Gemma spent the rest of the day as Mr. Fox's amanuensis, in the steel and glass kitchen that lurked behind a wall of vines. She was useful: she peeled the garlic cloves, opened the cans of tomato purée, pounded cardamom seeds, slivered salt pork, drained boiling beans, sliced sausage, and browned nuggets of mutton, deftly and prettily, as Mr. Fox started preparations for his own special brand of cassoulet, to be served at Friday's party. Did Mr. Fox want Gemma for her body, for herself, or as kitchen hand?

For myself, cried Gemma in her heart, for myself!

"When Marion dreamed her dream," Mr. Fox said casually as Gemma scoured the saucepans, "where did she stand to witness the event? Or did she float unseen, as if she were the guardian of the late and little-lamented Joanna First?"

"Down in the corner between the filing cabinet and the wall; it's all greys and blacks down there. Quite soothing."

"And she saw Mr. First's face clearly?"

"There's not much mistaking it, is there?"

"I hope she doesn't talk about her dream. It wouldn't be wise. It might make Mr. First quite angry."

"Yes, I suppose it would."

"Perhaps you should tell her so."

"I will if you want me to."

"What else would you do if I wanted you to?"

"Anything," said Gemma simply.

And Mr. Fox paused in the reading of a recipe book and said, "On Saturday week I am going to Tangier to see a client. He wishes to be fitted with gold thonging for his shins. Will you come with me?"

"What time on Saturday?"

"Do you only travel at certain hours on Saturdays, Gemma?"

"It's just that I have to collect my wages from the Agency, or I can't live. Between ten and eleven."

"One forgets. How one forgets!" Mr. Fox struck his white smooth hand to his handsome brow.

"They pay me twenty pounds. How much do you give them for me?"

"Forty."

"It's exploitation!" Gemma's face grew pink with indignation.

"Life *is* exploitation," observed Mr. Fox, who seemed neither surprised nor put out by the fact. "If one wasted time worrying about it, I'm sure one would get nothing done at all. Our plane goes at midday. You will be able to collect your wages before we leave."

A party invitation, and a weekend too!

"And Gemma," said Mr. Fox. "Don't talk to anyone else about Marion's dream, will you?"

"I won't," said Gemma. "I won't."

Gemma smiles at Elsa and says goodnight. Alice wheels her to her room.

10

Hamish comes to Elsa in the middle of the night. So King David came to his young wife, no doubt, to warm his old, cold bones. But whoever cared about her?

First, kindly Hamish typed the work Gemma had left for Elsa to do. One top, one pink, two blues and a yellow. Six letters to various London department stores—Gamages, Harrods, Harvey Nichols, Selfridges, Barkers and Bourne and Hollingsworth—requesting details of all models of dishwashers currently available on the market, specifying colours in stock and alternatives out of it, maximum and minimum measurements, method of water-flow, rinse-aid dispensing, and so on.

"I think Gamages has gone out of business," said Hamish, typing the first letter. "The trouble with Gemma is that she lives in the past."

"One of Gemma's troubles," he added presently.

And he typed on, a thin figure in a red-silk dressing gown and sealskin slippers. Elsa lay with the bedclothes up to her chin, considering her past and her future, the end of her dreaming and the beginning of reality. She was sleepy and warm and not unhappy. Hamish had brought an electric-fan heater with him, since the cen-

tral heating seemed to lose its efficacy on this floor of
the building, or had been turned off for reasons of
economy.

"I enjoyed being in the army," said Hamish over the
second letter, "much like the orphanage, but the food
was better, and I made my name as a typist. That's
what happiness is, so far as I'm concerned: a sense of
achievement. I feel I have achieved very little in life."

"Your money?" Elsa enquired.

"It means nothing."

"Then why don't you give it all away?"

Hamish's fingers paused for a second or so before they
resumed their efficient rhythmic dancing over the typewriter keys.

"It's never made me happy, so why should I inflict
it on anyone else?" he said triumphantly.

Over the third letter Hamish said, "I spent some months
in an open prison once. That was much like the army,
only without the typing. I didn't enjoy that. On the
other hand, I didn't dislike it all that much. Never
having had, in my life, a sense of freedom, the enforced
loss of it did not seem too distressing. Life itself is a
prison. I long for the end of it."

Now he turns and stares at Elsa, remembering why he
is here.

"Lovely thing," he says. "You don't feel like that
about life, do you?"

"No," says Elsa.

"You don't have to do this if you don't want to,"
he says. "I find it rather embarrassing."

"I don't mind," says Elsa, and she doesn't. She is
grateful that he is doing her typing, and flattered that
he has confided in her. Victor, she concludes, talks more
and says less.

"Just let me finish the typing," says Hamish.

Over the fourth letter Hamish says, "I am a nicer person than I used to be. Living with Gemma stretches the imagination. Gemma, on the other hand, is not so nice as she was. Sometimes I think the devil has got into her soul. She didn't lose her virginity to me, but to a rather bad man. A woman's first lover injects her with good or bad. Did you know that? Who was your first lover?"

"Victor."

"Really?" Hamish sounds interested. "Then I will be your second lover?"

"Yes."

"Well," says Hamish contentedly, "Victor should not be all that difficult to neutralise."

Hamish, stop typing. Come to bed.

Victor, thank you. You have revealed my true nature to me. You have peeled away the layers of love, fear, fidelity, dependence—call it what you like—and left me naked and unashamed.

Hamish, come to bed.

And indeed, Elsa is now consumed by an erotic energy, a desire to sleep not just with Hamish, but with all the men in the world.

Hey you over there! Man! Come to bed. Handsome, young, rich, powerful or otherwise fortunate—is that you? Excellent! Come inside. Because what I know and perhaps you don't is that by some mysterious but certain process of osmosis I will thereupon draw something of these qualities into myself. Don't run away—I need you! I must have you. I must sap your good fortune, drawing it into myself through the walls of my vagina, gaining my pleasure through your loss. Sex is not for procreation; it is for the sharing out of privilege.

You over there! Poor old man. Ugly, tired, crippled, half-witted—come along, hurry, quick, inside, out of the cold! I've something to give you; I am generosity itself; I will share my stolen goods with you; I will redistribute good fortune through the medium of my generative organs; I will make the world a fairer, better place, gaining my own pleasure through degradation, falling into a final shudder of wonder down there at the slimy roots of the world.

You and me, the outcasts of the world. Come to bed, Hamish.

I will take some of Victor's stolen energy and hand it on to you. I will take some of your power, your ability to control the world, which Victor badly needs, and pass it on to him tomorrow. I will mix his cheerfulness with your gloom, and balance the world better.

So long, just so long, as sex does not stop its dancing game and settle back grimly where it belongs; so long as I don't get pregnant. So long as my generative organs generate energy and not simply flesh and blood.

Well, that's easily managed. Since Victor seldom actually comes anywhere that could possibly make me pregnant, presumably I can manage matters likewise with Hamish.

Hamish, come to bed. Grey, dry, gloomy Hamish, difficult and kindly. Old Hamish, rich Hamish. Let me take some of that: something of your past, something of your power. I won't suck you dry; don't worry. Not quite.

"Will you let Victor have the library ladder?" asks Elsa as Hamish types the fifth letter.

But Hamish smiles his rare smile, and does not reply.

When Hamish has finished the sixth letter he says, "The trouble with Gemma is, she hasn't enough to do. We already have three dishwashers. Another of Gemma's troubles," he adds presently.

When Hamish has collated and piled the finished typing properly and neatly, he crosses to Elsa's bed and tentatively pulls back the sheet.

"Just call me Rumpelstiltskin," he says, "and you never guessed my name." He turns out the light, gets in the bed beside her, and lies cold and still. It is a very narrow bed.

"We could just lie here," he says, his voice unexpected in the dark. "If that's what you'd prefer. We are our own people as well as Gemma's."

She does not understand what he means.

"Do what you want," says Elsa. "I don't mind."

"I'll do what I can," says Hamish, "which is more to the point. My eyes are bigger than my parts—always have been. I've never been quite like other people. Always on the outside looking in. My mother didn't like me. She kept my sister at home; put me in an orphanage. She despised her husband, my father. She complained that I took after him. She only kept him to torment him—the way Gemma keeps me now."

This sudden spurt of bitterness stirs him into life. Elsa senses rather than feels his organ hardening, rising.

"Poor Gemma," says Hamish, "it's not her fault. The devil's in her. I should have saved her. I should have saved my sister too, but I didn't. I need women, I even love them, but I can't say I like them very much."

He sighs, quiescent again.

"I'm sorry," says Elsa kindly, turning towards him, enfolding him in soft, dark, maternal arms. "Really sorry."

"There's something unlikable about me, mind," Hamish complains. "That's why my mother never visited me when I was a child. She's still alive. She lives in poverty and misery, and suffers from hyperthermia, I hear. I don't care. Why should I care? She did nothing for me. Why should I do anything for her?"

"You must have loved her once. You have to get back to that," says Elsa with wisdom beyond her years, "or you'll be miserable forever."

"I suppose you love your mother," he says bitterly.

"Oh yes, yes!"

Of course she does. Loves her, fears her, pities her, resents her, escapes her, joins her, loves her, is saved.

"I might send her something one day," says Hamish cautiously, his head buried babylike in the crook of Elsa's warm arm. "Buy her love, if that's the only thing that works. Perhaps if you could help a little, Elsa? With my present predicament, I mean."

Elsa's large warm hand creeps down, persuades him for a time into automatic rather than willing vigour, and then she falls asleep. She is tired.

"I told Gemma I was too old to be a father," she thinks she hears Hamish say through vague dreams of Victor, and half waking later, finds Hamish is on top of her and inside her, and that she is lying relaxed, legs apart, arms crooked above her head, as a small child sleeps. Hamish, gaining confidence, covers her eyes, her mouth, her ears with unexpected kisses, blocking her away from her senses. His own face is wet with tears.

"Hamish," she wishes to say, remembers she ought to say, as she would with Victor, who is clearly altogether a more controlled, more experimental and less desperate man in his sexual behaviour than is Hamish, "let's do it another way, not this way, more exciting"—but Hamish is clearly beyond any rational communication, and as for herself, she is carried away now beyond reason, and the possibility of becoming pregnant is now a side issue, a bonus if it were to be so, the rare presence of the god, the amazing illumination, which repeated ritual entreats, and entreats, so powerfully and repeatedly, indeed, as to almost forget its own original intent.

Nor does Elsa feign orgasm, as she does with Victor. Old Hamish, unloved but desired, with his troubled prostate gland, his sad, unwilling organ, convulses her with an implosion of abandonment, as if streams of sensation, running strong again, the ground grateful after drought, had finally filled up and overflowed the black pool of desire and destiny: that same pool her mother bequeathed her at her birth, empty, dry, but waiting to be filled; as her own mother did for her, and her mother's own mother, back to the beginning of time.

"I like sex," says Elsa meditatively and gratefully after Hamish has finished and withdrawn, and lies, startled and gratified, beside her again. "That's the trouble: I like sex."

"No trouble," says Hamish. "No trouble."

"So long as I don't get pregnant," says Elsa, back in the real world again. Ah, sorrow. Victor waiting somewhere else; Gemma wronged; herself discovered; the antique shop waiting. Real life.

"But I thought that was the whole point," says Hamish, but again Elsa does not hear. She is asleep.

She wakes briefly when Hamish leaves the room. She thinks she hears him, or someone, turn the key in the lock, and means to get out of bed to investigate, but of course merely goes back to sleep.

Gemma goes to Victor's room in the middle of the night. He wakes, startled by some unnatural noise, and

turning on the bedside lights finds Gemma gazing down
at him from her chair.

"Let me in," Gemma complains. "I'm cold."

She wears a fine wool deep-blue gown. Her hair is pale
and smooth, her eyes large and bright, her skin young
in the lamplight.

What can Victor do? He leans forward and up and
stretches out his arms and she half-tumbles, half-falls,
to lie beside him.

He unwraps her from her robe, lays her white neat
body beside his and covers them both, for decency and
warmth, with the quilt.

"I'm so helpless," she murmurs. "And Elsa is with
Hamish. I don't know how you can sleep.

"One shouldn't mind such things," she adds, placing
his warm brown hand on her chilly white breast, "but
one does." She wears her mother's pendant. It falls between her breasts. Victor leans on his elbow and looks
down at Gemma.

"I won't hurt you?" he enquires.

"Oh no, no. It might even bring me to life," she as-
sures him earnestly. "The doctor said as much sex as
possible, but I'm afraid with Hamish that is very difficult, though it's recommended for him too. I am his
wife; he respects me. He requires a wicked woman."

"Gemma, you seem quite wicked enough to me."

"Victor, make me warm. Help me. Drive the devil
out of me, bring me to life."

To bring Gemma to life; to make her walk again! Victor is his parent's child.
How Victor's mother rescued things: wasps from jam,
woodlice from the flames, spiders from the bath. His
father was as bad: ancient monuments from collapse,

national institutions from disintegration, teeth from decay. In the end both moved to larger prey: the wasps, woodlice and spiders, the monuments, institutions and molars were left to their own devices; all Victor's parents' energies zeroed in on the wretched of Europe. They would save civilisation itself if they could.

And so they did, losing Victor on the way.

"I'll help you, Gemma," says Victor kindly, his large bulk moving over hers. How both to exert his strength and expend his own energies without crushing the strength from her? (So his mother pondered: how to wash the jam from the wasp without drowning the poor creature?)
Gemma smiles with icy invitation.
But surely Victor will melt the ice, or is it implacable, not ice at all, but chilly steel running the length and breadth of her, allowing her not even the physical movement of her legs?

Gemma's eyes remain open, wide and clear; her breath comes a little faster; she is otherwise composed.

"You must leave Elsa alone," says Gemma coolly to the flushed and impassioned Victor. "Leave her to me. She'll be upset enough when she discovers."
"Discovers what?"
"That her prince is a toad."

Gemma laughs. Victor pauses. But since his making love to Gemma is in spite of her and not because of her, he does not pause for long.

"Stop talking" is all he says. "You're not at the hairdresser's."

Gemma looks faintly puzzled.

"But I always talk," she says. "What's happening

between my legs is nothing to do with my brain. Is it supposed to be?"

Victor is incensed. He turns her over on her face. Her mumbled protests stop. She pants, she moans, she finally cries out.

He turns her over again.

"Good heavens," says Gemma lightly, "I feel like a pancake on a griddle—turned and turned again. Hamish only ever does it one way. I talk to him all the time. Is that wrong? How is one to know?"

"Poor bloody man," says Victor crossly, and then, happily if wrongly, "That won't please Elsa. One position!"

"That's enough," says Gemma, startled, as Victor lies her on her side with himself beside her; it seems calm and companionable to him. "That's more than enough. Stop it!"

"Stop behaving like the Queen," says Victor sharply. "You're only the typist, as you keep saying."

Gemma giggles. "Ah," she says. "I was happy then."

She feels almost warm to Victor. Or is it just his own heat reflecting off her smooth body?

"Gemma!" says a voice from outside; it is a deep, reproachful, powerful voice. "Gemma, are you in there? Gemma, I know you're in there!"

Victor lies still, startled. Gemma laughs happily and loudly.

"Gemma," says the voice, "oh, Gemma, how could you!"

Is it Hamish's voice, contorted by distress? If so, what price Victor's library ladder now? What price the furniture in the billiard room?
Ah, too dear, too dear. Careful now, or the deal will collapse. Deals are so easily upset. Go carefully! The combatants engage upon a structure flimsier than you

would believe: nothing more than the mood of the moment, propped up by past experience, sustained by future hopes, deep-carpeted indeed, and in rollicking fashion, by the cheerful instinct to trade and self-enrich, but undermined by self-doubt, remorse and a weary fatalism. I shall be poor; I shall always be poor; I am the wretched of the earth: the outsider, unloved, unliked. You may think me rich as Croesus, but you are wrong: what about tomorrow? You may believe me greedy as Midas: you misjudge me; I am throwing my wealth away doing you a favour, fool that I am. Unhappy as Hamish? Yes, ah yes! For the moment rich, for always poor.

Hamish, is that you knocking at the door? Then I must redress the balance, and you must win. Take my girl friend, keep your library ladder; make me pay through the nose for the pile of worm-eaten rubbish in the billiard room. I will accept your terms, allow you to profit from me. I will have to. I have cheated, taken your wife, though with the best motives in the world, and that was not part of the deal.

"It can't be Hamish!" Victor asks Gemma, imploring the heavens.

"Go away!" shouts Gemma to the door. "Of course it's not Hamish," she mumbles into Victor's ear. "It's Alice."

"But it's a man, not a woman."

"There you are, Alice," shrieks Gemma. "He thinks you're a man. You have a very male voice. You're unnatural. Go away and shave your moustache!"

Alice weeps great choking sobs of anguish into the panelling of the door.

"I can't stand her like this," complains Gemma to Victor. "She's so weak and wet. She just goes to pieces."

"Say something nice to her!" entreats Victor. "Put her out of her misery."

"I'm miserable," says Gemma into the pillow. "Why shouldn't she be?"

"I'm not crying for myself," sobs Alice to the closed door, "I'm crying for you, Gemma. How will you ever get better if you go on doing what you want, not what you ought? Your soul will begin to shrivel; your legs are beginning to shrivel already. Did you know that?"

"My legs are not shrivelling." Gemma sits up, doing Victor some injury, which she ignores in her passion. "They're just slim. Not great hefty pillars like yours."

Alice's sobs increase.

"Come inside and see what we're doing," says Gemma. "Come in and watch. I know that's what you want. You have to find out how normal people behave, poor thing."

Victor opens his mouth to protest. Gemma puts her hand over his mouth. She is smiling, animated, happy, almost alive. Does he feel her toes twitching?

"I'll open the door," says Alice cautiously, "but I won't look. I must talk to you, that's all. How could you, Gemma! We all loved you so; you were the only good thing in our lives, when poor mother was so depressed."

"She isn't depressed now! Why not just give in and enjoy it, Alice? You should have stayed at home and made up a threesome."

"I am perfectly normal," says Alice desperately. "More than you are. While your husband's with that girl, you're with him. It's disgusting. It's nothing to do with you wanting her baby. It's wife-swapping, that's all."

"Victor isn't married; how can it be?" calls Gemma. "Do go away and let me get on with my pleasures."

"What is it?" asks Victor, perturbed. "What is it?"

For Gemma gasps and cries. Has he crushed her, ruined her, is he killing her? Her breath, which should surely be warm, is icy-cold on his chest.

"I'm alive," cries Gemma, triumphant. "I'm alive."

But she isn't. She's as cold as the grave. Years ago.
"Gemma, naughty girl, come back to bed."
"But Mummy's here."
"Your mother's dead," said Great-Aunt May out of sleep. "And in her grave."

And again the shock and the pleasure, the cold and the fear. Mother die! Go.

"I'm alive?" asked Gemma, dazed.
"Yes, you're alive," said Great-Aunt May, "but you won't be for long if you stay out there in the cold."
"Alive!" repeated Gemma. Nothing else in the room. No one. But by the time she climbed back again into the bed and pressed herself against Great-Aunt May's lean dry side, little Gemma was so cold she might well have passed for dead.

"I'm sorry," says Victor.
"Never mind," says Gemma.

11 ·—◆—◆—◆—◆—◆—◆—◆—◆—◆—◆—◆—◆—◆—◆—◆—◆—

That night, too, Stan the Polish carpenter came to Janice, Victor's wife.

Janice had found him some weeks back through the Yellow Pages, the Post Office's official directory of tradesmen and services. The wardrobe door in her bedroom kept swinging open and Janice concluded she needed a carpenter.

Victor had changed his style of dress along with his mode of life, and left most of his expensive suits behind in the big mahogany bedroom wardrobe.

"Don't give them to the jumble sale," he'd beseeched his wife during one of the long wrangling telephone calls that followed their parting. "Try and sell them, or else don't ever complain to me or anyone that I keep you short of money. You can't just sit about and live off me for the rest of your life. You must make some effort. You owe it to yourself."

Janice had suggested that since Victor now had a retail outlet, he might be better at selling the suits than she, but he had accused her of being possessive and obstructive, and insulting his new profession, so she had

152

advertised the suits in the local newspaper and put "For Sale" cards in stationers' windows. But no one had replied, so there in the wardrobe the suits stayed. And something—either the dry summer and the subsidence of the soil beneath the house causing the whole structure of the house to tilt, or some alteration in the very nature of the suits themselves, which certainly seemed to get heavier with disuse and depression as the months of Victor's absence rolled by—had thrown the wardrobe out of true so that the catch would not hold, and the door would swing open even when the room was perfectly quiet, startling her—as if Victor himself was about to step out of the cupboard and fill the house again with his presence.

And what would he have to say about the state of the carpet? The dust under the bed? Strawberry jam spilled on the velvet chairs and rubbed in, not sponged off? Five of the glass brandy snifters broken? Well, presumably broken, since only seven remained of the dozen she'd bought him for their eighteenth wedding anniversary, out of housekeeping money saved over fifteen of those cheese-paring, housewifely, well-managed years.

No. Victor, stay in your cupboard. I don't want your vision of me anymore. I don't want to have to resist your disapproval, to struggle for my pride in the face of your contempt. Stay where you are. Please.
I don't want to have to intercede between Wendy and you: not anymore. I am tired of explaining to Wendy that you don't mean to hurt; you just can't help it. I am tired of explaining to you that it isn't Wendy's fault she is more interested in embroidery than boys, in the gaining of spiritual grace rather than the losing of her virginity. Wendy is yours as much as mine. You must take some responsibility. It is some hereditary factor working in her; it cannot be environmental. Not with you around, Victor.

She fears him. She sees him in her mind's eye, her

guilty eye, stepping finally out of the wardrobe, hears him speak, putting into words at last what his so reproachful look has for so long mutely suggested.

"Your child, not mine. My seed was far too much diluted. She didn't inherit her nature. I'm afraid she caught it."

For although Wendy was without a doubt Victor's child, inasmuch as one of Victor's sperm swam up to meet the egg deposited through Janice's Fallopian tubes, other men's sperm had also swum around inside Janice before Victor and she were married, and had, it was vaguely felt by both of them, left some disagreeable trace of themselves behind, polluting her procreative byways and highways, as it were, so that Wendy was not only Victor's child, but Alan's, Derek's, Mike's, Joe's, John's, Murray's and so on, and others whose names had been forgotten or never known, and probably took after the sum of all her mother's lovers rather than her acknowledged father.

Victor had always hoped to marry a virgin; expected to marry a virgin, as his father had done before him: someone as pure and helpful as his own mother. But alas, he fell in love with Janice. Or rather, having slept with Janice once, after a dark and drunken students' party, could not bear the notion of her sleeping with anyone else thereafter, and taking this for love, married her. Whereupon Janice, as if to reassure him, had silently and instinctively made herself as rigid, plain, clean, orderly and respectable as possible, bristling with defences designed to repel any possible sexual boarders, so that merely to look at her was to feel certain that here was a woman faithful to her husband.
Perforce, if nothing else.
Behold wild Janice, married! What we have here, ladies and gentlemen, is no woman, but a housewife. And what a housewife! Note her rigid, mousy curls, kept stiff by spray; her quick eyes, which search for dust

and burning toast, and not the appraisal or enquiry of
the opposite sex; the sharp voice, growing sharper,
louder, year by year: at home in a bus queue or order-
ing groceries or rebuking the garage, but hardly in the
bed. Does that suit you, Victor?

No.

But I thought that was what you wanted. How am I to
be desired by all, but still kept for your especial use?
My highways and byways unpolluted even by the
thoughts of others? Tell me! Victor! But Victor, I was
only trying to be what you wanted. It isn't fair.

Go to Elsa, then. I know her by heart, although I have
never met her. Who is wanted by all and desired by all,
her inner footpaths well trodden down by the thoughts
of men—and women too. Whose hair flows free and
spreads across pillows; whose eyelids rise and fall with
automatic erotic intent; whose voice is useless in the
grocer's shop but useful in the bed. Elsa, who is everyone's whether she knows it or not, in the imaginings if
not in the flesh. Go to Elsa, then, while I, Janice, remember who I am. While there's still time: before my
hair is iron grey, like my heart, and there is no turning
back.

Janice's wrist positively aches from slamming the wardrobe door. Presently she feels the task is beyond her,
and summons help. Janice sends for Stan, the Polish
carpenter. He is a small man; he weighs one hundred
and twenty-eight pounds (he tells her so); he trembles;
his eyes have the sorrowful appreciation of the immi-
grant: is he sorry for her or for him? Before she knows
it there she is on the bed, and him on top of her, hammering away with a quivering, nervous intensity. She is
to make it all better for him. The grand home of his
childhood, his family acres, lost to the state; his wife a
common working woman who cannot even understand
his degradation, cannot comprehend that carpenters

have poetry in their souls. Janice is to make up for it all. Not that he blames his wife. Her father was a prison officer, soulless, and beat all human aspiration out of her, leaving her merely English. Not her fault, but their mutual doom. He has always been doomed: angry, nervous, Polish and doomed.

Six times in one night; eight the next. This takes Janice back, like nothing or no one else: not even the plumber or the milkman. Is it mere physical exhaustion or the rebirth of her sexuality that leads her now to drooping round the house, careless of its appearance and her own? Slut that she's becoming, only fit to lie back upon the bed while Stan the Polish carpenter wreaks his nervous will upon her, expends his tormented energy and fills her dazed mind with the overflow of his complaints against the world, his wife, the betrayal of his past, his hopes and his country.

"It seems to me," said Janice, lying there, "that you do all right. If I'm anything to go by."

"You English," he cried, moving up to her mouth to stop her complaints, "all you English are the same. You understand nothing."

But Victor's kingsize bed with its orthopedic mattress is large enough for Janice to turn herself, so that his mouth, too, is presently stopped.

It seems to Janice, even from her comparatively limited experience with other men since Victor left home, that the physical activity of sex has become a great deal more varied since she was a girl and lay in missionary position beneath a variety of men. In those days tongues could only be used in mouths, and penises must only come in contact with vaginas, lest the word perversion be bandied about; and the involvement of hands or instruments carried with it the overtones of a horrid, secret masturbatory activity. And boyfriends, as she remembered, since the general consensus was that love must accompany sex, were supposed to come one at a time. But now, surely, there was a great tumbling of humans all together, and a more diffuse eroticism, which being limited no longer to certain parts of the person in ritual conjunction with certain other parts of certain other people, need hardly be so limited any more. Thank God!

Come carpenter, carpet layer, car mechanic, accountant; come one and all, since this sensation, this forgetfulness, is all we are after. What I think of you now, man, not what you think of me. Who cares? You'll be gone in the morning. Pray God.

And since my mouth, my comment, can be stilled not by your mouth, but right to the source of my objection with your erect penis; and I can stop your comment on me by using up your tongue between my legs; and I can obtain relief from self-observation by stopping thinking if only momentarily—and with this particular carpenter the law of diminishing returns seems to operate—after my fourth orgasm and his third the brain seems to work again. Dear God!

I am still myself, for all of you.

About the time that Alice comes battering at Victor's door, Janice wriggles free from Stan and says, "The wardrobe door is open again. Won't you for God's sake fix it? It's what you came for."

Her voice has lost its harshness of quality. Her hair, unwashed and uncurled for some weeks, has regained a natural sheen and clots greasily and heavily around her face. It pleases him and suits her. Her mouth has relaxed its grimness of line. She is abandoned, to all decency. She is herself again: heavy, sprawling and available, freely demanding of him and herself.

"You Englishwomen are cruel," says Stan. "You wish

to humiliate me. To remind me that I am only the carpenter. The useful little man around the corner."

But presently, singing and still naked, he takes his screwdriver and removes the lock and planes the length of the drawer, and by accident removes some beading, which he then has to hammer back. Bang-bang.
Janice sits up in bed, marvelling. Never has she seen such cheerful bungling. It is as if all his potential skill with tools has concentrated in the living one.

Wendy. Where's Wendy? How does Wendy fare while her mother relives her past and so thoughtlessly and selfishly redefines her nature?

Wendy's doing nicely, thank you. Wendy, the while, has been to the church choir social and eaten half a dozen fattening scones and drunk six small glasses of sweet sherry. Here she has encountered a postgraduate student from Milwaukee doing research into fading religious attitudes in Western Europe. His hair is curly, he is half her size; his face is lively and impish, as is his mind. Her slow head tries to follow his quick movements as he goes about the room making enquiries of one churchgoer and another. Wendy is patient, as is her nature. Finally he comes to her. He asks his initial questions, finds her replies promising, sits her in a corner, takes notes; he enquires about her attitudes to God, to sherry, to her mother, to her father, her sexual experiences if any, her parents' attitude to sexual matters. Presently his hand stops writing; he asks the question for himself, and not for his further degree. And Wendy, scarcely noticing the transition, continues to talk in a manner she never would have done had she not had so much sherry and believed herself to be furthering the cause of knowledge, science and truth. In so doing she offered herself to him as she was, and not, perhaps, as she would have liked to be, or her father might have wished she was.

The young man took her home, and it being a warm night, they bought fish and chips and sat together on a park bench to eat them; and he, knowing that her virginity was a bother to her and had driven her father from home, relieved her of it in the laurel bushes behind the bench, an episode disturbed only by a passing and indifferent policeman's torch, and then by a sudden change in the weather, making them scuffle through the undergrowth for their clothing. Neither, afterwards, had any desire to part, or felt any desire to be off and finished with the episode, but walked together hand in hand, bodies rubbing together at every opportunity. She asked his name at the front gate, and asked him in to share her bed, an offer he gladly accepted.

The noise of hammering came from the house. Janice's window was brightly lit and the curtains not closed. A woman sat on the front step. She wore a head scarf and spectacles, and seemed angry. She spoke with the flat sour accents of the underprivileged and defeated.

"My husband's in there with your mum," she said to Wendy. "Mending her wardrobe, like as not. If it's not that, it'll be her ceiling rose. Listen to him, hammering all hours of the day and night. Mind you, he's not English."

When Wendy, dazed by the suddenness of events, took out her front-door key and opened the door, the little woman in the head scarf ran in ahead of her and Kim —for that was the young researcher's name—and up the stairs and into Janice's bedroom, and flew at her rival, scratching and biting, as she sat naked and correct in the bed. It took Stan, Wendy and Kim together some effort to drag her off, by which time Janice was mauled, bleeding and shaken.

Stan's wife sat and cried in the kitchen while Janice

made her a cup of tea. Stan had dressed and gone home, but not before his wife spat at him.

"I'm not blaming you," said Stan's wife to Janice. "If it's not you it's someone else. I only wish women would stick together a bit. It's not for me I mind, not any more: it's for the children. He's never at home. He's either off giving his money away at political meetings or screwing the lady clients so his work never gets done. Then he quarrels with them or their husbands find out, so he never gets paid. I don't mind what he does with his cock; he's got to do something with it, that's for sure, and it's better than having it in me all hours of the day and night, God knows. It's a kind of nervous twitch he's got."

Stan's wife raised her head and looked about her, as if for the first time conscious of her surroundings. She looked at the unwashed dishes, the grime on the cup she drank from, the bottle caps and scraps of paper on the floor, the crumbs on the sideboard, the congealed fat on the table, the burnt debris on the stove.

"I'd be ashamed to live like this," said Stan's wife. "A real pigsty. Well, he likes a good wallow." And she left.

Janice, Wendy and Kim sat around the kitchen table for some time after her departure. Kim's hand itched with desire to take notes, but he desisted.

"You can't go on like this, Mum," said Wendy. "You'd better get Dad back."

"Do you want that?" enquired Janice. Her left eye was swelling, and her hands were trembling almost as much as had the carpenter's penis, erect. Stan's wife, she had noticed, trembled too. Her nose had been running, as if in her passion she had manufactured extra juices, and a drop had hung trembling unnoticed for some time on the end of her nose. The less she had to do with the carpenter and his like the better. A pity. It had all seemed so simple: summoning bed companions out of thin air, dismissing them again at will. All of them less than she, as she had been less than Victor.

"I'm all right," said Wendy with simple pride. "Now I've met Kim. I can take Daddy or leave him, if you see what I mean. Kim's coming to stay with us. He's only got a kind of self-service hotel in South Kensington, and he doesn't like it very much. It smells of cooked cabbage, he says. This place smells a bit too, but we'll soon get it cleared up. Won't we, Mother?"

"You clear it up if you want to," said her mother. "Nothing to do with me. But what will your father say if Kim stays?"

"Nothing I can't make good use of in my thesis," observed Kim in the constructive fashion that marked his passage through life.

"It's hardly up to Father to say anything," said Wendy, her hand travelling down towards Kim's crotch as naturally and easily as if she stretched it out to stroke a kitten.

Let Victor cope, thinks Janice, taking a tranquiliser and going to bed and sleep. The wardrobe door does not fall open, although Stan had no time to fix the bolt. Her orifices are still sensitive and uneasy from his quivering searches of them; her eye is hurting, as is the deep scratch, red-edged, that runs from her thumb to her wrist, and her mind thuds from the insults offered to her by his wife. But her head no longer aches. On the contrary, it feels well-healed and perfectly content. Even without the tranquiliser she would have slept well.

Elsa, too, sleeps soundly after Hamish's departure, but is presently awakened by a rattling of her door handle and the soft booming of Alice's extraordinary voice in the corridor outside.

Elsa sits up and shivers. The room is cold. The weather has changed in the night; the window is shut, but the wind has managed to find a crack and she feels it chilly on her cheek. Outside the night is draining from the sky, leaving it bleak and grey, yet streaked with a kind of shine, as if the bottom of the sky had been too harshly scraped in the new wind's scouring away of the night.

"Let me in," begs Alice, "let me in. I must speak to you."

"I can't," says Elsa. "I'm locked in. It's some mistake."

"It's no mistake," booms Alice through the door. "Victor's with Gemma and they don't want you to know."

Alice goes round to the back of the house, out into the kitchen courtyard, and climbs up to Elsa's window, using the library ladder to get her some part of the way; after that she relies on cornices, decorative alcoves and concrete gargoyles for footholds. She is a heavy girl, and in passing breaks the top rungs of the library ladder. Elsa winces at the thought of Victor's inevitable displeasure, and leans out to help Alice, and wonders whether perhaps it might not be preferable to topple down and end everything than to endure the pain that had clutched her heart at the thought of Victor with Gemma.

But when Alice, slipping, clutches at Elsa's hair and makes her cry out and all but pulls her from the window, Elsa knows that she wishes and means to live, and pulls herself back inside and Alice too, with an ease that surprises her.

Elsa closes the window and gets back into bed: her eyes feel stretched and wide with lack of sleep and too much untoward emotion, come too suddenly. Alice huddles at the end of the bed, under blankets.

"What am I going to do?" mourns Alice. "How am I going to live? Even Gemma despises me."

Elsa draws Alice in beside her. It is the nearest, for a long time, that she has lain next to a contemporary in age; she is surprised to remember the difference between stretching naked next to a young person, and next to one who is old. It is the whole difference between the sensation of immortality and that of morality. When she lay with Victor or with Hamish, death lay between them in the bed. They bridged him, but could not ignore him. Death waited, was made to wait, but clearly wouldn't wait forever. Is this the last time? Or this? Or this? Will I die before tomorrow night? A stroke, breast cancer, heart attack?

Elsa kisses young Alice, whose distress is merely that she will have to live forever as she is. She covers Alice with her body, lets her hands comfort and penetrate Alice as if it were her own body she thus cajoled. Alice, made like any other woman in detail, though not in broad outline, cries out and calms, and smiles in the cold light. Thus Elsa did with her schoolfriends on many an educational and recreational school journey to the Swiss Alps, the Italian Riviera and the Austrian Tyrol, until the exchange rate made such journeys difficult. Though Elsa worked weekends at the greengrocer's to save the money to pay for them.

"I'm not a lesbian," says Alice, "though Gemma thinks I am. I have trouble with my hormones, that's all. Is that my fault? I am as normal as the next person —just unhappier."

"You seemed so sure of yourself this morning," murmured Elsa, half asleep. "I was quite afraid."

"Come away with me," begs Alice. "Victor's too old,

and anyway he's married, and Gemma's spoiled all that for you."

"I shouldn't have gone with Hamish," Elsa reproaches herself, as if automatically. "Victor only went with Gemma to be revenged. And Gemma too. It's all my fault."

"You're so simple," says Alice. "It was all planned by Gemma. Everything always is. She means Victor to leave you, and Hamish to impregnate you, and herself to keep the baby so she can torment it as it grows up. And she'll get her way. She gets her way with everything except her own legs."

No, thinks Elsa. Surely not. I can't be pregnant. Can't be.

"If that were true," says Elsa, sinking backwards into sleep, "Gemma would be a very wicked person. And I don't know anyone wicked. So it can't be true."

"There was once a little spark of evil in her," says Alice, her voice now mixed up with Elsa's dreams, "and the wind of the world has fanned it into a great fire. It's consuming her and everyone."

But Elsa is asleep. Alice lies beside her, sleepless and miserable. Presently the door is unlocked and Gemma enters, as Alice had indeed supposed she presently would.

Alice smiles sweetly up at Gemma.

Gemma smiles sweetly at Alice. Behind her comes Johnnie with a breakfast trolley.

"It's stuffy in here," says Gemma. "Do open the window, Johnnie."

Johnnie opens the window, and stands behind the trolley. There is a glint of expectation behind his glasses.

So no doubt he stood, polite and expectant, in his native land, watching the tide of power sweep over the wretched and helpless of the earth; assisting it on its way, diverting it now and then to mulch the occasional head raised to block its path; listening, waiting, thriving on the cries of the tortured, the maimed, the burned. And now hot coffee, thick cream, fresh rolls, crisp bacon. Breakfast! What are good times without the bad? The pleasures of the privileged are much enhanced by the cries of the unfortunate.

Johnnie stands easily behind the trolley and watches and smiles.

"I expect you were cold in the night," says Gemma kindly. "I know I was. The weather's changed. Which of you kept the other warm, I wonder?"

"It was her," says Alice, thus displaying cowardice and conceding defeat all at once.

"Get out of bed," says Gemma, and Alice does so, naked, hiding her body from Johnnie with her large lean hands. She makes twice of him, but what has that to do with anything? Small men wield power, hold keys, apply electrodes, write execution lists, initiate policies. Before them the merely massive fall back powerless.

Gemma's chair whirs. She glides towards Alice, who backs towards the window.

"Get out of here," says Gemma, "the way you came." Alice half-falls, half-climbs out of the window, and half-climbs, half-falls to the ground, where she lies collapsed and crying.

"My eyes," she cries. "I've scratched my eyes. I can't see. There was a bramble—"

"That comes from seeing things you shouldn't," calls down Gemma, and drops Alice's jeans and T-shirt down after her from between distasteful fingers.

"You can open the gates for her," says Gemma to Johnnie. "We don't want her here. Run along."

Johnnie leaves. He does not run.

"Well!" says Gemma, alone with Elsa. "Well! Breakfast?"

She encourages Elsa to sit up in bed, and lends her a pink silk wrap to put around her shoulders. She touches each of Elsa's nipples gently with her cool finger.

"Breast milk can be deep-frozen now," says Gemma. "Isn't that useful!"

"I see you did the typing," she says, pouring coffee. "And so beautifully! You must have a deeply feminine nature. To type well is to desire to please."

"I hope Alice was merely trying to keep warm in your bed and nothing else," remarks Gemma, buttering toast. "I am afraid she has some kind of genetic deficiency and is sexually ambivalent. Her mother is a confirmed lesbian. There is a lot of it about. It is nature's answer to the population problem. I can't bear anything unnatural myself. Can you?"

Alice's motorbike can be heard to spit and sob and roar. The great wood-veneered gates open by Johnnie's remote command.

"I am disappointed in Alice as a person and as a physiotherapist," says Gemma, slicing the top off an egg. "She was very clumsy. And how could I have gone to Great-Aunt May's funeral? I have trouble enough getting to places I *want* to get to. The reason there was no one at her funeral was because she was so boring no one wanted to go. And she had no business sending me off to be a mother's helper, as if I were a skivvy."

Gemma's eyes are bright with remembered rage.

"My mother would never have allowed it," says Gemma. "And if Great-Aunt May had looked after my mother properly, had the roof mended so it didn't leak, my mother need never have died. I hate Great-Aunt May. I'm glad she's dead. She deserved to die."

She plucks the pendant at her neck.

"I'll leave you some more typing after breakfast," says Gemma, recovering her equanimity a little, although there are tears of passion in her eyes. "I would like you to stay in your room this morning and rest.

"Alice had a father," says Gemma bitterly. "All those Hemsley girls had a father. I didn't. I was a bastard, a skivvy, and everyone knew it. There's no excuse for Alice. She had every advantage. It doesn't matter how long ago your childhood was," she adds, by way of explanation. "It is never finished. Never.

"And now," says Gemma, calmer, "while you drink your coffee I'll get on with my story."

Mr. Fox's party, May 12th, 1966.

Gemma had borrowed Marion's mother's, white satin dancing shoes, circa 1930, and worn Marion's gran's white silk shawl, circa 1915, over a semitopless black lace dress bought from the now re-opened boutique at the foot of Fox and First's offices with money borrowed from Marion's dad, and had been to the hairdresser on her lunch hour to have her hair made bouffant and springy to the touch with lacquer.

"Ugh!" said Mr. First, touching it with a thin, dry

finger. "The more money you girls spend on your looks, the worse fools you make of yourselves."

Gemma cringed, as anyone might well do from a murderer—even if one thus defined only in someone else's dream.

"What do I do to deserve it?" rasped Mr. First, disappearing into his office. "No one likes me."

Mr. Fox's party.

Gemma was humiliated. Her breasts, by comparison with the minor swellings exhibited by the other women in the room, seemed to her own eyes to be gross, and Mr. Fox's earlier admiration of them was surely ironic rather than sincere. She was obliged to swathe them with her shawl and look rather like Great-Aunt May on a particularly cold day.

Mr. Fox set her to making champagne cocktails, spoke to her as if she were the maid, and otherwise ignored her. Oh, Mr. Fox!

As for Gemma's hair, all the other women had silky hair, close-cropped.
Gemma served champagne cocktails.

The party sank down upon soft cushions, pot-smoking, acid-popping; beautiful people rolled onto and over other beautiful people, limbs pallidly interlocked, without energy or particular interest.
Not Gemma. Provincial, uneasy Gemma.
As for the men, if that's what they were with their pretty, depraved faces, they took no notice of Gemma.

Gemma, who are you, after all? No one titled, or rich, or black, or amazing. You are a typist, and loving Mr.

Fox will not change that. Not this evening, anyway. Love's a trivial commodity here.

More champagne cocktails: a sugar lump doused in brandy at the bottom of each thick eighteenth-century snifter filled to the brim with champagne and adorned with a sprig of mint. Delivered into trembling, fastidious, manicured hands.

An oddly old young man, whose hair was dyed elderly grey, and with pupils turned red by means of contact lenses, pulled Gemma's shawl aside, peeked inside, laughed, closed the shawl again and offered her a drag on his reefer.

"Go on," murmured Gemma's mother in her ear, "go on. Join in! Or do you mean to let me down? Be a typist all your life? I left you everything I could: looks, ambition, a body to be used as a weapon in the world. I didn't make it, but you can, Gemma. Go on, accept!"

"Gemma!" whispered Great-Aunt May, shocked. "Don't you dare! Everything I've taught you! Virtue, obedience, self-control, submission to God's will!"

Gemma fingered her pearl necklace, which had looked appropriate in Marion's mum's mirror, but now looked merely pathetic, and hesitated. The young man raised what would have been his eyebrows had he not shaved them off and pencilled others in.

Mr. Fox left the party with two heiresses and a society photographer.

Gemma moaned. The young man, bored, moved on.

Gemma went home by underground. Round, on points, to Great-Aunt May. Mother scrabbles at the window, dead nails scouring the glass.

Mr. First, murderer, sister-slayer, raised his eyebrows and sneered as he passed through the office. Business was slack, and except for cleaning out the parrot cages there was little to do.

On Saturday Gemma collected her week's wages from a distraught Miss Hilary.

"It's all very well for you young girls," said Miss Hilary, taking a 50 percent commission on Gemma's week's work. "You have your life before you. Mine's all but gone."

On Sunday Marion's family took her to Kew Gardens. The first jumbo jet passed overhead on its way to Heathrow and everybody oooed and ahed. The azaleas were finished.

On Sunday evening Gemma wrote a letter to Great-Aunt May in her nursing home, telling her how she had left the North and was making a life for herself in London.

She never posted it. Years later Marion's mum found it pushed down the back of the sofa of the three-piece suite when she was replacing the upholstered furniture with cushions filled with polystyrene chips—something of a fire hazard, but no one knew that at the time.

Failing to get a reply, Gemma was of course hurt and angry.

Gemma dropped the pearl pendant in the wastepaper basket, but Marion's mum retrieved it. Marion's mum tried to put it in the top left-hand drawer of Marion's chest-of-drawers, which Marion kept for treasures of various kinds, but could not open it.

"Funny," said Marion's mum. "Stuck! I must get

Marion's dad to see to that one day. Smelly, too. What's she put in it now, the naughty girl?"

Gemma went home to shiver all night under the duvet, the latest notion fresh from the Continent, a feather quilt that replaced blankets, covered with pale blue cotton seersucker, as found in the houses of those in tune with modern living. Those who could afford to be really closely in tune with modern living also, no doubt, enjoyed central heating. Marion's mum and dad did not.

Marion's mum and dad had waited up for Gemma to return, the sooner to hear her tales of high life. Gemma could not even cry in peace.
Marion, not having been asked to the party, had gone to bed early with a sleeping pill and slept soundly.

"Such a wet blanket, that girl!" observed Marion's mum. "Not surprising she never gets asked out."
"She'll marry an undertaker and disgrace us all," said Marion's dad comfortingly.

When at last Gemma was in her chilly bed under the duvet, clutching the feathers around her, crying softly from pain and humiliation, Marion stirred in her sleep and wept a little herself, as if keeping Gemma company.

Mr. Fox then absented himself from the office for some ten days. Nothing more was said of the trip to Tangier. Gemma's bosom remained, as it were, expectant, thwarted and searching for someone to finger it. She could have sworn that in the interim it grew another couple of inches and tilted upwards, waiting. It began to seem to Gemma that her breasts had a life of their own, offering themselves insensately to the world, regardless of her wishes for them. She bound them savagely flat with the elastic bandages Marion's gran had used for her knees, and wore Marion's mum's sister's white satin wedding dress, circa 1928, to the office.

One fine day Mr. Fox appeared at Gemma's elbow and, bending sideways with dexterous charm, bit the back of her pretty white neck.

"I've lost seven pounds," said Mr. Fox, "and had a 22.25 percent increase in physical agility. See!" And he bent and nipped her again.

Nip-nip! Mr. Fox is back! Gemma's bosom swelled and heaved and burst its bandages.

"Ooh," cried Gemma, suddenly lopsided.
"Extraordinary," murmured Mr. Fox, and went to inspect the parrots.

Gemma blushed with shame and despair. But Mr. Fox's mind was still on himself.

"Do you think it's an improvement?" he asked earnestly. "I don't merely look haggard?"
"No, no," cried Gemma.

Mr. Fox cared what Gemma thought. Mr. Fox cared what everyone thought, but how was Gemma to know that?
Mr. Fox disguised need with a cloak of contempt, like many another before and since, but Gemma did not see it.

"I dined on lettuce leaves and water for ten days. The lettuce leaves were limp and the water came out of a tap. And how was horrid Mr. First in my absence?"
"Horrid." How smart Gemma is becoming! How she thinks now before she speaks!
Gemma, how I've missed you! Mr. First is in or out?"

"Out."
"Good. Come upstairs."

And Gemma followed Mr. Fox upstairs. So the world can turn upside down in a moment; thus, boredom turn to joy unconfined.

In a dark corner of Mr. Fox's penthouse, beneath a profusion of fern and a tangle of creepers, worked an elderly cleaning woman with dustpan and brush, feather duster, secateurs, watering can, fertiliser sprinkler and Perspex cleaner, genteelly cursing as hummingbirds swept beneath her nose or through the wisps of her white hair.

Mr. Fox behaved as if Mrs. Olsen wasn't there. So did Gemma, learning fast.

Well, the old woman got paid. What more did she want? Recognition? Understanding? Sympathy? She would have to pay them for that.

"You're getting fat," said Mr. Fox to Gemma.
"Two pounds," confessed Gemma. "It's Marion's parents. They're feeding me up."
"What for? The killing?"

Was there a glint in his eyes? The glint of Red Riding-hood's wolf or Serena's Bluebeard: wicked eyes peering out of a Disney forestscape?

Gemma laughed uneasily. Mr. Fox did not laugh.

"I hope Marion's been keeping her stories to herself?"
"Yes."
"And you?"
"Yes. Not a word to anyone."

"Wonderful to be home again! Health farms are such tedious places."

And Mr. Fox flung himself down on a leopard-skin sofa, and patted the cushion beside him. How lean and predatory he appeared, his body half sunk into feather cushions. He wore very tight denim trousers, open white shirt and a moonstone pendant.

Gemma sat cautiously beside him. Mr. Fox sat up and pushed Gemma so that she sprawled, not as elegantly as she would have wished, back on the cushions. Then he bent over her on one elbow, as Valentino inclined over his white, pure love.

Did Mr. Fox mean it? The romantic intensity of his gaze, the bright eyes searching her face, her throat, her body? Or was he joking?

Mrs. Olsen coughed in an alarmed fashion, but Mr. Fox took no notice.

Mr. Fox's weight was considerable, in spite of the recent loss of seven pounds, but his kiss was light, barely touching Gemma's lips. His lips moved over hers from right to left, from left to right, and then were gone. Mr. Fox's hand, however, was firm against her breast.

"A funny dress," he said. "All lumpy. Or is it you? Say it isn't you."

Gemma opened her mouth to explain, but now it seemed that her lips, like her breasts, were scarcely hers to control. They waited now for kisses; they had little time for words. If they spoke at all, now, it would be to utter protestations of love. Gemma kept her mouth tight shut.

"I do believe you love me, Gemma," said Mr. Fox.

"Which is only right and fitting, after all. Marion loves Mr. First, or she would have left long ago, and if you love me you won't ask for a raise, will you, because that would make me really angry. But do tell me, what are you wearing beneath your dress, and why?"

Mr. Fox stood Gemma up, removed her dress, unwound Marion's gran's bandage and dropped it into the wastepaper basket. Mrs. Olsen clattered her displeasure under the umbrella pine. Mr. Fox took the dress and the scissors and unsnipped a dart beneath the arms. Then, raising her arms above her head as if she were a doll, he replaced the dress.

"That's better," said Mr. Fox. "It is usually easier to fit the garment to the body than the body to the garment. And never, never let me see you again with your hair as you wore it to my party; next time I won't come back."

"Mr. Fox, are you serious?"

"Yes," says Mother in Gemma's ear, "deadly serious. Listen, learn, advance yourself. This is the way to live."

"Gemma," warns Great-Aunt May, "the man's an idiot. Your father was an idiot too, but your mother wouldn't believe me. Gawping and gazing over the footlights."

"Are you coming to Tangier with me?" enquired Mr. Fox.

"Yes," said Gemma's mouth, who was clearly on Gemma's mother's side.

"Are you a virgin?" he asked.

"Yes," said Gemma's mouth.

"The mixture is almost too strong to tolerate," complained Mr. Fox. "Love, Tangier and virginity."

Mrs. Olsen coughed less discreetly. Her gnarled hand

was outstretched, rough, red and old. That's what you want for me, Great-Aunt May. That's how you want my hands. I know you. You don't want me good, you want me miserable. My hands aren't for dishcloths and hot water. They're for the caressing of the male cheek; more, the male member. Look at my hands. Fold them in yours, Mr. Fox. See the cool, slender, nimble fingers, the rosy palm. Put your thumb there in the hollow of my palm, Mr. Fox; let me close my fingers around it. See! Not such a virgin but that I wasn't born to it. Such tricks!

Is that what you did, Mother, back in the old cinema in Maryport, Northumberland? Please say you did—that I wasn't conceived altogether without finesse? Not altogether!

"If I could bother you for my money, sir. It's three weeks now."

"Mr. First pays you, I think." Mr. Fox was vague and cold, his hands gone from Gemma's. But now her hands were his, with her heart and her mind and her lips.

"Mr. First isn't in until after lunch."

"Can't you wait, Mrs. Olsen? Surely!"

"No. My husband is crippled; he can't get out. He's waiting for his dinner."

"How much do we owe you?"

"Sixteen pounds plus fares."

"Sixteen pounds! It's incredible. And fares? Where do you travel from?"

"Whitechapel."

"Isn't that walking distance?"

"Not for me, sir."

"Really? At the health farm I walked eight miles a day and thought nothing of it."

"Could I have my money, sir?"

"I'll make a note of it. And Mrs. Olsen, I don't like being disturbed; will you remember that? And the spider plants have been allowed to become too moist; they're not flowering as they should be."

"I'm sorry, sir. There's rather a lot to remember; it's not as if I were a paid gardener."

"Any careful and reasonable person could manage. That will be all."

Mrs. Olsen left, rebuked, and without her wages.

"Treat them tough," said Mr. Fox happily, his money saved. "They love it."

"And now," said Mr. Fox, "now that we have had our interlude, Gemma, and I am reconciled to London and the office, which is not without its pleasures, though scarcely real life, you will perhaps earn your wages by doing some modelling for me. You may undress behind the bourbon-rose bramble, savouring its sweetness the while. Take all your clothes off, it you please: scraps of fabric merely distract the eye and distort the sense of proportion."

And while Gemma took off her clothes, Mr. Fox put on a white nylon coat and a French onion-seller's black beret, and presently sculpted around Gemma's white upper arms a mould for an arm-bracelet with jewel settings incorporated. Mr. Fox worked intently and happily; had he only been able to fill twenty-four hours of the day thus working, fulfilling his intended destiny, how admirable a person might he not have been!

When he was satisfied with his achievement, he put down his tools and sighed, and the far-off look left his eye and the glint returned and he blinked at Gemma's body, as if remembering it.

"Ah yes," he said, "Tangier."

Then Mr. Fox crossed to a coconut tree and unhooked from it a double coconut, which Gemma had believed to be simply growing there, and from a hinged drawer carved in its rather repulsive hairy shell drew out a single antique ring. A red stone gleamed in a silver snake's-mouth setting.

A ruby! At least Gemma assumed that it was a ruby, and not red glass. Mrs. Hemsley owned a massive gilt necklace whose whole purpose was to house a ruby chip. Gemma had been sent to Maryport on several occasions to pawn it, secretly, at the pawn shop there.

Mrs. Hemsley! Mrs. Hemsley had not written to Gemma since she left home, nor had any of the girls: not even Alice, who had sworn eternal devotion. That she had not let them know her address, and that their letters to the YWCA went unanswered, much to their distress, quite escaped foolish Gemma. Gemma was angry with Mrs. Hemsley and bitter too. Too bitter at not being written to to write.

"Hold out your left hand," said Mr. Fox. Gemma stretched out her hand.
"With this ring, etc.," said Mr. Fox, joking, and pushed the ring onto her third finger. The ring was too small, or her finger too large.
Gemma cried out in pain as it went over her knuckle.
"What's the matter?" asked Mr. Fox, surprised.
"My finger's gone numb," said Gemma. "It feels all cold."
"Never mind that," said Mr. Fox. "See how beautiful your hand looks with the ring upon it. You have perfect hands—or as perfect as nature can achieve. The artist, of course, outdoes nature. It is his function. The ring now on your finger belonged once to Catherine, Tsarina of all the Russias. Or so they say, and thus I paid. A very wicked lady. Wickedness comes expensive. Goodness is a far cheaper and more boring phenomenon, especially in retrospect."

Mr. Fox stretched out Gemma's arm, gently inclining

her hand so that it dropped slightly beneath the weight
of the ring. Both surveyed the effect.
He caught up the ringed hand and pressed it to his lips,
but lightly, jokingly.

"You may keep the ring," said Mr. Fox.
"Me? Catherine's ring?"
"For the moment."
"Oh thank you, thank you."

But how difficult it was to please Mr. Fox.

"You are not a little girl to say please and thank
you," said Mr. Fox severely. "I am not giving you a
treat; I am doing you an honour."
"I'm sorry."
"Never mind. Be careful with the ring, Gemma."
"Of course."
"Don't wash up in it."
"Wash up? Never!"
"Don't slap an admirer with it, however impor-
tunate the lout might be. It might loosen the stone."
"Of course I won't."
"And Gemma, don't let Mr. First see."
"Why not?"
"Because Mr. First lays neurotic claim to various
valuables about the building. But beautiful things be-
long to those who value them, not those who paid for
them. Don't you agree?"
"Oh yes, yes! I'll put it in my bag at once."
"You may wear it home, Gemma. It marks you as
mine. But go home now before Mr. First returns, and
take Marion with you. I shan't deduct the time from
either of your wages; I am a generous man. But I want
to be alone, to feel solitary, to let the muse flow. And
Gemma, once you have the ring home, keep it in a safe
place. Until I ask for its return."
"Of course, of course." Gemma, impetuous, leant

forward and kissed Mr. Fox on his cool, dry lips. Mr. Fox smiled, cool and dry.

Mr. Fox, Gemma loves you.

Well, of course that was what Mr. Fox intended.

"Gemma," said Mr. Fox, "remember to dress before you go."

12 ·—·—·—·—·—·—·—·—·—·—·—·—·—·—·—·—·—·—·

Gemma pauses in her tale. Victor stands in the doorway, the colour beneath his cheekbones heightened, chin pale beneath its stubble: thus he appears in times of illness and unusual stress. The top of his head seems more bare and more shiny than usual. His area of baldness crept noticeably down to meet his ears. This morning, washing his hair in the acid-green wash basin to clear away the sweat of the night, he was disconcerted to see what looked like seaweed floating in the water. Closer examination proved it to be what he feared: lanks of his hair come unattached in the night, and including those particular strands which he brushed across the top of his head to soften the line where haired skin and bare skin met. The discovery had a nightmare quality that failed to disperse even after the rhythms of the day had asserted themselves.

Stress, of course. Stress seeping today to the hair follicles, tomorrow to the heart or the brain, causing hemorrhage or coronary or both.
Careful, Victor. Things move too fast. Your body warns you. But where are you to pin the blame? Perhaps the sudden change of diet has unsettled your constitution? The shift from Yin and Yang to high cholesterol? Or the unexpected change in the weather? Victor's father

181

swore that on days the weather changed his patient
felt pain more acutely. Voltaire swore that when the
north wind blew the whole English race fell into a deep
depression, and no coffee house was worth visiting. Or
was it something worse; was it the loss of his love for
Elsa, which had acted as a kind of charm against age,
illness and the forces of decay? And did he in fact no
longer love her, or had he merely suppressed his feelings for her in the exhilaration of offering largesse to
Hamish, that sorry millionaire who had nothing to his
credit but worldly success, money and now of course
Gemma? Victor hardly knew.

Yesterday, had you asked Victor what love was, he
would have replied, "What I feel for Elsa. My attach-
ment to life itself." Today, locks of his hair lying
stranded on the bottom of the wash basin, he would
reply, "I don't know. An insanity, perhaps. Something
felt by the young." Or was it all Gemma's doing—
inciting Elsa, deceiving Hamish, sapping his strength,
tormenting his mind, stealing his bodily juices?

The sight of Gemma and Elsa together disconcerted
Victor. So he had worried at the sight of Janice and
Wendy together, wife and daughter, heads together over
the kitchen table. Plot and conspiracy!

"Elsa," says Victor, "aren't you even dressed yet?
Your train's in forty minutes."

If only I could come with you, Elsa. Abandon pride,
endeavour and my vision of myself. Never see Hamish,
much less Gemma, ever again. Forget my concern for
the artifacts of the past. Not care that a library ladder
lies out in all weather rotting to matchwood. See it for
what it is, and not just as a symbol. Agree with everyone else that it is our living that matters, and not the
manner of our living. Elsa, I am stranded out here, up-
stream, in the shallow tributaries of human existence,
floundering but still trying, while you go swimming
blithely, strong body tumbling along in the current,

downstream, midstream, to extinction in the sea. Elsa, understand me.

Both women stare at Victor.

"If only," observes Gemma, "we women could learn from one another. There's Victor telling you what to do. Will you do it? I expect so. I put Catherine's ring upon my finger, accepting Mr. Fox's version of the world. Love is such a laziness. So, of course, is marriage. Wives bring cups of tea to torturers, chiefs of police, army generals and advertising executives. It is expected of them, in the name of marriage, to pass no moral judgements, let alone take any positive action to disassociate themselves from behaviour which in any other man but a husband would appear monstrous. Mind you, they usually starve if they open their mouths—and the children too. Take the advice of a friend, Elsa; do not take the train."

"But you are my enemy as well as my friend," complains Elsa. "How can I trust you?"

"Because I spent the night with Victor, and you with Hamish?" enquires Gemma happily. "Does that make me your enemy? It should give us something in common."

Elsa's mouth drops open. Little, darling, sharp teeth revealed in all their imperfection: a lush red throat, leading down to cavernous depths.

"For God's sake," says Victor sharply, "shut your mouth and get dressed."

"Stay where you are," says Gemma. "I've iced her cake. It's her birthday. Happy birthday, Elsa."

Elsa has quite forgotten.

"I'm not taking the train," says Elsa, pale with the effort to learn, to accept, to change. "I'm staying until you go back."

"But I can't go back. Wendy and Janice are coming They'd be upset if I leave without seeing them. I'v caused them enough pain."

"Then I'll just have to meet Wendy and Janice," say Elsa.

"I'm sure they'll get on wonderfully," says Gemm brightly. "Do cheer up, Victor. We rely on you to kee us all cheerful. I've asked Hamish to let you have th library ladder. I'm sure he'll relent."

"I'd rather do my own bargaining, thank you," say Victor.

"But, Victor," complains Gemma, "you're so un grateful. I was trying to do you a favour. Hamish ha so much and you have so little. And you did me favour, or tried to, and I wasn't too proud to accept And Elsa is doing me an even bigger one. Has she tol you?"

Gemma must, thinks Elsa, mean the typing. She i tempted to confess that it is Hamish who does it, bu how can she? She has taken credit for a skill which both she and Gemma respect: a worse deceit, it now seems, than arranging to sleep behind Gemma's back with Gemma's husband. She closes her mouth.

"Elsa is having Hamish's baby," says Gemma, flush-ing with maternal enthusiasm, "and we're going to adopt it. Men do it for their wives sometimes: consent to artificial insemination. I don't see why wives shouldn't do it for their husbands."

Elsa's mouth drops open again.

"Elsa," says Victor calmly, "you did remember to take your pill yesterday, as I reminded you."

"I'm sorry," says Elsa. "I'm awfully sorry, Victor, but I forgot."

Victor leaves. The pink has washed down from his cheekbones to his neck, and up over the crown of his head. He forgets to incline his head as he leaves, and scrapes the newly shiny bald patch nastily. He doesn't even bother to swear.

"Let's get on with the story," says Gemma smugly. "Now that's settled. I thought he took it rather well. Though there's no reason why he shouldn't. If he can lend you out to Hamish, he can surely lend you out to me. He's not the squeamish kind, after all. You being pregnant by another man wouldn't put him off, would it? It would take quite a lot to put Victor off, I imagine."

Gemma smiles at Elsa, who is crying.

"Now where were we?" she asks. "Ah, yes. A Monday morning in 1966. Catherine's ring heavy on my finger. Marion in a tizz of jealousy and resentment because of it, and Marion's dad taking photographs of it with his new Polaroid camera."

Gemma sat on the armchair of the uncut velvet three-piece suite and thumbed through a copy of *Vogue,* and dozed, and felt her ring, and inhaled the thin cigarettes Marion's dad had rolled earlier in the evening from a new kind of tobacco sold at his workshop by the junior messenger, and thought of Mr. Fox, and the Ramsbottle voices drifted over her.

"I don't know so much about that syllabub," said Marion's mum. "It's on the heavy side after all that kertoffel. Perhaps on Wednesdays we could go back to jelly and cream, like in the old days. English cuisine. What do you say to that, Marion's friend? Wake up, Gemma! Lost in a dream, isn't she? It must be the Turkish cigarettes. You're sure they're nothing more sinister? Gemma, I was saying, any objection to jelly and cream on Wednesdays?"

"Leave the girl alone," said Marion's dad. "She's lost in love's sweet dream."

"Taking that ring home! The nerve of it. Mr. First

would be so upset!" moaned Marion. "It's one of their strict rules: no jewellery to leave the office without countersignature of the other."

"Be quiet, Marion!" said Mrs. Ramsbottle, offended.

"Such a stickler!" said Mr. Ramsbottle.

"It's Gemma I worry for. She'll get into trouble," persisted Marion, "with Mr. First."

"Rules are made to be broken, Marion," said Mrs. Ramsbottle.

"It's not often we have Catherine's ring in our house," said Mr. Ramsbottle. "Try not to spoil it for us, Marion."

Their daughter looked at them evilly. They waited.

"It's not the only ring in this house," whispered Marion, "and you know it."

The Ramsbottle parents jumped to their feet.

"She's having one of her fits, Marion's mum," said Mr. Ramsbottle urgently.

"We'd better give her a pill, Marion's dad, the way the doctor said. One of the strong ones."

"I'm not taking any pills!" cried Marion. "It will be shock treatment next."

"That it will," said her mother, "if you don't stop it, you naughty girl."

"Look!" cried Gemma, trying to ease the situation. "Here's a picture of Mr. Fox in *Vogue*."

Marion's mum and dad forgot Marion and turned to look at the glossy page.

"He's smiling," marvelled Gemma. "He doesn't often smile. He has a well of deep sorrow in his soul."

"She's a poet," cried Marion's dad, "a real poet. If only you'd taken your English O levels, Marion, you'd have something to occupy your mind. You wouldn't be in this state now."

"It was your fault I failed my English. All I ever heard throughout my youth was some bloody lingo. As for you, Gemma James, you're a bloody fool."
Marion's father put his hand over his daughter's mouth.

"Wash her mouth out with Lysol," said Marion's mum.

"No need to be harsh," said the father. "Kindness works wonders. But that's no way to speak to the lodger, our Marion. She's like a daughter to us."

"Better than me any day, I know." Marion was bitter. "You make that very plain. What would you say if *I* planned to go away for a dirty weekend in Tangier the way she has?"

There was silence while the family considered.

"What an old-fashioned girl you are, Marion," said Marion's mum at last, speaking for both. "I can't think where you get it from. A girl's got to get all the experience she can."

"Well, Gemma ought to be careful, that's all," Marion blurted, thwarted.

"Gemma's a lucky lass," soothed Mr. Ramsbottle. "You mustn't grudge her, Marion. It's people like her Mr. Fox who run the country now. It used to be the capitalists; now it's the glossies and the Sunday sups. Style, not revolution; that's the thing these days. Politicians don't make the rules any more, but people with style. What we're going to look like, what we're going to think, where we're going to go on our hols. And the telly commercials, of course. Après-sex, that kind of thing. The new London permissiveness, Carnaby Street, the Beatles. I like to see the foreigners here, myself, taking a look at good British navels. What else have we got to offer with a climate like ours and oil on our beaches and worse, washed up with every tide? Of course there's the matter of the balance of payments, our Marion, there always is. But British beauties like our Gemma here help the export drive one way or another. Look at the ring on her finger! That'll knock 'em in Tangier!"

"Yes, look at it," said Marion bitterly, her face cold, something in her tone now both final and dreaded.

"She's going, Marion's dad!"

"Fetch the doctor, Marion's mum."

"You fetch him, I'll kill him," shrieked Marion. "It's rings on fingers I can't stand. It's the nightmares I can't stand."

"It's always something," her parents chorused.

"Don't talk about the dream," begged Gemma. "Mr. Fox asked you not to."

"Quite right too," said Marion's mum. "We don't want to hear any more about the dream of Marion's. What an imagination she's got. As if anyone at Fox and First would do anything like that! Push a customer out of the window! And a relative, too. People have more respect for life than ever they used to—it was on telly last night."

Mrs. Ramsbottle spoke quickly and lightly, but there was a look of dread in her eyes, as well there might be.

And Marion was shrieking and clawing.

"I hate you all! You don't care about me. You never have. All you ever care about is holidays and I pay my share but you never go where I want. I wanted to go to Tangier last year but you wouldn't, and now I'll never go, because I'm sensitised to the sun. You didn't know that, did you? I went to the doctor and that's what he said. 'Sensitised to the sun!' But Gemma isn't and she's going to Tangier, and if you ask me you think more of her than you do of me, your own flesh and blood. Well, you can have her for a daughter if you like, only it won't be for long, because she'll be as dead as Joanna First if she's not careful, the way you want me to be. Dead and out of the way, saving you the third fare."

"Now what's she on about?" moaned Mr. Ramsbottle. "Get the doctor; I can't stand her like this."

"Look at that ring," shrieked Marion, and people on either side of the little terrace house started knocking on the wall. "Look at that ring! It's not Mr. Fox's to give. It's Mr. First's. He won't stand for it. You've got to be so careful at that place. No one believes me. Ophelia caught on. She got out just in time. Blood on the carpet! He had her modelling too, the way he's got Gemma. Standing there with next to nothing on—all in the name of art, I'll be bound. Till the next time."

"Not next to nothing," murmured Gemma, cool and provocative, disagreeable as only Gemma could be at certain moments in her life, not her father's daughter for nothing. "Nothing, unless you count the ring."

"Go on then," shrieked Marion to Gemma. "If you don't believe me, go up and look in my top drawer. It's in there. I can't bear to open it myself, only I catch the smell every now and then. You thought it was Gran's mattress, I know you did, but it's not. I can't even get at my clean knickers anymore. I have to wash and wash the ones I've got on, and they're damp every single morning and nobody cares."

"What do you mean, you dirty girl!" exclaimed Marion's mum. "What's in your drawer?"

"The finger," whispered Marion.

"Not again." Mr. Ramsbottle shook his head.

"It's so little," complained Marion. "A finger without a hand is so little. The ring's not little. It's worth thousands. We could all fly to Zambezi or somewhere."

"We can't take her to the funnyfarm," said Marion's mum aside to her husband, "not with Capri coming up. We can't go on holiday *and* hospital visiting at the same time, can we?"

"That's all very well," said her dad, "but we can't have her not changing her underwear. It's not nice for Gemma. It's self-neglect, and certifiable."

At which Marion screamed aloud and left the room, running, sobbing and slamming the door. A barrage of neighbourly knocks and raps swelled on either side of the room, and presently died away.

"I wish the pill had been around when I was a girl," said Marion's mum bitterly. "Kids are a dead loss, if you ask me. They grow up and what have you got—just more people, and all that work for nothing. Don't you ever have kids, Gemma. It's not worth the trouble."

"I'm glad you never took the pill, Marion's mum, in spite of what happened in the form of Marion," said Marion's dad warmly. "They do say it makes the female neuter, like worker bees, and I'd rather take risks and have a properly female wife, thank you very much, than any kind of neuter."

"I'll go after her," said Gemma, and though they remonstrated, saying Marion would calm down more quickly if left alone, Gemma did so, though more in the hope of a little peace than out of any real concern for Marion.

It was, alas, one of the characteristics of Gemma's love for Mr. Fox that it rendered her indifferent to others' troubles; like many a romantic love before and after, it was debilitating. Sexual passion requited invigorates the parties concerned, and enhances rather than diminishes the response to the outer world. An excellent patent medicine for all afflictions—curing madness, rheumatism, the bloody flux, anxiety, depression, warts and so on—at least for a time. Romantic love, on the other hand, works as a slow poison, making the sufferer egocentric, vapid, consumptive and hard to get along with.

Mr. Fox, Mr. Fox, Gemma loves you. Sleep sweetly on your circular jungle bed with its smell of olive oil, garlic and sweet crushed herbs. Sleep while you may!

At the top of the poky stairs, red-carpeted, Gemma went along the narrow landing, linoed, and tapped on the bedroom door, glass-handled, and softly, enquiringly called, "Marion, Marion," and hearing no response went on to the end of the corridor where the toilet was, with its woolly cerise cover and matching mat, and found that door shut and sobs coming from within.

Gemma crept back to the bedroom and the chest of drawers, and tugged at the left-hand drawer. It stuck. She tugged again harder. And a third time she pulled and this time it opened, and she rifled through Marion's Marks & Spencer undies, British Home Stores scarves and Marion's gran's old gloves, and found nothing remarkable.

Except one little white chiffon scarf at the back, rolled up and stuck in the crack where the drawer met its case, and she pulled at this, and it came up and away with her hand and something flew out of it and landed with a clatter on the floor. Gemma bent to look, and screamed and screamed, and felt a hand over her mouth.
It was Marion's.

"It's not real," whispered Marion. "Really it isn't. It's a dream. What were you doing anyway, going through my drawers? You had no business!"

But Gemma, eyes wide over Marion's broad fingers, could see very well that it was real: a finger without a hand, and a ring on it, lying at her feet.

"What shall we do with it?" whispered Gemma when Marion had set her mouth free again to speak.

"Put it in its proper place."

"Where's that?"

"Anywhere hidden!" Marion was wild-eyed. "They never believe me about anything. About Gran wetting her bed, about what it's like at work, about the pains in my stomach and my head. When I was a little girl my teacher used to take me behind the bushes; they wouldn't believe that either. Anything that's inconvenient. They'll take me to a psychiatrist—that's different. Get me put in a loony bin for August to save the fare. I'm surprised they don't have me put down, like the cat. Then we can have a nice little kitten in September. They only did that to me once, to be fair. Seychelles year. Put me inside, that is."

There was a little plop from the floor. The ring had trickled off the finger and now lay on the boards. The two girls stared at ring and finger, finally separated.

"I suppose flesh does shrink, once it's dead," said Gemma. "It would all dry up."

"It's not as if she was a nice person," said Marion. "She was greedy, and a nuisance. She was always eating buns and sweets; done up to the eyes in woollies even in the hottest weather. She could never leave anyone alone. She'd looked after her old mother all her life, she never married, and when finally the old woman went into a home, she turned up on the doorsteps. Mr. First was always very kind to her, though, in a sorry sort of way, until she started pestering Mr. Fox, and then he got angry. I saw him once trying to shut the door in her face, but she was pushing and struggling and screaming to get through to see him. Well, that's no way to go on. I was in love with a man once and I didn't behave like that. I just kept out of his way. It depends on the opinion you have of yourself, I suppose . . ."

Marion's voice trailed away as Gemma stooped and picked the ring up from the floor. It was a massive diamond, set in one of Leon Fox's settings: naked bodies twined in an erotic chain. The stone flung back the light from the overhead bulb, flyblown and bakelite-shaded, and turned it into something magical. The ruby on Gemma's finger glittered suddenly as if in recognition and welcome. Deep, deep red and brilliant white. Rose Red, Snow White.

"It's a wedding ring," said Gemma, enchanted. "It must be."

"Put it on your finger," said Marion in her new hard

voice. "It's what you deserve. It's what you want. You've worked for it."

And Marion thrust the diamond ring onto Gemma's finger over the knuckle, so that it lay next to Catherine's ring, and again Gemma cried out in pain, and then she smiled.

"See how the gems come to life," she said. "That diamond was nothing when it was on Joanna First's finger. Poor Mr. Fox. How he must have suffered!"

Still the finger lay there on the floor like some dried-up bean, reproaching them.

"It might be a bit of old chicken," said Gemma hopefully. "Or a very thin turkey's neck."

"Not possibly," said Marion. "We ought to tell the police."

"No," said Gemma. "I'm going away with Mr. Fox on Saturday. The police might interfere. I don't want anything, anyone in the world, to interfere. I don't care if Mr. First is a murderer; I don't care how you came to have this ring in that drawer. You're such a liar I don't suppose I'll ever know for sure; I just mean to get to Tangier with Mr. Fox."

"But, Gemma," said Marion. "It wasn't Mr. First killed Joanna; it was Mr. Fox."

Gemma opened her mouth to scream again, and then stopped. More of Marion's lies.

"You go down and say you're sorry to your parents," she said. "I'll put that horrible old turkey's neck down the loo. I'll pick it up with a piece of tissue. Otherwise one might get germs." So she had always instructed the Hemsley children to pick up, as pick up they would, the little dead creatures—birds, stoats, mice, gerbils—

which littered their path through life. Something finished, which once lived and exulted, held up by what remained of a wing, a claw, a tail. "Gemma, what is it? Gemma, Gemma, what will we do?"

Gemma bent and picked the object up.

"You only say such a dreadful, silly thing because you're jealous of me and Mr. Fox," said Gemma firmly when she came back from the toilet. "But it has no effect. I'm sorry."

"He's a homosexual; everyone says so." Marion's eyes remained piggy and mean. She was exhausted; she was undressing for bed. She wore at night the same white-to-grey vest and panties she wore by day. The skin on her body was dull and goose-pimpled.

"Everyone's everything nowadays," said Gemma as lightly as she could.

Great-Aunt May! To hear your little Gemma speaking so! But Gemma was shaken all the same.

"How can you love a homosexual and a murderer?" demanded Marion.

Easily, easily! Even if he was, which he wasn't. Of course he wasn't.

Love, in any case, as any young or even seasoned bride well knows, stands firm between the person loved and any seven or so deadly sins. Once we're married, my dear, why then you'll stop it. You'll stop drinking, gambling, stealing, fornicating, glutting, murdering, buggering; you only do these things because you're unhappy. And I will make you happy, yes I will. And you will make yourself wholesome for me—and for our baby.

Mr. Fox's baby. Tiny, bright, sharp eyes. Gemma shivered. The feel of the shrivelled object was still be-

tween her fingers. She went to the bathroom to wash
the feeling away with Permutit softened water and fabu-
lous pink Camay.

She returned, stunned.

"Marion," said Gemma. "Marion, wake up. The rings
won't come off."

Marion laughed.

"Now you've done it," said Marion, and so Gemma
had. Gemma's hand felt heavy now, and not with pride
and power, but with greed and guilt, lust and lechery,
thus publicly displayed. She was afraid.

Such fear and shame had Mrs. Hemsley felt, though in
lesser degree, when newly married: hiding her wedding
ring from strangers, seeing it not as the symbol of a
new honour, but as a visible token of her lost virginity,
her nightly disgrace. As well hold out the bloody sheets!
Nor did she care to go about in public with her husband, for fear that others might have too clear a vision
of them both locked in copulation. She felt brazen and
embarrassed when first required to wheel her new baby
out into the world for all to see; this mewling creature,
direct and living evidence of what she had surely done.

Gemma held her left hand under cold running water;
then she oiled the fingers and soaped the rings; she
tugged and pulled with her right hand; she tried levers,
nails and teeth, but neither ring would move. Marion
tried too, but to no avail. Only when Gemma's ring
finger was swollen and bleeding above and below the
rings did they desist. It was as if some essential chilliness
in Gemma's soul had transferred itself to the metal and
caused the rings to shrink. The silver snake clenched
its jaws yet more firmly around Catherine's ruby, and
tighter and tighter, locked in closer and closer embrace,

danced Mr. Fox's figurines around their diamond. The stone glowed brighter and colder than his eyes.

It hurts the poor to wait upon the rich. Mr. Fox's father had hurt, cold eyes, as did his son after him. Humiliation and the answer to it—revolution and murder—criss-crossed through the generations.

13

"I have a lot to do this morning," says Gemma to
Elsa, "so I shall leave you now. Mr. and Mrs. Ramsbottle are coming to Sunday dinner. This is a duty
weekend for Hamish and me, one way and another."

"A duty weekend?"

"When we do what we ought, socially, not what we
want. We have one every six months. I want you to
remain quietly in your room, so as not to dislodge any
possible pregnancy."

Gemma means to have a perfect baby. It will be Hamish
as he could have been and not as the world has made
him: herself sent out into the world to run, laugh, love
and multiply, free in movement and response. Everything she once was and now is not. She will nurture the
baby through its growing period as Hamish nurtures a
delicate but genetically sound specimen of some new
variety of pot plant: by a mixture of science and close
attention, until it blossoms into profitable life.

"There is more profit in people than in things," murmurs Gemma to the bemused Elsa. "If only Victor
realised that! They can be renovated and polished up,
just like Georgian bureaus and Victorian sideboards.
It's much more fun! And Elsa, try and think nice
197

thoughts. The egg needs to grow in a hormonally benign environment. We must keep you calm and happy, and Annie will bring you some milk mid-morning. I've brought just a little typing with me. Will you do it by lunchtime? I don't want to tire you, for your own sake. There's nothing more pleasing to the spirits than doing something you're really good at."

She locks the door behind her. She does not want Victor diffusing, as it were, any possible pregnant brew. Presently Elsa gets out of bed and looks at the work Gemma has left. Gemma needs lists, in triplicate, of the ingredients needed in the making of, variously, *dashi* and *owanrui*, *bento* and *zensai*, *sashimi*, *gohan*, *sushi*, *menrui*, *mushimono*, *yakimono*, *nimono*, *nabemono*, *agemono* and *sunomono*. Nor is her handwriting good. Lists have to be sent in triplicate to various exotic food importers, and a copy of the entire correspondence to date, with estimated prices, sent to an educational trust for the disabled, whom Gemma maintains are obliged, under the terms of their endowment, to ship the ingredients by air from Tokyo at reduced rates. Gemma means to take a course in Japanese cookery in the near future.

Elsa retires to bed, and waits for Victor to rescue her. He must. Or else Hamish will have to divorce Gemma and marry her. She does not doubt but that she is pregnant; she has a kind of curling, tickling feeling inside, and a muffling blanket between the world and herself. And just as well. Elsa's mother Sheila always knew within hours when she was pregnant, and thus described the sensation: "Here comes the blanket!" As if nature tossed a faintly disagreeable tranquiliser in her direction, as an old lady might toss a covering on an over-noisy parrot's cage.

Abortion? No. Elsa has seen too many slides and leaflets issued by the Society for the Protection of the Unborn to fancy that. She has even marched in their parades beneath the banner of the wretched fetus.

Hoist, yet again, by their own kindly, obliging petard.

Presently Hamish unlocks the door and sits down to do the typing. Will he declare love, offer marriage, suggest a settlement?

No.

"Marriage is a very strange institution!" observes Hamish, typing out a recipe for Temple of Jade *nabe*, offered to the educational trust as typical of the difficulties to be surmounted, especially if the *harusame* (or transparent noodles) were to be home-made, and real *ichiban dashi* used, rather than mere chicken cubes. "You think you're marrying some empty-headed girl, rather against your better judgement, and what do you end up with? Gemma! I'm not worthy to lick her boots. I started off being sorry for her. Now I worship her. Why she puts up with me I can't imagine."

"Perhaps it's your money," says Elsa unkindly.

"She despises my money," says Hamish sharply. "Everyone does. Gemma is generosity itself. Not many wives would make such a sacrifice. To offer their husband a baby through another woman!"

"Not many women would agree to it," remarked Elsa, blanket up to her chin.

"I think they would, if you made it worth their while. Gemma and I have decided to offer you twenty-five pounds a week from the day pregnancy is established until six weeks after the birth. I think you'll agree that's very generous."

Elsa's look must show that she considers it a very small payment indeed, for he quickly adds, "and full board, of course."

"I'm not going to live here, whatever happens!" protests Elsa.

"I think Gemma wants you to. She can keep a proper eye on you if you're in the house. Things do go wrong. Look how poor Annie lost her baby when Johnnie turned up. Gemma was most upset. A little girl, too."

Hamish finishes the typing and leaves with a polite nod, locking the door behind him.

"I'll take Gemma the typing and say you've done it," he says as he goes. "You and I have our little secrets, don't we. In the face of such perfection, I find one has to."

Over Sunday late-morning drinks Hamish offers Victor the contents of the billiard room for one thousand pounds, with the library ladder thrown in.

"I'll give you a token ten pounds for the lot," says Victor. "And think yourself lucky. It was not part of the bargain that you should impregnate Elsa. If you have, which I doubt. If you can, which seems even more unlikely."

"There is no need to get heated," observes Hamish. "And you may well be right about my diminished fertility. I am an old man and obviously not as virile as you, but by Gemma's account you did no better with her last night than I have recently. Disappointing."

Victor falls silent.

Presently bargaining resumes at about the thousand mark.

Elsa is allowed down to Sunday lunch. Brown soup, roast beef and Yorkshire pudding, roast potatoes, carrots and peas, followed by apple tart and cream. Like a dinner on a railway train, Elsa thinks. She is very hungry.
Embarrassment is saved by the presence of Mr. and Mrs. Ramsbottle, and the ex-vicar of the parish and his young church-worker wife. He has been asked to resign from his position, not on his divorce but on his remarriage to his young parishioner, then fifteen.

"Hasn't our Gemma done well for herself," says Mrs. Ramsbottle confidentially to Elsa. "And not one bit proud! She remembers her old friends. She lived with us when she first came to London. We were like a mother and father to her. She never had parents of her own. And she was like a daughter to us. We had one of our own, of course, Marion. But I'm afraid she didn't turn out well."

"Where is she now?"

"In a hospital, dear, with her nerves. We visit her on the third Sunday in every month. We put her off today to come here. I know she'll understand; she's a good girl at heart . . . She doesn't complain anywhere as much as she used to; of course, the tranquillisers help."

"Gemma still sticks to the English cuisine, I notice," says Mr. Ramsbottle. "Well, I'm coming round to it myself. We've been everywhere, Marion's mum and me, tasted everything. There's nothing like home, young lady, in the end."

"We booked up on the first flight of the Concorde," says Marion's mum, "and that just about finished us. It wasn't just the expense; it was seeing the earth so little below. Such a little place!"

"Times were better when we didn't know so much," says Marion's dad sadly.

Marion's mum gulps the sour local cider, served in cut-glass cider mugs.

"We have a man of the cloth amongst us," says Marion's dad. "Perhaps you have a word or two of comfort to offer?"

"What about?" asks the ex-vicar, startled.

"I just wonder where things went wrong," says Mr. Ramsbottle.

"The outside world is much as it always was," says the ex-vicar briskly. "We project into it our own state of mind, that's all."

He picks a juicy piece of meat up from his plate, and

quite without self-consciousness pops it between his young wife's firm, pale lips. She has, at the best of times, a slightly reproving look. She accepts the tidbit, however, as the lesser of various possible evils, and even seems to enjoy it.

Marion's mum and dad, disconcerted by the vicar's lack of spirituality, have a change of heart after the coffee and mints, and decide that after all they can just fit in a visit to Marion.

"After all," they say, not without a hint of reproach, "it is our day for visiting, and she is our daughter. Our own flesh and blood. And what a lucky girl she is: such a lovely view from her window. Rural England at its leafy best."

While Gemma, at her most gracious, waves the Ramsbottles good-by, Victor takes the opportunity to manage a few minutes alone with Elsa, who has been forbidden after-dinner coffee by Gemma, but allowed to telephone her friend Marina from the sedan-chair booth, provided she reverses the charges.

"Christ, I'm sorry, Elsa," says Victor. "We'll get out of this somehow."

By sitting her on his knee and leaning backwards he is hidden by the faded antique curtains and can penetrate her without being seen.

"What's the matter, Elsa?" Marina keeps asking in one ear. "Your voice keeps fading. Is something the matter?"

"We're both being used," complains Victor in Elsa's other ear. "Abominably used! Hamish actually told me this was a duty weekend. Those extraordinary people to Sunday dinner! What an insult. A calculated insult. The whole thing's calculated. He only asked me here to con me into buying his billiard-room rubbish. Friendship! If you look at it closely there's not a single piece that's right. I'd make a great mistake buying it at all. And Gemma only asked you here because of her harebrained maternal schemes."

He falls silent at last, his mind eased by Elsa's unchanging warmth: his own again, now cleansed of the trespasser. He closes his eyes and sighs with the relief of it all, however temporary. Elsa, still trying to detail the contents of Gemma's typing to Marina, gives up the attempt.

"It's no use wasting the phone bill like this," complains Marina. "If you're going to talk nonsense, at least don't reverse the charges." And she puts down the telephone.

Victor is back in the drawing room before Gemma can become alarmed at his absence.

Janice, of course, is Gemma's trump card. She arrives triumphant, as Gemma knew she would, one eye black and puffy, and with her daughter escorted by a personable young man.

"Dear God," cries Victor, seeing his wife thus damaged, leaping forward to take her hand. "What happened?" Janice withdraws her hand coolly.
"Really," she says, "it's nothing to do with you."
"Who's this?" demands Victor of Wendy.
"We're living together," says Wendy flatly. "In my room."

The cake is on the central table in the tearoom; frilled in silver, embossed in pink and white icing, with the message "Happy birthday twins!" upon it in little yellow furry balls.

"I had to place each ball with a tweezer, separately!" says Gemma proudly.

The cake is flanked by plates of tea-time delicacies: little ham sandwiches, tiny sausage rolls, delicate éclairs. The cups and saucers are Spode, the teaspoons sterling silver. The chairs and table are of flimsy bamboo, Japanese-style, and uncomfortable. A plinth is set out with music chairs and stands, as if for a small orchestra, but in fact the background music, of the soothing Palm Court kind, comes from a cassette player.

Elsa is fetched down from her room. Janice and Wendy view her benignly. Kim has his notebook out.

"I'm so pleased to meet you," says Janice. "I hear you make Victor truly happy. The sooner we're divorced and you two married the better."

Elsa opens her mouth to say she does not believe in marriage, but closes it again.

"What fun to have a stepmother one's own age," says Wendy distantly, leaning back into Kim so that he can hardly control his pencil. "I could knit you a wedding dress in silver rope. They're quite fashionable at registry offices, I believe. I saw one in *Vogue*."

"You have to be thin," says Elsa.

"Isn't it amazing," says Gemma to Victor, "that your daughter and your new wife should have birthdays on the same day! I know there's a year between them, but even so, what a coincidence."

Kim grunts something beneath his breath.

"What did you say?" demands Victor sharply.

"Nothing," says Kim.

"You did," says Victor. "Come on! Speak up like a man."

Victor's cheekbones turn pink. The chairs provided are obviously too small and weak to support his bulk. He strides the room, hovering with menace over this new usurper's comparatively frail form.

"I said," says Kim, giving in, "not all that amazing. Merely incest fantasy acted out. Not unusual in men with unclaimed daughters beyond the age of consent."

Silence falls. Janice and Victor both blush. Elsa's mouth falls open. Kim and Gemma smile. Only Wendy remains unperturbed. But she takes out her knitting and keeps her fingers busy, lest, as Kim remarks afterwards, they were tempted to stray where they had no business. It was not advisable, Kim said, for children to see parents of the opposite sex—or indeed the same sex—walk naked about the house. So had Victor and Janice walked for Wendy's benefit. So had Victor's parents, for him.

"Do cut the cake!" suggests Gemma. "Both of you together, since you're both birthday girls."

Elsa and Wendy overcome their reluctance to touch one another, and together slice the cake. It is light and fragrant.

"Both big girls, aren't they," says Kim, making a note of it.

"What happened to your eye?" asks Victor again of Janice, covering his confusion.

"Nothing to do with you," says Janice, cool as cool.

"There's nothing to be ashamed of," says Wendy. "Nothing in our own nature should disgrace us. That's what you always used to say, Father, though I know how ashamed you always used to be of me. But I don't mind now. Mother has a black eye because one of her lovers' wives beat her up. One of her many lovers, I mean; not one of that particular lover's many wives. One must be precise. This one was a carpenter. He came to mend your bedroom cupboard."

There is an edge of complaint in Wendy's voice. There are now tears in both her mother's and her father's eyes. She is not unpleased to see them.

"That's a very fine cupboard," says Victor presently. "An excellent piece of mahogany. There was nothing the matter with it when I left."

"The door kept swinging open."

"So what did you do? Find some bloke in the yellow pages who shaved down the frame instead of re-hanging the door?"

"Yes."

Janice is unafraid where once she was fearful.

Victor's tears brim over; he sobs and clutches Janice's hand. This time she does not draw it away.

"I'm sorry," says Victor. "I'll go to my room for a moment. I'm not up to this."

He leaves. Janice follows. He is tall and she is short, but they move alike and clearly one is an extension of the other.

Elsa's mouth falls open.

"Happy Birthday," says Gemma, triumphant. "We must sing 'Happy Birthday.' "

14 ————————————————

"I've been so lonely," says Janice from beneath Victor. "I've enjoyed it in a way, but it's been so unnatural."

"I can't stand being an antique dealer," says Victor. "It's all right as a hobby, but as a way of life it's too frightening."

"The house is in a dreadful mess."

"I don't mind. What about this young man of Wendy's?"

"I don't know. She only met him yesterday. What about that young girl of yours?"

"She'll be all right. She's not particular as to who or why or where."

"Then she'll get what she deserves," says Janice, looking up at Victor with one clear eye and one puffy one.

Victor slept. So did Janice.

Victor, waking, was restored to himself. He woke with a sense of relief, as one does from a bad dream, to find the real world again, and with Janice beside him. He shook her awake, and walked with her down the mock-marble stairs and along dim corridors to the kitchens, and through them to the courtyard, where he found the library ladder still leaning against the wall beside the dustbins. He sighed over its freshly broken rung, closed it and tucked it under his arm.

"Are you stealing it?" asked the newly delinquent Janice.

"Yes," said Victor, and they walked round through the back and into the garages, where his car was trapped behind closed doors. He folded down the back seat and laid the ladder tenderly in a blanket he kept for just such a purpose.

He started the engine, let it run for a few seconds, reversed as far as he could, and then drove the car at the garage doors. They were made, as he had surmised, of the same flimsy wood-simulating plastic that Hamish used to manufacture windowboxes, and splintered easily. Janice got in beside him, and Victor drove round to the front of the house and parked outside the French windows of the tearoom. He beckoned Wendy, who rose obediently, came to the car and got inside. Kim followed. Gemma came after them, but her chair could not traverse the step down from the French windows.

"You can't go," called Gemma. "I shan't open the gates till I'm ready."

But Victor, his family safely inside and the library ladder saved from further dilapidation, aimed the car at the gates, and they gave before him, as had the garage doors, like a block of Greek halva before a determined spoon.

Elsa remains sitting with her head in her hands.

Presently Gemma rejoins her.

"Never mind, Elsa," says Gemma. "I'll look after you. You have nothing left, really. No family, no home, no job. No clothes, I suppose?"

"Not to speak of."

"Of course not. You travel light. Nothing left; all

gone with Victor. Nothing but remembered love. Well, it's all any of us have in the end," says Gemma, her worldly domain stretching high and wide around her. "Have another piece of cake. Didn't it turn out well! I'm glad Alice didn't make it sink; she might well have. And weren't the Ramsbottles terrible! How dreadful the past is, and all its inhabitants. I'm sure I don't know why I go on tormenting myself with it. One will never understand it, much less oneself."

Gemma fingers her mother's pendant.

"I would like to change, Elsa," she confides, "but I don't know how."

And Gemma continues her story.

1966.
Gemma's ring finger is swollen and sore, and the two rings are still upon it. Nevertheless Marion and Gemma set off for work with their bits and pieces in one of the new psychedelic plastic carrier bags. Gemma wore Marion's gran's gloves to make the rings on her fingers less conspicuous. The gloves were of special stretch open-weave, the better to enclose swollen arthritic joints. Mr. Ramsbottle gave the girls a lift to the station in the Ford Cortina.

"I've been thinking," he said. "After all that to-do last night. Perhaps you shouldn't go off with Mr. Fox like that, Gemma. Call me old-fashioned if you like, but you should work up to grand holidays; otherwise you'll spoil things for the rest of your life. Succession, that's the secret of holidays. Who wants to go to Dieppe when you've had a good time in Monte Carlo? But Dieppe, if it's only been Bournemouth before, appears as a seaside paradise. You're welcome to come with us, Gemma, to the Isle of Capri. We could even see our way to advancing the fare."

"That's very kind," said Gemma in her most refined voice, "but no, thank you. I wouldn't want to presume."

What, Gemma go on holiday, on a package tour, with ordinary chip-eating, tea-drinking people? Leon Fox's true love? Someone wearing the Tsarina Catherine's ring on her finger, not to mention another she'd really rather not think about, but which a jeweller would surely manage to get off. Without cutting, of course. Mr. Fox's erotic circle could not be rudely broken. Stretched, perhaps, but not broken.

"I think," said Marion while they were strap-hanging on the underground, "you'd be wiser to have your finger cut off than go to the office wearing those rings."

"It will only be till lunchtime, when I can get to a jeweller. Mr. Fox will sleep all morning, and I'll hide my hand if Mr. First is about."

And so he did, and so she did, and panic subsided.

But at lunchtime the jeweller was leaving for the pub just as Gemma arrived, and though she pleaded and cried, he would not deign to open up his workroom for her. He'd do it at five thirty-five, he said: stay in especially for her. And he looked briefly at the rings, and then with rather more interest at Gemma, and said, "Where did you get these from? Never mind, tell me all about it at half-past five. I can do it without filing, if I put my mind to it."

"I hope you can," said Gemma.

"Depends on the degree of co-operation," he said, and off he went: beer-and-sandwich first, sex afterwards. Easy enough to deal with when the time came, thought Gemma, safe in the spiritual arms of Mr. Fox.

During the morning Mr. Fox had come bouncing down the stairs, nodded briefly to her—how her heart pounded!—and gone out. Shortly after lunchtime he returned. This time he appeared preoccupied and not to see her.

Marion remained closeted with Mr. First. Presently she came out and went off to buy fresh coffee beans, and soon Mr. First emerged from his office. Gemma smiled brightly and falsely and sat on both her hands.

"Gemma smiled at me," croaked Mr. First. "She smiled! I wonder if she thought I was someone else! You did, didn't you! Yes. Do you hate me, Gemma James?"

"No."

I fear you, but I don't hate you. I wish I did. Hate is the easiest, most invigorating emotion of all—next, of course, to despising.

"That's something," said Mr. First. "Not hate. But what do you think of when you think of me? When someone says 'Mr. First,' what vision comes into your head?"

"Your hands."

Mr. First was pleased.

"Yes, I have nice hands. They're very nimble. I'm quite a good typist, you know. Very good, in fact; better than you, and you're not bad."

"A man! A typist!" sneered Gemma quite openly, and for the first time Mr. First appeared alarmed.

"You don't think that's a manly thing to do?"

"I don't. It's just silly. Anyway, I was thinking about the skin on your hands."

"What about it?"

"It's old."

"And you are young, you mean."

"Yes."

"May and November can live together. I've known it to happen. One gives wisdom and the other gives strength. Would you marry me, Miss James?"

"No."

"I only enquired to hear the tone of your voice, which quite lived up to expectation. Horror and disgust. I am a lonely man, Gemma, and don't know how to behave. You should have some pity on me. You could even marry me for my money. I have quite a future, even if this business fails, which I quite expect it to do. Money lies in the mass market, not the elite. Too many bad debts. I'm going into pot plants. Yes, marry me for my money, Gemma. I've known girls to do that. Not many, in actual fact, not as many as you'd expect, but a few do manage."

"I have some pride," said Gemma, hoity-toity.

"Pride! Remember the girl with the new red shoes! She flung her mother's loaf of bread into the mud and used it as a stepping stone. And it sunk with her upon it, down, down, to the Halls of the Bog King, and she was compelled to dance before him forever in her new shoes, in the mud and the slime. Why are you sitting on your hands?"

"It's a habit of mine."

"Ask me a favour, Gemma. Anything. At least be grateful to me."

"Never."

"Show me your left hand, Gemma."

"No."

Her heart beat strongly. She had never been so frightened, and yet she was brave.

Mr. First put out his grey hand to hold her arm. Her flesh shuddered at its touch; it seemed to do so of its own volition, quite disregarding the normal circuit of sensations to the brain and back again.

He withdrew his hand and smiled.

"We could have lovely children, Gemma, you and me."

So men have spoken to women from the beginning of

language, against reason, against hope, driven by the steady wind of instinct onto the rocks of humiliation and disaster.

"I see you as mother of my children. Marry me, Gemma."

The rocks were sharp indeed. Spite and malice showed in Gemma's face.

"You're mad. You're disgusting. Pay someone to have your horrid children. All you'll ever have is money. I'm never having children, anyway. I hate children."

Oh, Gemma! How could you! Great-Aunt May withdrew her protective strength, turned away in sorrow, bitterness. So, follow your mother. She never wanted you, Gemma. It was you who kept her there with me, an old woman even then; you who trapped her in a miserable hovel to catch her death of cold. You, not me.

Mr. First was angry, full of a hate that echoed Gemma's own. He caught her left hand and exerted his full strength to turn it and open it: yet it was not his strength but her nature that caused her flesh to surrender.

"Two rings!" observed Mr. First mildly. Now he had her in his power his anger evaporated. "Greedy Gemma."

"I can't get them off."

"I can see that. Your poor little finger!"

His dry hand caressed hers.

"Marion put them there."

"Don't tell tales," said Mr. First. "It isn't sporting. I was brought up in an orphanage. I got the cane for telling tales, and the cane for not telling tales. Life can be very difficult. What you have there, Gemma, is the Tsarina Catherine's ring, which should be in the bank as part of our security. And the one and only Diamond Dance. I offered it to Woolworth's as a prototype for mass production."

"One of Mr. Fox's rings! For Woolworth's?" Gemma was horrified.

"That was rather Mr. Fox's reaction," observed Mr. First. "And the ring promptly disappeared. But now it's rediscovered and we must waste no more time. I need it. Now."

And Mr. First caught up the paper knife and brandished it in a friendly suggestive way, and she thought her end had come. Her throat first, her finger next.

"How pale you look," said Mr. First. "And so you should, you naughty, silly girl. These are dangerous games you're playing."

But when she had well and truly shrunk into her chair with fear, he put down the knife, turned on his heel and went up the circular staircase to Mr. Fox's penthouse.

"Stay there," he said. "Just sit. Don't move, on peril of your life. I'll be back soon."

And Gemma just sat. Nothing kept her there at her desk waiting for mutilation and death: nothing except her own nature. There was the door, just there. All she had to do was get up and run out of it, to freedom and life.

Gemma stayed where she was, as requested. Likewise she had lain on the doctor's examination couch, as requested, although the door was half open, and the doctor's wife and decency only a few short yards away.

Don't despise her. Thus we have all stayed to endure when we need not. While teachers caned us, parents scolded us, meals upset our digestions. Sat at dinner and been abused; lain in beds, likewise. The door is there, and partly open. We seldom go out of it.

Gemma stayed and waited for her destiny. Marion clumped up the stairs, red-faced and breathless, holding not coffee beans but sharp pottery fragments in her hand, and a long, trailing, withered plant.

"I was nearly killed just now," complained Marion. "Someone dropped a flowerpot on me from the penthouse."

"An accident." But Gemma knew it wasn't, even as she spoke.

"We're going to die," said Gemma calmly. "We're both going to die. Mr. First's up there. He's going to kill us both. He found out from Mr. Fox about your dream, and what you saw. He tried to kill you with that Transylvanian vine."

"Not Mr. First," shrieked Marion, "Mr. Fox."

"You only say that because you're in love with Mr. First," shouted Gemma.

Their raised voices set off some kind of alarm amongst the parrots, who surged squawking out of their cage to flounder about the room. The sea gulls outside, incensed, fluttered and banked against the window panes: one broke and the gull that had caused the breakage blundered blindly inside, to be mobbed and pecked by the parrots.
Marion stamped and shrieked and cried.

"Yes, I do love Mr. First. It's my secret. You're not to tell my mum and dad. I respect him and he respects me, and he's terribly, terribly kind. He's protecting Mr. Fox because Mr. Fox is an artist, only quite mad. Murderous. Only now he wants me to have his baby with-

out being married to him, and I've no one to confide in
No one. And he makes love to me on the floor when
it's hard, because that's what he likes; he's a bit funny
but it's not his fault, he had this dreadful childhood—"

The parrots fly up, united at last by some common in
stinct, and are off through the window, up and away
Some two thousand pounds' worth of birds. The solitary
sea gull sits peacefully nodding, eyes glazing.

"Mr. First is the murderer," whispered Gemma into
the sudden silence. "He tried to kill me. It's he who's
mad. Not Mr. Fox. And if you want to know, Mr. First
wants me to have his baby too. He asked me just now."

Marion was silent. Great tears of real sorrow swelled
in her puffy little eyes.

"Oh no," she said. "Oh no."

And for once she wept real quiet peaceful tears, as a
girl does when what she has always known can no
longer be hidden. And Gemma crossed to her and
stroked her slightly greasy hair (Marion had to wash
it three times a week) with real affection and concern,
and the jewels on her heavy left hand glinted with some
kind of promise, some reassertion of happiness and
good times to come; if the sorrow of the moment could
be survived. Well, they were both young.
Gemma murmured something to this effect and Marion
sighed, and sighed again, and the sobs slowed.

"A pretty sight," said a voice from above. "Whatever
can be the matter?"

Mr. Fox, smiling with all his teeth, dressed in pearlised
navy blue, descended the circular staircase. How light

upon his feet he moved! How bright and sharp his eyes!

Gemma put her left hand behind her. Had she been betrayed? Did he know? Had he seen?

No. Still Mr. Fox smiled. There was no anger in his eyes, only kindness and sympathy.

"Someone dropped a Transylvanian vine on my head," complained Marion.

"But it was terribly ugly," said Mr. Fox. "It had to leave the office. It was a disgrace. Rampant at the best of times, and then it started to die for no reason at all."

"You might have killed an innocent passer-by."

"Passers-by are not necessarily innocent. They may well deserve to be killed. From this height, in any case, they are all insects, and hard to believe in. I'm sorry if I upset you, Marion, but I was upset myself. Mr. First has a passion for mass production and was threatening to proliferate the Transylvanian vine. Can you imagine it? The lounges of the vulgar choking with the dreadful weed? I had to get it out of his hands. And I see the parrots have left! Well, they were noisy, messy birds, and ungrateful, though I always did my best for them. Perhaps we should try fish, next? Porpoises or sharks— the fish of the future, I feel. Gemma, will you come upstairs with me? Now?"

Gemma said nothing, did nothing. Love and fear struggled for supremacy.

"What's the matter? Mr. First? Horrid Hamish? He's left by the back stairs," Mr. Fox assured Gemma. "There is nothing to be afraid of. You are far too good a typist to lose. And I shall always look after you, you know that."

Behind Gemma was the door. Before her was her love,

whose hands had rested on her naked breasts and gently fingered her navel, that untidy hole, linking us back and back, through our mothers, to the beginning of mammal life.

Gemma stepped forward; how could she not? Thus Mr. First earlier had hurled himself upon the rocks; so did Gemma now. Mr. Fox! Mr. First! One or the other! What did it matter? What is a murderer but a man who makes the world safe for his own? And she was his own. Yes, she was.

"I want to make a coleslaw for supper," said Mr. Fox. "I need someone to shred the cabbage paper-thin. Such a boring task! I shall let you mix the salad, Gemma, as your reward. It must always be done with the hands, so as not to bruise the leaf tissues unnecessarily. Let me see your hands, Gemma. A salad can't be mixed with ringed hands. Both suffer. Gold and silver tarnish in the vinaigrette; the salad becomes tainted."

Gemma held out her left hand. Mr. Fox smiled, gazed, lifted it to his lips, kissed the rings and not her fingers. Then he tried to remove them with his own chilled, accustomed fingers. He failed.

Mr. Fox's eyes narrowed; his breath expelled.

Marion uttered a little cry and ran out of the door. Gemma heard her footsteps running down the stairs to safety, running away, avoiding her destiny. Treacherous Marion! False friend.

But oh, Mr. Fox, Gemma loves you. Pierce her with knives or with your own body; it is all the same. Make your mark upon her; carry her off towards death, towards life; it is all the same. What's done cannot be undone, in this world or the next. A long-lost spirit gazes at her through familiar eyes. You have known each other through all eternity. Mr. Fox and Gemma. Hand in hand through the corridors of heaven and hell.

"Something so dreadful happened," said Gemma. "I wasn't going to show you until I'd got it off. I thought you might be angry. You told me not to wear Tsarina Catherine's ring where Mr. First could see it, but of course now he has, and we all have to be terribly careful because he's quite mad and murdered his sister, and I'm afraid he'll murder all of us. We must go to the police at once."

"Come upstairs," said Mr. Fox, "and watch me make the perfect vinaigrette. Be cool, be cool, my dear. If you accuse people of murder do it with some style. Jokingly, I think would be appropriate, though I must say I haven't had much practice. Where did you find the other ring?"

"On a finger."

"What, with no hand attached?"

"A wandering finger," Gemma volunteered, following Mr. Fox up the iron staircase.

If one tripped, if one fell? But girls in love do not fall. They are protected by magic.

"That's better," said Mr. Fox. "There's the beginning of a conversation with some style. So Marion's dream was true?"

"Yes."

"I am glad I have you safe up here," said Mr. Fox, shutting the door behind them. "I must look after my rings. I can't possibly let you go, my beautiful Gemma."

"Mr. Fox, we have to do something about Mr. First. If he killed his sister."

"Mr. First is my partner. I'm sure a man's entitled to kill his own sister. It's not as if she was a perfect stranger."

"Stop teasing me!"

"When you lift your hands to your head like that,

you give me an idea. One could have a kind of golden chain on the upper arms. A lacing. It would do well in Germany. Dearest Gemma, if you could just remove your blouse and bra while I find the calipers."

Obediently Gemma did so.

"Gemma, look at yourself in the mirror. A skirt is a most unsightly garment when worn with nothing else. You should know that by now. Do your boyfriends teach you nothing?"
"I have no boyfriends."
"Poor Gemma. All alone in the world."
"Yes."
"No one to miss you?"
"Marion and her family would."

Mr. Fox frowned. Mr. Fox's frown cleared. Presumably he had thought of a way round that. Mr. Fox measured Gemma's upper arms. She had obligingly removed all her clothes. Gemma, you are too bold!

Then Mr. Fox measured Gemma's neck, and around it placed a heavy gold collar, on which was embossed a frieze of artistic if orgiastic couplings.

"I don't care for it myself," he said. "Too heavy and too uncomfortable, I imagine."
"Yes. It digs me in the back."

Mr. Fox stepped forward to take it off.

"Oh, dear," said Mr. Fox. "The clasp seems to have jammed in some way. How on earth am I going to get that off."

Where does one thing stop and another start? Where does desire end and murder begin?

Poor Mr. Fox with his sad, cold eyes and his lost and

horrible world. Where are his clients now? Dead and
gone, early to their end from drugs, excess and malnu-
trition; or washed away by the rising tides of necessity,
mortgages, children, boredom.

Mr. Fox, who could not be content with just killing himself, took out an axe: a pretty axe, its handle made of
pink lacy plastic, but its blade pure shining steel.

"Mr. Fox," wailed Gemma, "my Mr. Fox."

"Don't wail," said Mr. Fox, "it isn't a pretty sound.
The cabbage leaves will wither from shock. They have
been flown in from Algeria. You have a soft and lovely
voice. Don't abuse it."

"But you killed Mr. First's sister. She got your ring
stuck on her finger."

"She shouldn't have eaten so much. It was her own
fault. Nor should you. I did warn you, Gemma."

"It's not a sin to be fat. Not a crime punishable by
death."

"Yes, it is."

And Mr. Fox advanced like some jungle beast on Gemma, crouching white, naked and glittering beneath a
gently waving palm tree. Gemma shrieked, and ran to
the door and tugged and tugged, and tugged again and
this time it opened, and running down the stairs, no
longer protected by love—for Mr. Fox was clearly mad,
and who can love a madman; what does that make of
oneself?—tripped and fell over the edge and round and
down, and caught her necklet in a bannister as she fell,
and at the bottom lay helpless, unable to move, her left
arm outstretched, and the rings glinting on them in
their marriage, or was it their sisterhood, of red and
white. Rose Red and Snow White and their friend—or
was he their enemy—the bear? Sent by their mother,
alarmed on their account, shuffling out into the snow,
gruffly growling, sorrowful.
Mr. First, Hamish: fumbling, kindly, dangerous beast.

Mr. Fox, predator: sharp with his teeth, his knives, his smile, wounding, piercing with his you-know-what.

Gemma, you should not have loved Mr. Fox, now dancing on light feet down towards you, round and round, pretty lacy axe high in his hand.

"I would have preferred to love you to death," says Mr. Fox, "but want must be my master!"

15 ━━━━━━━━━━━━━━━━━━━━━━━━━━━━━

"I missed the birthday cake," says Hamish, coming into the tearoom. "Why did no one tell me? Where is everyone?"

"Gone," says Gemma happily. "Victor went off with Janice and Wendy. Wendy has a boyfriend now. Fancy that!"

"And that leaves Elsa with us." Hamish cut himself a slice of birthday cake. "I hope you sang 'Happy Birthday.'"

"Of course."

"What a delightful cake. You must let Gemma teach you to cook, Elsa."

Elsa looks from Hamish to Gemma. A little seed of anger roots, sprouts, swells, driving out grief.

"I hope he didn't take the library ladder," says Hamish.

"I'm afraid he did."

"A man of direct action," says Hamish sadly. "One has to admire it."

"You'll instruct your solicitors?"

"Of course."

"They're better than his?"

"Naturally."

"Good. I'm afraid he hasn't behaved very well to Elsa. Her prince turned out to be a positive toad, didn't he, Elsa?"

Still Elsa does not reply.

"Sit down quietly, Hamish. I'm just finishing my story. Of how I met you, my dear."

"I hope it's true."

"It will do."

And Gemma continues.

While Mr. Fox pursued Gemma with his lacy axe, Marion went in search of help. She rang her father at his office.

"Dad! It's Marion. Mr. Fox is murdering Gemma."

"Speak to your mother." Marion's dad handed his wife the telephone. Mrs. Ramsbottle often visited her husband's office; together they would tour travel agents in search of new brochures.

"Mum, Mr. Fox is going to murder Gemma."

"You naughty girl! You'll be in prison for libel if you go on like this."

But something stirred in Marion's mum's mind. Floating on top of the scented blue water in the toilet bowl this morning—what? Flush and flush, but still it floated. Hideous, horrible, this vindication of their daughter.

Marion's mum and dad came round in a taxi, and at the bottom of the Fox and First building found an agitated Mr. First trying to summon the lift, with Marion beside him.

"He's left the lift doors open," said Marion. "He sometimes does that. As a joke."

"No joke," said Mr. First. "He was in no joking

mood. Such genius! Such tragedy! We'll have to walk. Quick, quick!"

So while Mr. Fox raised his lacy axe above poor Gemma's head and she lay helpless, rescue was on its way.

Up and up, round and round. Would it come in time? Or if it came, would it be effective? Could the imperfect unison of such imperfect parts—Mr. First, Marion, Marion's mum and dad—contain sufficient goodness to combat Mr. Fox's concentrated villainy?

Up and up, round and round.

"Just one more flight," begged Mr. First, bringing up the rear. "I'm afraid she's in great danger. I never thought, never dreamt—" but he needs all his breath to make his thin legs work, and Marion's mother likewise, to make her fat ones move.

"Like being back in the Dolomites," she panted. "Just the same feeling in the back of the legs. It will be hell tomorrow. Why are you going so fast, Mr. First? He's not really going to murder her, is he? It's just Marion and her tales again. Such a nice man, Mr. Fox. Always such a charming smile and such clean teeth. You ought to clean your teeth more, Marion, you might have more success with the boys."

"I clean them twice a day, Mum. I can hardly take a toothbrush to the office."

"I'm sure Gemma does."

"Well, look at Gemma now!"

Look, indeed.

Down came the axe on the third finger of Gemma's left hand. She had been quite right; never again would the hand be fit for the ordinary tasks of everyday life.

It hardly hurt; it hardly bled. Mr. Fox removed the

rings, slipped them on his own fingers. How easily they fitted, lubricated as they were by blood.

"You see," he cried. "A nice slim finger! If I put on a pound in weight I go for a week to the gym and lose five. That's self-discipline, Gemma. You should have developed it. Now as to the neck, that may be more difficult!"

He bent to investigate the golden collar, but his fingers travelled down her body, exploring. Gemma fainted, and just as well. She had some memory afterwards of a sudden personal pain, felt as the loss of her finger still was not, but likewise hazed by shock, and looking up and seeing Mr. Fox's eyes above her, near and far, near and far, red and narrow with the exercise of his lust or love or whatever it was; and in her own heart, her own body, welling up, the ineradicable stubbornness of love, so that she cried out aloud from fear and joy, pain and pleasure mixed.

Now die, Gemma. That's all. That's enough. That's what it was all about.

"Up you go!" cried Marion's dad, pushing his wife from behind. "Let's just hurry, shall we? Let's be on the safe side! I too found a human finger floating in the loo this morning. You could flush and flush, but it wouldn't go down. You know what some objects are like—something to do with specific density, I believe. Come on, old dear. Pretend you're in an avalanche run and it's just begun to snow."

And the noisy, clattery, ridiculous party arrived on the landing to find the fire door locked and entrance to the Fox and First showrooms barred.

"We keep it locked," said Mr. First faintly, "in case of burglars."

"I don't want to go in," shrieked poor Marion. "I don't want to see. Don't you understand, everybody, I've had enough?"

But they didn't, couldn't, never would understand.

"The neck will have to go," said Mr. Fox. "No other way. Sorry about that. I was carried away."

Marion's father opened the little leather case, bought in the Algarve—which he referred to jokingly as his "in case case"—and took out a bent piece of wire and a plastic plaque with which he quickly and simply picked the lock.
The wind blew in through the shattered glass, fluffed the tail of the dead sea gull, and spattered water from the fountain across Gemma's face.

Mr. Fox stayed his hand and withheld the axe while he admired the effect.

"The fountain plays a rainbow of grief across your face, poor Gemma. If I could only make a necklace of your tears, or of my own . . ."

Mr. Fox laid down his axe and knelt beside Gemma's unconscious form; he tried, indeed he did, to find another way of removing the collar without cutting the neck, and it is to his credit that he did so. But finding none, he again picked up the axe . . .

"None of that rough stuff," said Marion's father behind Mr. Fox's back, and Mr. Fox turned and paled, and his hand sank down, and Mr. First removed the axe while Marion and her mother hurried to Gemma's side.

"My dear Gemma," said Mr. First, distraught. "I told you not to leave your desk. I knew that staircase was a deathtrap. Now see what you've done! And Leon, is there no controlling you?"

Gemma moaned and stirred and moaned again, feeling pain now in her back and in her finger.

"I can't move," said Gemma, and so it seemed.

"I must ring the police," said Mr. First. "You understand that, Leon?"

"I understand very well. The barbarian hordes have arrived. The package tourists. It is time for me to depart. You won't have a business left, you know that. You can't survive without me. It's the end of Fox and First."

"It's the end anyhow," said Mr. First. "We couldn't really have mass-produced that ring. There isn't a market for it. Ordinary people remain as respectable as they ever did; all this is surface froth. The bottom's dropping out of the erotic-jewellery market. After the surge, the recession. Time I was getting out of Carnaby Street and into something more serious. More natural. There's going to be a swing back to wholesomeness, mark my words."

"Then ring the police," said Mr. Fox. "Let them come for me with dogs and sirens. I wish I could hang. A glorious barbarity! But even that is not allowed. Now begins the whole dreary business of paper mugs and instant coffee, probation officers, head-shrinkers, social workers, open prisons and the smell of boiled cabbage forever and ever . . . I knew it would come to it in the end."

Mr. First rang the police. Mr. Fox peered at Gemma.

"You are a silly girl, Gemma. There was no need to

run away. I was only joking. We could have been happy together. When you'd been trained, of course."

Mr. First raised Gemma's head and pressed his dry lips to her soft ones. Marion cried out in grief.

"Don't they make a lovely picture!" said Marion's mum, head on one side. "Gemma and her millionaire. It's what she deserves, I'm sure."

Gemma's cool, sad voice stops.

"Have you finished?" enquires Hamish coldly.

Elsa, looking through the French windows, can see the small figures of Johnnie and Annie clearing the debris of the front gate, as to the manner born. Annie sweeps patiently with a wide broom. Johnnie raises the splintered blocks and beams shoulder-high and tosses them to the side of the drive. The weight is as illusory as that of the chunks of foam and balsa that bounce upon the crowds in films of earthquakes and tornados.

Good-by, Victor. Shattering barriers that scarcely existed, in the final impulse of familial generosity.

"And that's the end?" asks Elsa brightly, bravely.
"Not quite," says Gemma, fingering her pendant. "When I woke in the ambulance Hamish was sitting next to me. He asked me to marry him and I said yes. Well, for a girl without working legs and a ring-finger missing who'd just been raped, it seemed a good offer. As good as any I was likely to get."

Hamish's grey face is greyer yet with pain. I could

make him happy, thinks Elsa, but I could never make him suffer. What good am I to him? To anyone?

Hamish reaches forward and tugs the pendant out of Gemma's fingers.

"Horrible cheap thing," he says. "Why do you wear it? You only do it to annoy."

He uses so much force that the chain cuts into Gemma's neck; she cries out in pain and anger; the chain snaps. The pendant falls.

"See what you've done?" she weeps. "My mother's pendant."

"Don't believe a word Gemma says, Elsa," says Hamish. "The only truth in it all is that she came down to London as a young girl and got a job modelling jewellery at Fox and First. Mr. Fox was a homosexual, and later did his boyfriend to death in a rather horrible way and had to be restrained in Broadmoor, which played on my poor wife's mind. And my unfortunate sister fell accidentally from the window, and it's true that the other typist, Marion, was somewhat disturbed and stole one of the rings. We did not press charges. And that's all."

"But my finger! How do you explain my poor hand?"

"You caught your finger in the lift door. It had to be amputated. I proposed to you in the ambulance; that much is true. You loved me then; we loved each other. The present is bad enough without you blackening our past as well."

"And my legs? What about my legs?"

"The paralysis started later, on the day we were married. You fell on the steps of the Registrar's office after the ceremony. You have not walked since. There is no organic damage, the doctors say. Only an emo-

ional disturbance for which you will accept no treatment."

Gemma cries, head in hands, nine-fingered. How old
she seems! As fantasy drains from her veins, decay
creeps in.

"One story or another, Hamish," she says, "what's
the difference? It is all the same. It's the one-way
journey we all make from ignorance to knowledge, from
innocence to experience. We must all make it; there
is no escape. It's just that love and romance and illusion
and hope are etched so deeply into all our hearts that
they can never quite be wiped away. They stay around
to torment us with thoughts of what might have been.
For you as well as me. We are fallen creatures; we
never quite lose sight of grace, and the pain of our fall
is always with us."

"I didn't do the typing, Gemma," says Elsa into the
silence. "Hamish did it."

Gemma turns her old and spiteful eyes upon her husband.

"You have such a humble heart," she says. "How
you wish to be of service! It's what I most despise in
you."

Hamish says nothing. How haggard Gemma looks, and
how malevolent. A witch!

"You deserved to lose Victor," says Gemma to Elsa.
"Little liar, little slut."
"I know," says Elsa.
"You had no right to him in the first place. You're
just a bit-part player in other people's dramas. You'll
never amount to anything else. Do you realise that?"
"Yes," says Elsa.
"I lost Mr. Fox and all my future too, whoever he
was and however I did it; it's all the same. This is a

living death I have here in this chair. And don't think that because others are worse off than me, that's any comfort. It's not."

Gemma, you should have died when your mother did. Great-Aunt May, you should have let Gemma go; not nursed her through her infant illnesses; saved her against a rainy day. What good did it do you in the end? You died lonely, and were buried alone.

That's why you did it. Yes, you did. That was the end you feared. You had no child of your own, so you stole your sister's daughter's child.

Back and back through the generations goes the good and evil in us. Proliferating as the peoples of the world increase, raising the banners of their struggle high.

"Never mind," says Gemma softly, to Elsa. "Sit here beside me in the sun and we'll look through Harrod's baby-linen catalogue and choose the nursery furniture. Hamish will find it a sixteenth-century rattle. Won't you, Hamish."

"If that's what you want, Gemma." Hamish sits, mournful and depressed, his energy evaporated.

"Gemma," says Elsa tentatively, "we don't even know if it's conceived yet."

"Then you will stay at Hamish's side, in Hamish's bed, until it is. We will rear your child, Elsa, as the living evidence of the renewal of grace."

"But what about me?"

"You? You can go back to your typing pool, or wherever you're happy, six weeks after the birth."

Gemma stops talking. Elsa stands beside her chair like some living puppet. Her mouth gapes wide.
But Gemma frowns, and now seems to address herself.

"What are you saying?" she asks, and her face is contorted, and an old-lady croak comes out of her mouth to match her old-lady face. "You're being very naughty, Gemma."

Great-Aunt May's words, Great-Aunt May's voice. Great-Aunt May perhaps. Hamish is on his feet, startled. But it is to Elsa he goes, not Gemma, as if he were afraid the spell might break and she might escape. He clutches her upper arm in his hand. Later she is to find bruises upon it. But Elsa shakes him off disdainfully and easily, and gives him a quick look, and sees nothing more than a sad old man with strong fingers, a lecherous eye and a failing prostate gland. She looks at Gemma and sees an old lady in a wheelchair.

"Run, Elsa, run," says Gemma in her new, old, cracked voice, herself transcended. "The door's open. Just run. Please run."

Elsa, mesmerised, backs towards the French windows, fumbles with her foot by the sill, finds it, steps down. The sun strikes low over the horizon, large and red.

"Run!" cries Gemma once more, and her voice is her own again, light and hopeful. It is the voice her mother gave her, and which Great-Aunt May preserved. "Run, Elsa! Run for all you're worth. Don't fall. Please don't fall, the way I did. You can do it; go so far and then draw back. I know you can. You must! You must run for me and all of us."

And Elsa runs, though whether for herself or Gemma she is not quite sure. She runs towards the splintered gate, stops to unlace her platform heels, and then runs on; her head spins, her side aches.

"Stop her!" calls Hamish from the terrace. "Annie and Johnnie! Stop, thief!"

What is it I have stolen, wonders Elsa. His child, his

heir, his vision of himself? His hope for a different future?

Annie and Johnnie stand together, arms akimbo, in the gateway. Still Elsa runs. She trips, she falls, she is at their very feet. She cries out in pain, gasps her distress. Johnnie raises the broom as if to belabour her, but Annie bends and takes Elsa's arm and helps her up, pushing her husband aside.

"Run along, Missie. Quick," she says. "Out of here!"

But Elsa, standing again without breath to move, turns and stares back at Gemma and Hamish, and what she sees is etched forever in her mind.

Gemma is on her feet, out of her chair. She is reaching, craning, walking forward. She is unsteady, but she is over the step and onto the terrace and past Hamish, as if she too would, could, might perhaps somehow reach the gate and freedom. Annie and Johnnie run back towards Gemma. But she shakes her head; she needs no help from them. She turns back to Hamish instead, and takes his arm and stands swaying beside him.

Gemma laughs. Gemma walks on her husband's arm. One step forward, one step back. Collapse. Then up again, off again. Gemma smiles her triumph; he smiles his. They are each other's child; they do not need Elsa's. Never did.

Gemma and Hamish walk side by side back into the house. Annie and Johnnie follow.

Elsa, forgotten, turns away and limps out of the gate. She has stubbed her toe and scraped her arm in falling. Her feet are bare. Thorns and brambles scratch her.

Not far from the gate is a telephone box. Elsa reverses the charges and speaks to her mother—or rather, cries